HER GLASS
HEART

Mary Cantell

WIPF & STOCK · Eugene, Oregon

38212007353086
Rodman Main Adult Mystery
Cantell, M
Cantell, Mary, author
Her glass heart

Resource Publications
A division of Wipf and Stock Publishers
199 W 8th Ave, Suite 3
Eugene, OR 97401

Her Glass Heart
By Cantell, Mary
Copyright©2013 by Cantell, Mary
ISBN 13: 978-1-5326-4164-0

Publication date 11/17/2017
Previously published by OakTara Publishers, 2013

* * *

To my beloved husband,
all my love and gratitude,
and
to my precious mother,
who nurtured the writing bud in me.

Prologue

As long as anyone could remember, nothing of any consequence ever occurred in the quiet town of St. David's until the summer of 1966. When the little girl died. A small enclave, it was a peaceful community where the serenity was only gently roused at hourly intervals by the tolling of the church bells, or when the metallic scratch of the local train ground along the tracks, announcing its arrival by steam and whistles. The sweet call of a resident red-winged blackbird could also break the morning silence, but this was more of a blessing than an interruption of the peace. St. David's remained restful and solemn—reminiscent of an aging queen who had retained her noble position throughout the years. And like a queen, it would one day hold a royal secret.

1

Early fall, 1980

WHEN JORDANNA GOT UP THIS MORNING, she didn't have a good feeling. While there was nothing outwardly wrong, she didn't have the sense that all was right with the world. Whatever it was, the mood followed her throughout the day, bearing the stigma of an unwelcome shadow.

The Paoli Local sped along the westbound tracks toward the last remains of a persimmon sun draped at the horizon. Jordanna focused on the moving landscape until her eyes strained under the weight of the swiftly shifting patterns. Red building, white warehouse, graffiti-covered walls. The staccato of colors popped among the dim clusters of spindled shoots and overgrown brush.

The train stopped and started along the 22-mile track between Philadelphia and Paoli before reaching St. David's, wresting her from a lulling half-sleep. The conductor announced the names of the stations—*Bryn Mawr, Radnor, Villanova*—in bold syllables. As the doors opened for the exiting passengers, a blanket of air, hot as a campfire, pushed through the car. Evening had brought little relief from the Indian summer heat. Her silk blouse, an early morning choice she now regretted, clung by a layer of perspiration. A cotton blend would have been a wiser decision, but taking the time to listen to weather reports was not on her radar...more akin to something her mother would do. Living on campus precluded the motherly touches—packed lunches, freshly folded towels smelling like a meadow, and being told what to wear.

"Saint David's..." came the familiar, sonorous call of the conductor from the back of the car. He placed a funny emphasis on the word *saint* that always sounded oddly comical to her. After years of announcing train stops up and down Philadelphia's Main Line, he must have had to entertain himself somehow.

Just before dusk, Jordanna stepped off the train. She rushed across the platform and down the wooden stairs to the road that led to her college campus. With barely enough time to stop off at the dining hall before her evening class, she stepped up her pace. The only sound on the quiet street was the rhythmic crunch of her heels on the gravel, like horse's hooves on a riding trail. In her haste, a shoe slipped off, sending her tumbling onto Chaminoux Road. The gritty surface stung. She hobbled to retrieve it, and although no one else was around to witness the awkward fall, she flushed, thinking windows always have eyes.

A hidden, narrow path nestled between two residential properties—a white clapboard and a brick colonial—and paved the way to the back entrance to Colton College. Easily overlooked, it was marked by a thin, wrought-iron railing and used mostly by Colton students or those in the neighborhood who knew of it. As she started up the pathway, a cool pocket of pine scent enveloped her and she savored the sweetness of the greenery. While some thrived in the big city with its eclectic mix of energy, Jordanna felt hollowed by the amalgam of grime and noise, preferring the quiet confines of a small college town, like St. David's. Up ahead, there was a flash of red—someone at the other end, most likely walking a dog. Everyone had a dog in this neighborhood, it seemed. A lone wasp hovered around the bushes. Hoping not to distract it from its meandering, she moved cautiously over the mossy fieldstone.

At the end of the path, the formal campus emerged into a large grassy knoll dotted with oaks and maples. The canopy of leaves overhead spread generously, dispelling the light. While absorbed in the calm seclusion, she was drawn to the bordering shrubs—a stirring, not wind driven, just a few yards away. In a glance, there was an image that didn't fit the pastoral setting.

A man. He crouched at the edge of the clearing as though readying for a race. His eyes bored into hers, lips pressed into a tight line. Her blood tingled. What was he doing there...and where was his dog? Was there ever a dog?

In a heartbeat, the peaceful setting turned awry. Every instinct said to run. Adrenaline surging through her body, she pressed her books firmly against her chest—and bolted.

Jordanna weaved through the mass of trees like a sprinter pulling out of the pack. Hurtling over jutting rocks and fallen branches, she clenched her toes to the soles of her shoes that were on the verge of flying off. *Not now, Lord. Please, not now.*

The old stucco dormitory in the distance was never more welcoming; it beckoned as an oasis. Yet the safety of Dane Hall seemed so far away, as though in a dream. Would she be able to get there? Her heartbeat pounded in her ears. Was he gaining ground? Like fire to her chest, her lungs burned. Although she ran for what seemed to be a safe enough distance from him, she dared not turn around for fear he'd be right behind her. In that tiny second

4

would be his chance—to grab her.

Then the door came into focus . . . the bright red door. She never noticed the color of the door handle before, but now she mentally embraced the worn brass fixture, wishing to feel its smoothness in her palm. Where was Fuzz, the gentlemanly custodian who'd usually be standing there holding it open for her? Of all the times for it to be closed. If only the door could swing open and swallow her inside.

Now, within just a few feet, she lunged for the handle. It slipped from her grasp. The force knocked her back into the railing. She groped for it again. More adrenaline pulsed through her. Locked. All the doors were locked after six o'clock. *Was it after six already?*

She scrambled around the side of the dorm and tore onto the path that led past Walden Pond. The green circle of water at the foot of the hill that once lent a charming serenity now appeared indifferent to her struggle. Her heels cracked hard on the pavement—the echoing reminder that she was still in danger.

In the distance, a glint moved through the trees. Coming up the driveway, was the silhouette of Sarge, the campus watchman, behind the wheel of his blue Chevrolet.

"Sarge!" she called across the pond.

He wore a startled expression as he exited the car. His lean body moved as though in slow motion as she closed in on him. "What's going on?" he said, moving toward her, placing his brown-from-the-sun hand on his hip.

"A man...up in the clearing just past Cott Hall—before Dane," she managed between gulps of air.

"A man?" His eyes narrowed under his visor as he peered in the direction of the two buildings. "What happened?"

With her breath heaving, she explained the course of the last few minutes. "...and then I turned and saw this guy crouched down looking at me. He looked so odd, like he was about to dart out and jump—"

"Are you all right?" he said with a frown.

She nodded and swept the hair from her eyes.

"What did he look like?"

"Dark hair—and a beard. That's all I could tell, really. He was mostly in the bushes."

"How old was he?"

"Not sure." Her heart still pounded. "Maybe a little older than me...I couldn't tell, really. I thought it was someone walking a dog at first, but—"

"Between Cott and Dane Halls?"

"In the clearing."

"I'll go check it out," he said, turning for his car. "Are you sure you're all right?"

"I'm fine."

"Do you want a ride back to the dorm?"

"It's right across the soccer field," she said, pointing to Key Hall, where some students ambled up the path on their way to the dorm. "I'm fine, really."

Sarge eyed her for a long second and then turned to get into his car. A spray of dust shot up from his back tires as he sped toward the upper end of the campus. With her nerves still rattled, she decided to skip dinner and her evening class. It had been enough for one day.

On the way back, even the familiar gurgling of water from the waterwheel could not calm her spirit. The toll of the church bells rang out—usually comforting to her, signaling God was near, but she was too out of sorts to appreciate it. She hurried across the soccer field before glancing back at the cluster of trees where Sarge was headed. A shiver ran through her. She couldn't shake the feeling of his eyes still on her.

2

A FEW STUDENTS SAT AROUND THE TELEVISION IN KEY HALL absorbed in the evening news. The volume of the television was too loud, but no one else seemed to notice. Not in a social mood, Jordanna breezed through the lounge, hoping her presence would go unnoticed. The sound of Dan Rather's voice followed her down the hall as she hurried down a flight of steps to her room halfway down the long corridor on the ground floor. Plopping onto her bed, the day's events circled in her mind.

Soon the sound of familiar voices, one by one, filtered from the hall. Damaris Lopez just got a kitten that promptly soiled her brand-new comforter. Her mild disgust could be heard all the way to the fire escape. Karen Kraemer recently became engaged and excitedly chirped about it to her mother by phone. Footsteps reverberated down the hall as other voices came and went.

What brought them all to Colton? Damaris, dressed to the nines every day, had come for her Mrs. Degree, no doubt. Karen...Julie...Beth. She compared herself to them. Not as smart as Beth, who'd been in the honor society in high school. Not as pretty as Julie, whose clear complexion rivaled the flawless essence of a baby peach. Now they shared their lives with each other—books, tapes, perfume—in side-by-side rooms. Jordanna vicariously engaged in the snippets of conversation until the precious moment of sleep took over and the voices dissolved.

*

Shortly before ten o'clock, Jordanna awoke, still wearing her street clothes. Forcing herself to get up to change, she groped in the dark for the reading lamp above her bed. The light revealed the presence of her roommate, Beth Briscoe, asleep across the aisle. Her steady breathing filled the room.

Jordanna peeled off her blouse, cringing at the inevitable sweat stains now indelibly imprinted, no doubt, and put on a nightshirt before heading to the bathroom.

Soon back in bed, she placed her hands under the cool softness of her pillow and tried to fall asleep again. Every volt of electricity in the room drew itself into her veins. Unable to sleep, she recanted the Twenty-third Psalm over and over. Her mind spun, keeping her wired. Well past midnight, she shifted and turned.

She got up. A thin light lined the bottom of the door. Opening it, the brightness of the hall light assaulted her eyes as it bounced off the yellow walls and white linoleum. The hall had the sub quiet sound of deep sleep and the distinct scent of disinfectant near Damaris's room. At the end of the hall, an old white Freeze-King refrigerator rattled inside a tiny open closet. Several brown paper lunch bags had collected on the shelves with unfamiliar names scrawled on them. Another shelf held a bruised apple, a can of Lipton iced tea, and two cups of yogurt. She picked up a yogurt and headed back to her room.

The door stood ajar. She thought she'd closed it but wasn't certain. Inside the room, she turned on the small lamp above her desk, hoping not to disturb Beth. While reaching for a spoon in the desk drawer, she startled at the sight of a man sitting on her bed. Dark hair and a scraggly beard. His lips twisted into a grisly smile....

*

In a panic, Jordanna woke up and bolted upright.

"Jordie, are you okay?" Beth said from across the room. She switched on the lamp by her bed.

"Oh, gosh," Jordanna said, "I just had another dream."

"Like the one last time?"

"Worse." Her neck ringed with sweat.

"Want to talk about it?" Beth said with concern as she propped herself up with one arm. "It might help."

"It was awful."

The imprint of his face festered in her mind. Across the room, the window shade was half open, and the insufferable thought of the real man watching from outside hit. Perhaps he skulked just beyond in his car, or by the trees at the edge of the parking lot, past the eye of the floodlights. She got up and pulled the shade down, then peeked through the side.

"What are you doing?" Beth said.

Jordanna surveyed the murky silhouettes of the cars in the parking lot, straining to see if she recognized them. "Nothing, just looking," she said, attempting to hide her fear, hoping that if she didn't talk about it, the problem would go away.

"Do you want me to get you anything?" Beth said. "I have a leftover banana in my drawer, I think."

8

"No, I'll be okay. But thanks, Beth," she said as she crawled back into bed.

Beth was sweet, but the last thing she wanted was a warm, speckled banana.

"Try to think about something pleasant...maybe you and Jeff at the Four Seasons, or something," said Beth. "That'll make for some sweet dreams." She grinned as she turned out the light.

"Sorry I woke you."

"Don't worry about it," said Beth. "Are you sure you're okay?"

"I'll be all right," said Jordanna, wishing she could mean it.

Jeff would make a pleasant dream right about now. It wouldn't be the first time she'd thought of him right before falling asleep. If only her dreams about him would come true.

*

By morning, with the sheets wrapped lightly against her legs like the tender folds of a rose, she fought to break free of the sweet repose until she remembered she had a Shakespeare exam at 9:00 a.m. She pushed the sheets aside and hurried out of bed. She should have studied harder and didn't feel anywhere near being prepared for the test. She wanted so much to please her professor, Dr. Bradley. So passionately he lectured, his thick lips protruding prominently through his thick salt-and-pepper beard and seeming to grow fuller by the very syllables he spoke. It looked as though his thoughts and feelings for the old seventeenth-century bard came from a place deep inside him.

Grabbing her notes, she gave them a quick read-through before taking a shower. When she got back from her shower, the room was empty. The lingering scent of Beth's signature perfume hung in the air.

*

Jordanna stepped outside as the sun crept up behind the pines. In the distance, a white morning mist hovered above the dewy fields near the security building where Sarge stood with Toby, his dog. If not for the gold stripe running down his pants, his dark blue uniform could have been issued by the Navy. His tanned skin resembled a sailor's, having spent too many days in the sun. He had a stiff and deliberate gait, as though he'd get there when it pleased him...encumbered, it seemed, by his own inner struggles. The dog ran ahead of him, yanking the leash as he sniffed the ground.

"Morning, Sarge!"

He looked up as she hurried toward him.

"Hey, just wondering... did you find that guy yesterday?"

He shook his head as though disappointed with himself. "I checked out the upper campus—didn't find anything."

Toby waddled over to her, his tail wagging. His sad eyes stared up as though he wanted to join the conversation.

"You didn't see anyone?" she said with a frown.

"I searched all around the clearing and along the perimeter...walked all around Cott Hall back to Chaminoux Road." He pointed into the distance, sketching his route in the air with his finger.

"That's so weird," she said, shielding her eyes from the glare as she visually followed his course, wondering where the man could have gone.

"He may have been a birdwatcher—you know, one of those bird-types checking out a rare species or something. Or maybe he dropped a contact."

"Maybe," she said, thinking otherwise. Deep in her gut she felt certain it wasn't any of those things.

Sarge gazed in the direction of Cott Hall. "I'll keep an eye out for him. A dark-haired guy with a full beard, right?"

"Yeah, and kinda scruffy."

"I'll be on the lookout. Don't worry."

"Thanks, Sarge."

He gave her a long look before turning away with Toby at his heels.

As the sun came up over Walden Hill, Jordanna got back on the path again and headed for the dining hall. She tried to forget about the stranger.

3

JEFFERSON JAMES LOOKED LIKE HE'D JUST STEPPED OUT OF THE SHOWER—his hair and face slick with sweat. A second-year sophomore, he moved with a confident stride across the soccer field. Jordanna's temperature spiked at the sight of him. Even soaking wet, his good looks would not waver. Jordanna watched him from the crest, hoping he'd soon catch a glimpse of her. In her daydreams, she imagined sitting across a table from him by candlelight, where she could feel pretty with the help of soft lights. For now, she had the harsh morning light of a thousand candles—and little makeup. Yet she didn't want to take the chance on his passing her by.

"Hi!" she called, feeling the familiar rush that always followed when she was close to him.

"Hey, what's up?" He beamed the smile of someone who'd just won a prize.

"How was practice?" she said as he neared, feeling a delicious anxiety.

"Rough. The coach worked us hard—even in this heat."

He plopped down in the grass next to her. Her stomach fluttered, and she didn't know what to say next. He wasn't a stranger, but the extent of her vocabulary and social skills suddenly melted. She searched his face. Aside from a cluster of sweat beads and a slight overgrowth of facial hair, his looks were intact. Without even trying.

"You can sit on the blanket." The words came out fast, surprising her.

"I'm drenched. You want this sweat all over your blanket?"

"I can always wash it."

He eased his way onto it and lay back, flashing an easy, milk-white smile.

"You want something to drink?" She feigned a casual air.

"Sure, what do you have?"

A small green bottle of mineral water, dripping in condensation, lay at her side. "It's kinda warm by now. Sorry." She opened the bottle she'd brought for herself and handed it to him.

"Thanks." His fingers brushed hers as he took it from her. "How's it going?" he asked several gulps later.

"Okay, except for this heat. I came outside to study, hoping for a breeze."

"I'm guessing you didn't find one."

"I love Indian Summer," she said, trying to come up with something that didn't sound lame.

He took another guzzle and gave her a look while she pretended to read. "Man, it's brutal out here," he said, wiping his face on his sleeve.

She agreed the heat was almost unbearable. But she'd endure just about anything to find a way to talk to him. As the temperature outside climbed to match the one inside her body, she wondered how long it would be before he'd carry the conversation to more than just small talk. Maybe this time he'd ask her out. She kept her head in the textbook, but the words on the page eluded her.

"That pool looks great over there, don't you think?" Jeff said.

In the distance, the aquamarine water held the glimmer of a gemstone at the foot of a cluster of maples.

"It'd be nice if the pool were still open," she said.

"Open? Look at it. It couldn't be more open." He grinned. "Let's take a dip."

"Now?"

"Sure."

"We can't. The pool is closed."

"So let's hop the fence." His eyes twinkled.

"Sarge's office is right around the corner." She pointed to the security office. "Not to mention that I'd like to retain my lifeguard job again next summer. How would it look if I broke the rules and—"

"Oh, Jordie, it's so hot. Let's just sneak in for a quick dip." His expression resembled a little boy whose bike was stolen.

"I don't know…" She hesitated again, knowing full well that she longed to break the rules with him.

He took off his shirt. His chest glistened in the sunlight. "Let's go check it out," he urged, grabbing her arm.

She delighted as she felt his skin on hers. He may as well have grabbed her heart as she bent to gather the quilt. Together they scurried down the hill and across the soccer field to the beckoning water. Jeff approached the fence first and took hold of the bar, pulling himself up and over with the agility of a pole-vaulter. Jordanna still struggled with the idea but, not wanting to disappoint him, followed his lead. She tossed her textbook and the quilt over the side and then climbed up and over but not before snagging the hem of her T-shirt that clung to one of the links in the fence.

"Darn it," she said with disgust.

"What?"

"The fence wire. It caught my shirt."

Jeff reached out to help her down. Taking his hand, she didn't want to let go. They walked to the deep end, half-shaded by a large tree, where she laid down the quilt. Shimmers of white reflections danced on the blue pool. Jordanna slipped her feet into the cold water.

"Ah, that feels nice." She playfully splashed him with a spray of water while he feigned annoyance. "Hey, you're the one who wanted to cool yourself off," she said, laughing.

Moments later, he dived under the water. "Man, this is great," he called from the middle of the pool. "Come on in, Jordie." The water slurped through his mouth. He plunged under and popped up like a seal. "You coming in?" he asked, bobbing up and down.

"I'm okay." She gathered handfuls of water and poured them on her body, cooling herself down a little at a time. "I'm fine, really. This is enough." She ran her wet hand along her neck and back.

He eyed her while nearing closer to the edge, as though he were determined to get her into the pool. "I could pull you in, you know," he said with a grin.

She quickly pulled her legs out of the water. "You wouldn't dare, Jeff James!" she said from a safe distance away on the grass.

He smiled and ducked under the surface. After a few laps, he got out. He lay next to her on the quilt she'd stretched out in a shady spot under the trees. His back shone with beads of water that trickled onto his hard biceps. A slight breeze broke through, gently rustling the thick leaves overhead.

"I love the breeze…feels great." The gentle air grazed her freshly shaven legs.

"You should have come in." He rolled over to gaze up at her with the curious gaze of an intrigued cat.

"Getting my feet wet was just enough. Besides, we shouldn't be here," she said, peering past the fence. In the distance, several people were coming down the path, and a couple more walked across the soccer field. She recognized two of them as Beth and her boyfriend, Dan. "Oh, no!" She scrambled to her feet.

"What's the matter?"

"People are coming. We've probably been spotted." She bounced up and began to gather her things.

"Spotted? You make it sound like we're criminals or something."

She began to fold the quilt. He bent and took the other end, and soon their fingers touched as they brought the quilt ends together. He let his hand linger a second before pulling away. His eyes glimmered in the sunlight, and she felt her insides swirl.

"Well, I guess I'd better hurry. I have duty at the nursing home later this afternoon." She picked up her book. "Are you going to lunch?"

"Actually, I have a paper due." He shook the water out of his ears.

"Oh, okay. Want me to bring you back something?" she asked, testing the boundaries of their newly made bond.

"I have a leftover tuna grinder back at the dorm. But thanks, anyway." He picked up his shoes.

She felt a sudden weight in her chest and hoped he wasn't closing down. This was their first real date, of sorts. Hopefully, it wouldn't stop here.

Just then, Kingsley Willoughby, along with two of his frat brothers, came strutting around the gym toward the pool. He swaggered like he owned Colton College.

"Hey, you were on fire today, James!" Kingsley Willoughby's voice bellowed. "Great game, man!" His tall, husky body towered over the others as though he were the Alpha Dog.

"Hey, what can I say?" Jeff gave him a sideways grin.

"You guys hot or what?" Kingsley said as the trio ambled closer.

"The water looked too good to pass up," Jeff explained as he and Jordanna climbed over the fence.

"It must be nice having a lifeguard for a friend," Kingsley said with a wink.

Jordanna pretended not to notice him. She drew back to catch her reflection in the glass of the gymnasium window a few feet away. After some preening, she noticed Jeff still talking, uttering words like *scores* and *stats*. They used shrugs and spit as punctuation along with towel whips and light punches. Guys. They were a whole different breed to her, especially Kingsley. She didn't know what Jeff saw in him. How could he stand to be roommates with such a blowhard?

"I'll see you later, Jeff," Jordanna said with a wave.

Jeff turned and broke away from the group. "Okay, later!"

"Hey, where ya' goin', Jordanna?" Kingsley's voice boomed.

"Lunch," she said over her shoulder while keeping her stride.

"All right...but watch out for Susie Colton!" He chuckled.

Jordanna braced at his remark. *Susie Colton. Her dead cousin.*

4

THE REMINDER OF SUSIE LEFT JORDANNA STARTLED. She knew of the rumor about her cousin on campus and heard the story once too often after arriving at Colton. *Watch out for Susie Colton. Her ghost is alive and living in Walden Hall.* It chilled her every time she heard. It. Not wanting the negative attention, she kept her feelings to herself, never revealing to anyone her relationship to the Colton family.

Haunting thoughts of Susie had been a big part of her consciousness for a long time until she finally put them to rest years ago. The memories had comfortably settled like fine layers of sediment, but now their stirring seemed imminent. The decayed recollections were beginning to find life again—all in a hazy kind of reminiscing that left Jordanna with mixed feelings.

Whenever Susie's name popped up, she ignored it or left the room and sometimes thought it had been a mistake even to transfer to the college from Sarah Lawrence. But it seemed so right to come back to a familiar place. The home of her aunt and uncle, John and Adelaide Colton. The place where she and her mother had been invited to live for a while after her father passed away when she was just a child.

Jordanna recalled the day last spring when she and her mother came back to visit the place they once called home for the first time in 14 years....

*

"This place is still so lovely, isn't it?" Jordanna said. "I can't believe God put so much beauty into one place."

As they neared the pond, she marveled at the buildings that usurped old verdant fields of grassland, the growth of the trees, a parking lot in place of what used to be a garden or a field...she couldn't remember which. Dormitories and other structures dotted the landscape where pheasants once roamed.

Above it all, Colton still held an intangible spirit, a reverence, palpable along the paths winding through clusters of brush and fern and over the sparkling stream that cut through and over jutting rocks. The nearby waterwheel, attempting gracefulness, churned awkwardly amid its cupping and sluicing. Just above, a smaller pond sat in shadows under the earnest bow of the quiet, yet mighty willow, and the tender wave of the daylilies dipped in the breeze.

"Look, Mom...in the water!" She pointed to the Mute swan floating by a cluster of tall reeds. Its elegant simplicity drew her in.

Her gaze danced over the pristine landscape. Above the pond, the old Spanish-tiled estate home rose above the towering oaks and sentry-like maples. Flourishes of red and yellow blossoms and bold lavender swells of wisteria draped along the back stone wall. Jordanna and her mother remained still, absorbing the resplendence of a come-to-life picture postcard. At the foot of the hill, the pond shimmered back the reflection of the large stone mansion sitting royal and persuasive above it.

"Mom, I want to go to college here. I want to go to Colton," she said, standing at the waterwheel. The spray of water flew off the buckets and sprinkled the stones on the banks. "I feel drawn to this place."

Her mother, Sarah Bronson, shifted her cane and sat on a nearby bench along the path. Her face grew serious. "Jordie, remember, that's what you said last year about Sarah Lawrence," she said, an edge to her voice. "I hope you won't be changing your mind every year."

"No, it's different here. I think this is where I'm supposed to be. It just feels right."

"It's a small college—less than a thousand students." A line grew between her mother's eyes and the light went out of them.

"It doesn't matter. I need to be here, Mom."

"I'm sure your Aunt Adelaide would be very pleased," Sarah murmured.

Jordanna clearly remembered what she'd said to her mother that picture-perfect spring day they had come to visit the campus last April. She'd felt so sure she wanted to come back. Something was calling her to attend Colton College. Her words had resounded over the water and back again that quiet morning. Even the Mute swan content in the shadows on the water seemed to nod in approval. It had been so clear to her. But now she wondered if she'd made the right decision.

How had Kingsley come to spreading such a false rumor about Susie? How could he and the others be so callous as to taint the reputation of the Colton family by their flagrant assumptions? *Watch out for Susie Colton. One day she committed suicide by jumping out of her bedroom window.*

The girl was barely seven when she passed away. How ridiculous to assert she caused her own death! Jordanna was determined to defend her cousin's reputation and set the record straight, as though it was her own pardon she

16

yearned for. Yes, she would quell the rumor and enlighten them. If only she knew herself what happened that tragic August morning. If only she could remember...

*

"Hey, you okay?" Sarge said as he approached her on the path.

"Sure, why wouldn't I be?" Jordanna said, startled by his presence.

"You don't look so good." He studied her as a concerned father would inspect his daughter after bruising her knee.

She cowered at the thought of him peering through to her soul. "It's nothing, really," she replied, hoping to convince herself.

"You sure? You almost walked into the pond." He whipped off his sunglasses and peered down at her. His steel blue eyes seemed to observe past her skin, her protective shell.

She winced that he could possibly perceive her private thoughts. Her mother had warned her never to wear her heart on her sleeve. But how could she not? It wasn't some deliberate action or something she could control. Just where was she supposed to put her feelings?

"It's just—well, nothing really. Something I heard. About Susie Colton."

"Susie Colton?" His voice turned sharp.

"Yeah. I'm not too fond of ghost stories."

He remained silent.

"Oh, I'll get over it," she said. "But thanks for your concern."

He put his sunglasses on and lent a quick glance to the pond before looking back at her.

"Well, I'm running late for work." She forced a tiny smile and turned back to the path. "See you later, Sarge."

Thoughts of her only cousin pushed at the surface—circling, wanting desperately to get out. The long-buried feelings stabbed again. Walks by the pond usually lent her serenity, but now the impact of the past crushed her. She yearned to dive into the water and drift to the bottom, letting the water settle over her, to quench the remorse dormant for so many years.

As she neared Walden Hall to pick up a quick lunch before going to work, she increased her pace. Her thoughts turned back to Sarge. He didn't look too well himself.

*

The air hung stagnant in the brownstone nursing home in Waynesboro. Caseworkers maneuvered smoothly past each other through the narrow hallways with the agility of minnows as they tended to their patients.

"Hello, Miss Jordie," said Doranda Welling. The short, rotund woman dwarfed behind her desk that swam in tall stacks of paper and miscellaneous clutter.

"Hi, Dorrie, how are you?" Jordanna said brightly.

"Can't complain, can't complain. What's it like out there, child?"

"It's gorgeous." Jordanna headed for her locker. "I walked today, it was so nice out."

"Sure looks good from in here." Dorrie craned her neck to see beyond the lobby window. "One last hurrah b'fore fall really sets in, I guess."

"Have you been outside today?"

"No, but I shoulda took my break long ago. Lordy, I been here close to ten hours."

"You need to take a break." Jordanna reached for her white medical jacket.

"Good idea, child…soon as I finish writin' up this report."

"Oh, how's my favorite patient doing today?"

"Mr. Upland? He doin' alright…seems like he's holdin' his own."

"That's good, I guess. I was hoping he'd be walking by now."

"The man had a stroke. Give him time, child!"

Jordanna smiled as she smoothed her hair and tied it back with a barrette.

"He's a tough ol' bird. That's what I've heard."

"Yeah, and stubborn," said Jordanna.

"Well, I haven't gotten no bad reports about him since you were here last…at least not yet." She winked and went back to her paperwork.

"See you later, Dorrie." Jordanna buttoned her jacket and walked down the hall.

Inside the therapy room, a great equalizer was at work. Patients, therapists, and caseworkers were all rendered equally sallow by the unforgiving light. The overhead fluorescents had no sympathy. Empty wheelchairs sat staggered on the dingy gray floor, their owners working on various stages of rehabilitation. A makeshift kitchen unit enabled patients to go through the motions of life at home—should they be able to return to living on their own.

A short white-haired woman tried to balance herself at the pretend stove. A two-quart stainless steel pot sat on the backburner while a fake toaster held a piece of rubber toast. Across the room, several others leaned over a round

18

wooden table where blocks of varying shapes and colors were stacked in the middle. Judy Fallow, the therapist in charge of the participants' hand-eye coordination, watched every move the patients made and took notes on a writing pad. Her lips pursed as she stood tall above them. A scruffy faced man in a wheelchair sat next to her. His eyes focused on her like dull stones.

"Hello, Mr. Upland!" Jordanna spoke louder than normal to get his attention. A dank odor rose up from his red-and-black-checkered shirt as she bent to hug him. "How are you doing today?" She took a napkin from a nearby tray and wiped his mouth.

He nodded. "Doing okay, I guess."

"That's great. Glad to hear it." She forced a smile into her voice.

He rubbed his palms together, ready to begin.

"So have they been working you hard when I was away?"

"Oh, yes, it's been a picnic," he said dryly. "Pass the potato salad."

Jordanna grinned at his sense of humor. "That's a good one, Mr. Upland!"

A white-haired man sitting nearby looked over at them. His pink face puckered into a frown. In a far corner, a woman wore a black shawl and a flimsy floral dress. Toothless, she begged with her eyes. Jordanna didn't recognize either of them.

"How's your walking been?" she asked Mr. Upland. "Do you want to get out of the chair today and try to walk across the room?"

"I can walk fine. It's the balance I'm having trouble with," he said with frustration.

"Okay, let's see what you've got." She locked his chair and helped him step out.

While holding his arm, she guided him to the bar. He took it with an unsteady hand that revealed prominent blue veins under his onion-thin skin. Jordanna ached to watch him. He stood for a moment with the stance of a child about to dive into the deep end of a swimming pool for the first time. Gathering his courage, he took one step and then another. By the third step, he began to sway.

Jordanna jumped up to spare him from almost toppling over, but he grasped the bar in time to secure himself. He paused to regain his courage, breathing in and out through his mouth. Jordanna held her breath while he began to move again, mentally, taking each step with him. With every few steps, he reached out to clutch the bar, sometimes just letting his hand linger over it. His tongue drifted out of his mouth as he concentrated on his task. His pace was slow, yet he was able to walk the entire length of the bar and back. Cheers erupted from those who witnessed his performance.

"Very good, Mr. Upland!" she said with every ounce of conviction she could muster. "I'm proud of you!" She clapped louder and longer than anyone.

He stood motionless at the bar as he eyed the wheelchair.

"Okay, I guess that's good enough for now." She reached for his hand.

"No, no. It's not good enough. Not at all." His face contorted into a grimace, and he began to shake his head.

"Mr. Upland, it's okay. You're okay," she soothed.

"Everything okay?" asked Judy, who was still standing at the table.

Jordanna gave her a quick nod.

"No, it's not good enough. It will never be good enough until I can walk again." He gripped the bar. "Not until I walk again, without the bar...by myself!" The words were punctuated with spittle.

"You need to be patient with yourself, Mr. Upland. Look how much you've improved since my last visit."

"Hmmph," he said under his breath.

"I'm sure one day you'll walk on your own, but for now, you need to practice. Give yourself time." Jordanna took him by the arm for the few steps toward the wheelchair. He sighed as he plopped himself onto the leather seat.

The sight of the struggling people desperate for life as it used to be cut into her soul. She could have bled all over the room if it would lend more energy to their tired, wrinkled faces. She wanted to grab the markers from the knobby hands at the craft table and shove the blocks to the floor...take the residents by the hand and whirl them up and away. She longed for them to stand up. To dance. To walk. *Enough of this!*

She wanted the woman at the stove to throw away the rubber omelet and place a real egg inside the pan. *Enough! Stand up...stand up, everyone!*

On the table several newspapers with headlines popped—*Phillies Near Title...Carter Signs Peace Treaty*—while a dismal hum surrounded it all as though none of that was important. On the verge of tears, she wanted the slow motion to end. It was like a carnival ride out of control, and she longed to make the ride stop. If only she had the power to put everything back where it once had been.

"Good work, Mr. Upland. I think we've accomplished something today," she said once more, masking the ache in her chest with a cheerful expression. "I'm so proud of you!"

Mr. Upland sat with his head in his hands. His mottled hands slowly raked through his matted hair like sticks through a bird's nest. "It will not be good enough until the day I can walk out of here," he said bitterly while pressing his eyes shut, shoving the napkin to the floor.

5

SARAH BRONSON LIVED ON A QUIET CUL-DE-SAC in Mullica Hill, New Jersey. The lemon yellow Cape Cod sat back from the road in the shady comfort of a cluster of old pines, bordered by a worn driftwood fence. A row of crimson roses spread generously between the fence posts. In front, the mailbox hung askew and threatened to drop its contents at any moment. The precarious angle annoyed Jordanna, who wished the wind would upright it, or topple it over all together.

"I'm back, Mom," Jordanna called out from the foyer. "Got the mail."

"I'm in here," her mother's sweet voice answered from another room.

Jordanna, home for her monthly weekend visit, caught a glimpse of her reflection in the hall mirror. Her hair never stayed in place no matter what she did to it. She pulled out a brush, irked by its imperfection. "Such thick hair," hairdressers always remarked, as though it were something special they didn't see every day. Jordanna wished for a more manageable mane and would rather have thin hair than what she'd been blessed with, which was enough for three women.

"Mom, when are you going to get that stupid mail box fixed?" she asked, inspecting her face.

"Mr. Higgins said he'd take care of it," Sarah said from the kitchen.

"I'll believe it when I see it." Jordanna searched for a barrette in the bottom of her purse.

"He's very busy, I hate to bother him." Sarah hovered by the dishwasher.

"I know. But how long has it been? Also, the garage handle is loose again. I don't know if you noticed."

"I did, but—"

"If we had the right tools, I'd do it for you myself. Where do you keep the toolbox?"

"Oh, it's not important, Jordie. He'll get to it."

"You need to remind him, Mom."

Sarah puttered at the kitchen sink, moving slower now because of the palsy. Jordanna smoothed her hair, clipping the wind-blown strands back.

"You look best in short hair, Jordie." Sarah watched her from the kitchen.

Jordanna hoped her mother would not start harping about her hair again, feeling another unnecessary argument about to brew. But hair was not worthy of a fight. She knew her mother loved her. Almost too much sometimes. Sarah fussed about every square inch of her daughter's life. Being an only child, Jordanna found it hard to bear all of her mother's excessive devotion, sometimes wishing for a brother or sister to help spread her mother's laser-like focus on her every move.

"What's wrong with it long, Mom?" she said, trying to hide her annoyance.

"I just prefer short on you. A pixie."

"I look horrible with short hair."

"That's what you think."

But her mother didn't know of the times the kids at school made fun of her. Their mockery thrummed down the halls and out into the playground. *Monkey face, monkey face!* Of course, her teacher, Mr. Cohen, had complimented her haircut in front of the whole fifth grade class. Even as much as saying her new dress looked nice as well. But to Jordanna, having short hair was the bane of her existence. Upon entering sixth grade, she had hair caressing the top of her shoulders—resembling a mop, as her mother called it. But the mocking stopped.

Jordanna attempted to sway her mother off the subject. "Your cheeks got a little sunburned from walking the boardwalk yesterday.

"They did?" Sarah patted her face. "They do feel a little warm." She opened a drawer and pulled out a tube of cream. "That kid with the beach ball...you know, the one whose bathing suit was hanging half off? She kinda reminded me of Susie." Sarah applied a smear of white cream on her cheeks. "Remember the summer we spent in Beach Haven when she lost her bathing suit in the surf?"

"I remember," Jordanna said with a half-smile.

Sarah moved to the living room and sat down, reaching into her knitting bag to draw out a bright ball of yarn. She stopped to open an eyeglass case and put on a pair of glasses.

"I didn't know you wore glasses, Mom. When did you get those?"

"Shortly after I started this." She held up the yarn project she'd begun. "All this close work has ruined my eyes. I never should have started it."

She wished her mother had chosen a more flattering pair. The thick brown frames, more fitting for a man, deadened her mother's beauty. Her mother was still beautiful, though. High pink cheekbones off set by almost jet-black hair that her mother insisted was dark brown, lent a semblance to Elizabeth Taylor. Why would she deliberately choose such an awful pair of glasses?

"I know they're not attractive, but they'll do," Sarah said as though reading Jordanna's mind.

"What are you making?" Jordanna stared at the yarn, the color of cotton candy.

"I'm attempting an afghan."

"I hate knitting."

"You mean you don't *like* knitting," he mother reproved. "We don't *hate*."

Her mother obviously hated the word *hate*. "You have no patience, that's why," she said, her fingers lost in the yarn.

It wasn't so much patience. It was just plain boring. The last time Jordanna had done anything like it was in an eighth-grade home economics class, where she tried to begin a macramé project and ended up borrowing her friend Gail's macramé belt, turning it in as her own.

"Is there anything else I can do before I leave?" Jordanna glanced at the clock while playing with the ends of her hair.

Her mother raised her head and pulled off her glasses. "Oh, Jordie, there's always something to do around here." Sarah sighed as she panned the room. "But for now, I think I'm all right."

"How about the roses? They look so wild and overgrown. Do they need watering?" she asked, gesturing toward the patio.

"I haven't gotten around to them lately."

"They need to be clipped back for the winter. Do you want me to do it before I leave?"

"That would be wonderful. I meant to do it yesterday and then I got too busy."

"I don't mind doing it."

"You'll need gloves."

"Where are they?"

"I'm pretty sure I have a pair out in the shed," said Sarah as Jordanna was already one foot out the door.

Sarah's garden stretched along the back of a long railroad tie wall where tall fluffy grasses and several rose bushes nestled alongside clusters of spent baby's breath. A few budding mini roses sat unassumingly between several large boulder-sized rocks. The lone oak tree at the side of the house loomed larger than before. Its branches now grazed the edge of the roof and dwarfed the house by comparison, lending the yellow Cape Cod to more of a toy box. Overgrown hedges…chipped driveway. How many other things would soon be in need of care that her mother would not be able to handle?

Her mother said she'd been too busy even to tend the garden. Did that mean too tired? Jordanna didn't want to think about her mother aging. She went to the small shed in the back yard and brought out a pair of clippers and gardening gloves. One by one, she clipped the thorny rose branches back, wincing at the imagined pain she was inflicting. Plants had feelings, she always sensed. Why else would people talk to them? She snipped and trimmed until the bushes were half the height they'd been during the summer. Jordanna gathered the fractured limbs and placed them in the compost heap in her mother's garage. Afterward, she gave the garden a good soaking.

"It looks very good." Sarah stood at the patio door as Jordanna came inside and went directly to the bathroom to wash her hands. "Thank you, sweetheart, I really appreciate it. I hope it wasn't too much for you."

"The gardening? Not at all. I love it."

Jordanna came back into the room and gave her mother a hug. The citrus scent of her mother's Jean Nate perfume drifted up from her moist skin.

"Are you leaving now?" asked Sarah.

"I guess." Jordanna pulled quickly out of the embrace.

"Thank you for coming, sweetheart. Do you have enough money for the train?"

"Uh-huh."

"Oh, and don't forget the fruit." Sarah pointed to the bag on the dining room table. "You forgot it last time."

"Okay," Jordanna said flatly. She felt her mother's eyes lock on her.

"What's wrong, Jordie?"

"Nothing…why?"

"You have that look on your face."

"What look?" She examined the contents of the bag.

"Every time you get ready to go back to college, you have that same expression." Her mother's eyebrows furrowed. "Is everything okay?"

"Of course. Why wouldn't it be?"

"It doesn't sound so."

"I'm fine." She gathered her things. But things weren't fine, Jordanna knew.

"Is everything all right at school? Are you having any trouble?" her mother pressed, eyes imploring. She shifted her weight on her cane while keeping her eyes fixed on Jordanna. "I'm getting the feeling that you're unhappy there."

"No, it's not that I'm…unhappy."

"What is it, then?"

How did her mother probe her mind so well? Jordanna resolved not to tell her mother what was on her mind. Her mother had enough of her own problems than to bear hers, too.

"I don't know," she said, knowing that the truth was just on the verge of coming out, despite her not wanting to bring it up. It's just...that I keep thinking about Aunt Adelaide and Uncle John."

Pallor came over her mother, and she moved to her chair.

"And most of all, Susie. I think about her all the time lately."

Sarah bore a worried frown.

"It'll be all right," Jordanna said, resting a hand on her mother's shoulder. "Really, I'll be okay." Jordanna gathered her books and slung her handbag over her shoulder, noticing her mother's familiar drawn expression. "Mom, please don't look so upset."

"I just want you to be happy, Jordanna. It's all I've ever wanted," she said with finality.

"I'll be fine, really. Please don't worry so much, Mom. It's not healthy. And when you worry, I worry—about you." She offered her mother a weak smile before closing the door.

6

ON A COOL, NOVEMBER EVENING, heavy bass notes thumped across the Colton campus. The usually quiet college grounds, where night cricket chirping had been the featured music, had livened to the upbeat strains of rhythm and blues, courtesy of Delta Pi Epsilon's annual fraternity fundraiser dance. Jordanna and Beth, along with several others, walked down the path toward the gymnasium and entered the lobby where a crowd had gathered.

"I'll be right back," Jordanna told Beth before heading to the ladies' room. Not wanting to enter dances or parties too early, she preferred to arrive later—after the buzz started so as not to call attention to herself. On her way, she peeked inside the gym. A shiny disco ball cast flecks of sparkling light around the room. The only other source of light came from inside the snack bar, where sorority sisters Michele Lynd and Cheryl Pollock stacked soda cups. A few figures lined up against the wall.

Jordanna exited the ladies' room minutes later, wearing fresh lip gloss. "I'm sorry Dan won't be here."

"I know. Me, too." Beth grimaced as if she'd eaten cold vegetables.

They hung in the lobby for a few minutes until the booming of the DJ, whose amplifier was ramped up for a stadium, broke in. His voice cut through the semi-dark interior in a metallic decibel overload as the music started. A few people began to stir and move toward the middle of the floor. As the mixer came to life, Jordanna's insides fluttered thinking about Jeff. Would he be coming?

Resembling moving fish in dark waters, people maneuvered to find their bearings. Some gathered at the snack bar as moths flocking toward the light; others lingered along the walls and bleachers.

Kingsley Willoughby stood tall near the main door—a self-appointed sentry. When Debbie Hale walked by, he reached out and grabbed her arm. She spun and flashed her Chiclets-white teeth, pretending to be surprised. It reminded Jordanna of a toothpaste advertisement. Minutes later, they were on the dance floor, gyrating to the upbeat rhythm of the Jackson Five.

"Look at Kingsley," Beth said.

"You'd think he owned the place." Jordanna watched him dance. "He could use a lesson."

"I think he's cute...oh, there's Sharon. "Hey, Sharon!" Beth waved. "I'll be right back."

Couples gradually moved from the background shadows to the dance floor. Two by two, their bodies came together like butterflies in a summer garden. It took Jordanna back to her first junior high school dance, where she and her best friend stood awkwardly at the edge of the dark gymnasium. Insecure about their place in the social world they'd been thrust into, they clung together, wondering what would happen if they were actually approached and asked to dance. She'd watched enough of American Bandstand to know how to swing her hips. All fast dancing looked the same. "It's easy," she'd say when having to defend herself and prove that she knew how, before snapping her fingers and shaking her hips like crazy.

"Hey, Jordie," Jeff said.

Jordanna came alive at the sound of his voice as the mercury in the thermometer of her body climbed higher. He wedged both hands into his pockets in schoolboy fashion.

"Hi!" Momentarily self-conscious, she smiled her best smile. "I didn't know if you'd be coming."

"Hi, Jeff!" Beth walked up from behind him.

"Beth, how's it going?" he said with an upward nod, rocking back and forth on his heels as he looked over askance. "You thirsty?" he asked Jordanna.

"I'm fine for now, thanks." Her insides were bubbling.

She felt more than fine. She'd landed the attention of Jefferson James. Smart and good looking—that was a rare combination. Most of the guys on campus were nice, but most were not her type. Mike, one year her junior, caught her eye once, but somehow she lost interest—or didn't really feel comfortable having to tower over his short frame. Jack, a guy she'd met at the library, had made eyes at her—until she found out he was almost 20 years older and a flake. Perfection in a guy would be hard to come by. That's why she couldn't understand the good fortune to have someone as good as Jeff paying her attention. What had she done to deserve it?

"Kingsley's crazy." Jeff pointed to him gyrating in the center of the room. "He's tearing up the place. They should clear the floor for them." He winked at Jordanna.

"That's only for ballroom dancing." She giggled. "I guess he thinks he's John Travolta."

Kingsley jerked frenetically to keep up with the beat, swishing his hips awkwardly like he'd just learned to dance. He clapped his hands and then suddenly went down into a split on the dance floor. Jordanna squirmed at his foolish attempts at being cool. It was a daring move even the Temptations wouldn't have attempted. When the music stopped, Kingsley was still on the floor. He grimaced. Debbie Hale extended her arm to help him up, but he waved her away. He slowly managed to get up on his own. *Show off. He got what he deserved.* As he passed the snack bar on the way out, he forced a smile at some of his fraternity brothers, who lined the wall. His humiliation was evident. Jordanna flinched at seeing his chagrined face in the light of the snack bar. He limped out of the gym with Debbie not far behind.

Over the next hour, the DJ spun the familiar beats of the latest Top 40 records. Jordanna and Jeff danced nearly every song together, and she'd never felt more proud to be seen with him, hoping everyone noticed. Her happiness overflowed, turning into giddiness and rising somewhere above the twinkling disco ball high over their heads. She'd been here before—with others—the height of her affections reaching far beyond her grasp to rein them in. It was dangerous, she knew. But the natural high came so easily to her. What could she do but just enjoy the ride? She never knew when it would be over, but for now, she let it sweep her away.

At the beginning strains of a ballad, Jeff took Jordanna by the hand and brought her out to the far corner of the dance floor. He moved in to hold her, clinging tightly to her waist, and she put her arms around his neck. Her body melted into his as she lulled in the moment, breathing in the rich amber of his cologne. The song lyrics pulled her to another dimension: "We'll fly away…just you and me." The song could have played forever. Caught up in the moment, she lost track of time.

Suddenly, the scene on the sunny beach of her mind ended abruptly. She jolted as the DJ's mega-watt voice broke her reverie with his pronouncement the dance was over. When she unclasped her arms and the lights came on, she saw softness in Jeff's eyes. Was he in love? She could only hope. Her heart lifted and began to float inside her. He took her by the hand as they walked back to the bleachers to retrieve their coats when Tom Harkness, one of the Delta frat brothers, came toward them.

"Hey, Jeff!" Tom said.

"Tom…what's going on?"

"We're heading over to Minnella's. You coming?" he said.

"You want to go?" Jeff looked at her.

She shrugged, hoping her indifference would speak for itself. She had no intention of spending the rest of the night with his rowdy friends he could see anytime. Tonight she wanted him all to herself and hoped he felt the same way.

"Not sure, yet," Jeff said.

"Okay. Well, you know where to find us." Tom turned away.

"Yeah, later, man," said Jeff.

Jordanna tried to contain her joy…so happy that Jeff chose her over his friends.

"I'll see you back at the dorm," Beth told Jordanna with a wide smile.

Jordanna mouthed, *Thank you* to her friend, then reached for her coat—and Jeff.

*

Chimney smoke lingered in the cool night air. Hand in hand, Jeff and Jordanna took the long way around campus, past the baseball field and over the footbridge to the overhanging rock at Walden Pond. As they neared the rock, he stopped. She felt something good about to happen.

As though by instinct, they turned toward each other. With his arms around her waist, he pulled her in, pressing his lips lightly against hers before pulling them away. He moved to kiss her again—letting his mouth linger a moment before parting his lips wider. She mirrored what she felt and melted into him as his arms grew tighter around her. As he lifted his lips away, she longed to press into them again. Electricity rushed down her body. He kissed her once more before moving back to look in her eyes. His expression made her feel that she could have been the loveliest thing he'd ever seen.

He took her by the hand, and they began to walk again. She couldn't feel her feet as they followed the winding path back to the dorm. The moon shone like a slice of hot steel.

"I'm glad we didn't go to Minnella's," she said at the door to Key Hall, where he gazed at her with tenderness. "Sometimes your friends can be—"

"I know. Wild and crazy, right?" he replied with a tight grin and locked his eyes on her. "So, I'll see you soon?"

"That would be great." With a big smile, she nearly danced back to her room.

7

LIGHT STREAMED THROUGH THE DINING HALL. It fell low across the tables in long narrow chunks the color of butter where a few stragglers from the dinner crowd lingered. From a far table in the corner, someone's cackling laughter peeled across the room. Nothing could be *that* funny, Jordanna mused. She picked up one of the few remaining trays and scanned the hot bins of food, settling for a crusty chicken leg and a side of rice. The server scooped up the dregs of rice clinging to the bottom of the pan with the same type of utensil used for ice cream. Perhaps it was some sort of subliminal message? Cafeteria food needed all the favor it could get.

Soon she found a seat at the window with a view of the courtyard. The window of the newspaper office, one story above, looked gray in the retreating light. Remembering she'd left her journal there, she made a mental note to retrieve it later.

Leaving the dining hall, she rounded the corridor that led to the marble steps in the heart of the old mansion. As she caressed the coolness of the polished mahogany banister, she remembered the childhood times she'd slid down the rail as though it were a play ride. So many lovely days had been spent climbing up and down these marble steps. Glancing down from the top as a child, she'd shudder with an overwhelming fear at the thought of falling over the edge of the railing onto the white marble floor below.

After a stop at the mailroom to check her mail, she left by the side exit to head back to her dorm. Two steps outside the door, she remembered she had forgotten her journal just as the door slammed shut and locked itself behind her. She walked to the front of the building and went back in through the main entrance.

Upon entering the foyer, she plunged once more into the past. The image of the magnificent mansion when she was a child superimposed itself onto the present view, like a photographer placing a negative over another still picture in his darkroom.

All of the rooms had once been so extravagantly fashioned in the discriminating taste of her Aunt Adelaide Colton. Now they were stripped down to mere pragmatic function. Students passed in and out, oblivious to its former beauty and the tiny details her aunt had so meticulously ordered in an effort to make the house a home. The cherry wood artifacts, indoor fountains, pure gold fixtures. If only they knew how special this home had been. The furnishings had been imported from Spain or Cairo, or wherever Adelaide felt the longing to buy something and ship it back home. The long entry and marbled foyer had housed the finest artwork of Matisse and Chagall. Hung in fat gold frames, the pictures came alive in the shadows. Adelaide seemed to live for the finer things, Jordanna once heard her uncle say.

There was always a party or social event that Adelaide hosted at the estate. She organized social gatherings as easily as most people would plan their evening suppers. The upper crust in St. David's and Philadelphia, as well as around the globe, had been her guests. Rumor had it she had once dined with Matisse's daughter, Marguerite, one afternoon in Corsica after the war.

Now the walls were devoid of artwork and painted lackluster beige, resembling dirty lace. The most inspiring thing hanging in the foyer was the Dean's List.

Jordanna climbed the stairs to the east wing where the former bedrooms had been converted to more utilitarian functions. The master bedroom was now the cashier's office, and the sitting room now housed the president's office. Farther down the hall, the other bedrooms were converted into the yearbook and newspaper offices as well as the guidance office and the chaplain's facilities. Her aunt had kept some of the rooms locked back then, instructing that no one was allowed to enter. She and Susie had peered through the keyholes several times, wondering what could be so sacred inside.

Jordanna unlocked the door to the newspaper office. The room was quiet—as quiet as the library had ever been, so now was as good a time as any to do the English class assignment. In the half-light the fireplace loomed as foreboding as a foxhole. Jordanna moved toward the desk and picked up the journal right where she'd left it. The blank pages looked naked. She flicked on the light and sat down at the desk.

A half hour later, she finished her work and stretched before getting up to leave. Before she reached the door, an odd sound seemed to come from the window. She froze. Thoughts of Susie immediately flashed, drawing her back into the private world they once shared together....

"Look! There's a hand at the window!" Susie once had whispered from under the covers. They'd both squeal and pull the bedclothes over their heads.

"Stop, Susie, you're scaring me!" Jordanna said, all the while realizing it was just pretend.

Yet the plausibility lingered, and with it, a touch of fear. Jordanna countered by telling Susie there was a monster under the bed. Soon they would be safely asleep, yet the image of the hand at the window left a deep impression.

The sound came again, and the imagined hand at the window loomed in her mind. If only she could be that little girl again, playing make-believe safely under the bedclothes...the days before things changed forever in the Colton household, the day the family was torn apart.

The silence met with the rush of her own heart pulsing inside her ears. She held her breath and waited for the sound to come once more. If only it would come more repetitively, in an effort to give her more a sense of what it was—to give itself away before her imagination took over. It seemed to know her apprehension. Kept her waiting.

Was the man from the clearing out there? Could he have climbed up on the stone wall and managed to climb onto the upstairs veranda? She fought the desire to look over at the window—afraid of what she might see. "Walk through your fears," someone had told her once. "It's just a mind over matter situation. Push through and don't let your fears overtake you. It's all in your mind. Control it."

With anxiety rising, she aimed to distract herself. She focused on the desktop, its surface chipped and marred from age. She studied the embedded lines, pictured it when her Uncle John was still alive when he sat behind it reading his law reviews. She tried to rise above her fears, but her imagination had a mind of its own. Perspiration trickled from under her arms as the clock ticked in the shadows. Why did she have to forget her journal?

The wind howled and sent a low whistle through the trees. Moments later, the heavy scratching came once more. Soon she exhaled a sigh of relief at the realization of what had propelled the fear. It was nothing more than the wind lifting and rubbing a tree branch against the glass. An incoming storm maybe.

Ah, Susie.

After she locked the door and headed for the stairway, an impulse came over her to turn back in the opposite direction from where she came, farther down the hallway that curved back into the dark recesses of the wing. The only lighting was in the form of brass sconces that lined the walls in small pockets of light. They shed merely a few feet of light in each direction, barely piercing the long hall, leaving it mostly in yellow-gray shadows. The hallway looked different to her now. Not like the earlier days when she'd climb out of bed late at night for a glass of water, the hardwood floor cool on her feet. She'd try not to look at the shadows on the walls, fearful that they would evolve into faces, or worse, shift and follow close behind her. By morning, the sconces had looked different, more like the heads of sentinels, lending a somewhat less foreboding aura.

The clanging of dishes in the dining hall kitchen had ebbed by now to an intermittent clinking. The muffled snippets of conversation had all but ceased as well. She found it curious as to why this sudden urge to reverse her course had come over her. She passed the yearbook staff office tucked in its own mini-wing and, directly across from it, the marble-tiled bathroom with the huge claw-foot tub that had once frightened her. Up ahead was a tiny staircase that led to the attic.

It was at the end of the hallway...Susie's room. Uneasiness gripped her. Slowly walking toward it, barely breathing, she became all too aware of the imagined power ascribed to the darkness...and the unknown. The door shone in the same dark umber as she remembered. Kingsley Willoughby's words echoed. She didn't believe in ghosts, yet she wished she had brought someone along with her now. Alone in a dark hallway, the old horror stories she had heard at camp flooded back to haunt her, further empowering her own sense of dread.

The doorknob gleamed in the likes of a giant diamond. It was the original faceted crystal enclosed in brass. All of the doors in the wing had the same crystal doorknobs. She'd been inside all of the upstairs rooms at some point while she lived there and wondered how much had changed inside the room she shared with Susie.

Reaching for the door, she found it locked and let out a sigh, unaware she'd been holding her breath. As much as she wanted to go inside, she was relieved she couldn't open the door. Turning to leave, she cast her eyes ahead, and instantly her stomach tightened. At the top of the stairs stood the silhouette of a man. She didn't know what to do—stop, turn back, or just keep walking toward the stairway, closer to the person in the darkness.

The figure moved toward her. "Jordanna?" he asked, coming closer.

"Sarge? Thank God it's you."

"What's the matter?"

"You scared me." She raised her hand to her chest.

"Sorry, just making my rounds. What are you doing up here?"

"My heart. First the window and now you..."

"What window?"

"Oh, nothing. I left my journal in the newspaper office and then heard something—at the window. It was nothing, but you know..."

"I'm not a ghost," he said with a wry grin.

"When I heard something at the window, I nearly jumped out of my skin." She moved toward him. "Why is everything scarier when you're alone?"

With her journal in hand, she headed for the stairs. Before descending, she called back over to him, "Hey, Sarge, would you happen to have the key to the room at the end of the hall?"

Sarge stared at her for a moment without speaking. He appeared ghastly white by the light of the sconce peering down over him. "I might, why?"

"Oh, I was just curious as to what was in there."

Taking off his cap, he smoothed his hair before placing it back on his head. He gave her a strained look. "Curiosity killed the cat, Jordanna," he replied as he headed down the hall.

8

THE AFTERNOON SUN BOUNCED OFF THE NEWLY FALLEN SNOW and cast a brazen glare into the room. The light warmed Jordanna as it filtered through the window, caressing the back of her neck and shoulders while spreading over the floor in a warm mat. The ambiance of the newspaper office was especially nice now, during the holiday break when few were around. Other than the occasional purrs of a copy machine or muted fragments of conversation, which seeped through the heavy walls, the room remained silent. It was the perfect place to write the paper for her Winterim course in Christian-Marxist dialogue.

The hot cup of Earl Gray warmed her cold hands. As she breathed in the steam, her thought processes ebbed and flowed, moving languidly from the present to the past. People and places floated through her mind: Aunt Adelaide...Susie...summers on the estate. Thoughts of Jeff were never more than a beat away.

*

"More butter?" Hilda, the sweet Austrian caretaker, would ask them at breakfast while hovering over the table where Jordanna and Susie gobbled stacks of bread with generously sweetened tea. Hilda was up early every morning during Jordanna and her mother's summer visits to prepare breakfast for the family much the same as a loving grandmother, keeping the girls quiet and occupied while the others slept.

"Yes, please," the girls said, sometimes in unison. "And more tea, too."

Hilda's homemade bread and chutney butter were all they could want on those languid summer mornings before going outside to ride their bikes, racing each other in the cool of the shade trees. Their childhood days seemed to pass so slowly. An hour car ride would feel like forever. But at the same time, so fleeting it was....

How many years ago had that been? Yet it felt like yesterday, Jordanna mused. She wondered if Hilda were still alive. She couldn't have been much older than her aunt but probably had moved on to another home or gone back to Austria by now.

In the hallway, faint voices drifted before disappearing into the thick walls. She felt drawn, once again, to the end of the corridor and got up from the desk. Her footsteps echoed softly on the wooden floor as she drew closer to Susie's old room. Face to face with the door, she knew it was locked but reached for the doorknob anyway. It turned! Sarge must have unlocked it for her. He was so nice when he wanted to be, underneath his rough exterior.

Cool, dank air poured through the crack. Jordanna halted, riveted at the threshold, hesitating to go inside, yet intrigued as to what lay beyond. Visions of the beautiful pastoral mural, which once brought the walls of the room to life, came to her. Was it still there?

For a brief moment, she peered into the murky darkness. Something pulled from deep inside her. As much as she longed to go past the door, she closed it. Memories of her past lay just beyond the door. She wasn't ready to confront them.

*

By the end of the holiday break, the campus rhythm pulsed once more. A renewed energy flooded the dorms and classrooms, and once again, the novelty of another semester lay before them.

Jeff and Jordanna walked arm in arm along Chaminoux road on a quiet Saturday morning. A strong sun rose in the crystalline sky. Snow had fallen, and slushy remnants of the plowed streets clung to the curbs. Some of the lawns still had a fresh, virgin coating. Everything gleamed in icicles. The trees and pergolas resembled crystal-coated objects on a giant frosted birthday cake. The breath of joggers and dog walkers left trails of vapor as they made their way down the snowy streets—everyone bundled up in fur and flannel, like packages tied up neatly by flowing scarves. Curls of smoke wound out of the chimney tops of the Queen Annes and old Victorians. Their projecting oriels appeared to be coated in white gloves.

At the curbs, forlorn pine trees lay waiting to be picked up and tossed away, their purposes fulfilled. It amused her to see Christmas trees in their beginning stages of adoption—newly picked and anchored atop car roofs.

Once objects of admiration, gaily festooned in tiny sparkling lights and ornaments, now they lay abandoned with shreds of tinsel still attached. They rested on the curb in the image of praying hands adorned in silver bracelets.

The quiet of the morning hung thick and serene. The tranquility was gently roused when the church bells of St. Peter's tolled across town, its steeple rising sharply against the ice blue sky. Jeff ran ahead of her and scooped a handful of snow. He molded it into a ball and threw it at her.

"Hey!" She bent to dig her gloved hands deep into a thick pile of undisturbed snow, molding her own ball. "I'll throw it, don't you worry. When you're least expecting it, I will get you, Jeff James!"

Their playful banter grew into a more teasing exchange as they began to roll and wrestle on the snow-covered hill outside of Dr. Porter's house.

"Get off of me!" Jordanna feigned an indignant look as he grabbed her and pinned her to the ground.

"Now I've got you." He grinned as he climbed on top of her.

"Jeff, stop!" She faked a cry.

"What? What am I doing?" He had both of her arms in his firm grip, holding them above her head. "I'm not sure I see what all of the fuss is about." His eyes danced.

"Jeff...please." She was halfway to tears at this point and dropped the snowball she'd hoped to use for payback.

Down the hill came Dr. Porter's dog, Sandy. The Yellow Labrador had become a fixture around St. David's, as the dog could often be seen just about every day wandering the streets and occasionally popping up unexpectedly on campus. A friendly dog who rarely barked was now barking—at Jeff.

"Sandy, help me!" Jordanna said between bursts of laughter. "He's killing me. Sandy, help!"

In a matter of seconds, Sandy leapt up onto Jeff with her two front paws and managed to get herself on top of him. She straddled him flat on the ground.

"Get off me, you stupid dog!" Jeff half-chided, half-laughed. "Sandy, get off. Bad dog!"

The sight of the dog—now silent with its wagging tail—and Jeff underneath brought even more amusement to both of them.

"Sandy, it's okay. You can get off of him now." She pushed the dog gently out of the way. "Isn't that the cutest thing you've ever seen?"

"Oh, yeah, real cute," he said, getting up.

"He must think I need protection." She grinned.

"Crazy dog. You're a crazy dog, you know that, Sandy?"

The dog seemed to understand and gave a reply in the form of a single bark and ambled back up the hill, tongue hanging and tail wagging. Jeff got up and brushed the snow from his jeans. Jordanna found it odd that the dog had honed in like it did, coming to her rescue, somehow thinking that she may have been in danger.

*

St. David's business district stirred with early morning shoppers. Several storefront windows held strands of holiday gold and silver garland ceremoniously tacked up along the perimeters. The faint tinkling of bell chimes rang as customers went in and out of the drugstore. On the hill by the train station, a plastic blow-up replica of Santa Claus lay spent and lifeless on the ground by an evergreen, his job done for another year.

Jeff and Jordanna entered the corner café. The air smelled rich with espresso.

"Oh, good, our table is empty." She pointed to the corner where the private table was partly obscured from the rest of the café.

The glazed windows cast a diffused, other worldly light into the room. Jordanna felt more at peace than she had in a while as she snuggled into the booth, gently warmed by the sunlight. Glancing across the table, she watched Jeff, already perusing the menu. Did she have a place in his life? What were his intentions after graduation? There was a mystery about him that she couldn't quite read. She longed to hear the words *I love you* and wondered when they'd come. Most guys would have said something personal by now. They always had. He was different than the others.

"Are you taking Economics this semester?" She put down her menu.

"Uh, huh, I've got Inwood."

"Did you know that Dr. Inwood travels all the way from California to Colton just to teach here?" she said, hoping he'd be impressed with knowing the bit of trivia.

"Yeah, I heard. It's pretty cool."

"It's amazing. He's so dedicated to his teaching."

"I can't figure out what drives him."

"Probably an airplane," she said with a mock grin.

His eyes lit up from behind his wire frames as he smiled at her across the table. A waitress came to take their orders. A moment later, she felt his stare again. "You look good," he said.

"Thanks." She felt herself blush and wondered what he really meant.

Her hand lingered on the table, and he reached over to cover it with his own. "You still thinking about law school?"

"Not sure now." She took a sip of water. "I had hopes of following in my uncle's shoes, but the stories about law school seem to make the task of becoming a lawyer a trial in itself."

"I'm sure."

"Besides, I think we've got enough lawyers in America."

"You'd be great, Jordie."

Jordanna smiled. "You think?"

"Well, you fight for every underdog."

"I'm just a softy." She chuckled. "The other case lawyer in court would probably make mincemeat out of me."

"No, you'd beat them to it." He grinned.

"What's going on with Dr. Belden's class?" she asked.

"He wants me to do a project for the annual business show. He buttonholed me in the hall the other day."

"He always looks wound up and running at full tilt."

"He's a ball of energy. Never quits."

"How's the class coming?"

"It's a cake course."

"Are you going?"

"Well, Joe Thompson and I are putting something together, but I don't have any concrete ideas yet."

"I can help, if you want," she said. "That is, if you want the help of a lowly English major."

"Right now, we can use all the help we can get."

The scent of hot food wafted up as the waitress came back to place their food on the table.

"This soup is good," Jordanna said. "How's yours?"

"Great." He scooped his clam chowder.

"I wish the college had food like this."

"Doesn't everybody?"

They hungrily ate their soup and grilled cheese sandwiches.

"May I?" he said later, eyeing her untouched potato chips.

"Take all of them. I'm trying to stay away from fried foods."

"Health nut?" he asked while crunching.

"Kind of...but I wouldn't go that far."

"How'd you become so health conscious?" He popped another chip into his mouth.

"I don't know, really. I guess pretty much since my mother never let me have too many sweets as a kid," she said, hoping she wouldn't get too caught up in her words and risk boring him. "The time I came home from a neighbor's birthday party and felt nauseated later that night from eating too much ice cream and cake...well, it changed things."

"Your mother's efforts sunk."

"Actually, she didn't say a word, but I learned my lesson. I haven't had much cake since then."

He lifted a brow. "Not a bite?"

"Well, not the way I ate it back then as a six-year-old. You know, five pieces shoveled in, followed by a pint of ice cream."

Jeff smiled.

"But I sometimes have trouble resisting a nice, warm, chocolate-chip cookie. Speaking of which, can we stop at the health food store on the way back? It's right across the street."

"Sure, why not?" He signaled the waitress for the check.

"They have the coolest stuff in that store. And the best cookies, too. I think they make them right on the premises."

"Don't shovel them in too fast," he said with a decided grin.

"Funny." She slipped on her coat.

*

The buttery walls and lacey curtains of the health food store resembled a large, old-fashioned kitchen rather than a place of business.

"I love this store," she said as they entered.

The ambiance was as warm as a hug to her. They perused the aisles where shelf upon shelf held quirky items she'd never seen anywhere else—certainly nothing that would be offered at the college dining hall.

"I think I'll buy some carob-chip cookies...and some dried papaya sticks," she said as she turned the corner. "Do you want anything? My treat." She glanced back to where he stood perusing the dried fruits. "Maybe some chamomile tea? Or green?"

He shrugged an okay.

"I'll get both, and we can share it," she added as they approached the counter. The words hung heavy. For a moment, she felt embarrassed at the familiarity of her remark. It sounded as though they were perhaps already married. She peeked back to see his reaction, but he'd gone farther down the aisle. Hopefully, he didn't hear. What would he think if he knew that she'd

40

already envisioned them married? She'd muse over her name and his together on address labels and Christmas cards. She loved the alliteration of it—*Jeff and Jordanna James.*

"Hi, Mr. Sweeney," Jordanna called to the proprietor as he came from the back room.

"Hello," he replied before ringing up the purchases. His face keenly bent over the cash register in an effort to read the numbers. "Did you find everything you need?"

"Yes, thanks. I could browse your store all day," she said, her eyes still roaming.

A minute later, he handed her the register receipt before mumbling good-bye and hastening into the back room as if there were something more pressing he had to do.

Outside, the cold air had mellowed to mild. The sun sparkled as they journeyed back to campus.

"This day is perfect for skiing." Jordanna inhaled deeply.

"Actually, I've never been on skis," he admitted.

"No skiing…ever? What about ice skating?"

"The last time I did that, I fell on my butt. They gave me my brother's skates that were way too big. My ankles kept wobbling, and I kept falling down."

Jordanna laughed. "I can just picture that!" They sauntered down the street, past Dr. Porter's house. "Hey, where's my guard dog?"

"I don't know where he is, but you're going to need him soon." He grabbed her and nuzzled her neck. "I guess he wandered off to attack another innocent victim or something."

Jordanna broke free. "Sandy, where are you ol' dog? I need you," she called in a mocking, desperate plea for Sandy's help. Then she broke into a light jog, looking back at Jeff to see if he were joining her.

"You won't find him," he shouted to her as she increased her stride. "I gave him a bone when you weren't looking, and now he's my friend. We've bonded, Jordie, so you're on your own now. No more protection for you!"

With that, she giggled and ran down the hill. "Oh, Jeff, but I still have you, don't I?" she jovially called back to him.

He reached down to pick up a handful of snow. "I don't know," he shouted as he ran to catch up with her, unobtrusively placing the snowball into her hood as he strode up to match her pace.

"You're not my protector?" she said.

"You keep running away from me." He shoved her hood up over her head and ran past her.

"Jeff!" she cried as the snow fell down her back. "I'm going to kill you!" She raced to catch up with him. As they rounded the curve toward campus, some children were tobogganing down the hill by Dane Hall.

"Oh, look!" Jordanna pointed. "That looks like fun."

Jeff slowed his pace down just enough to let her catch up with him. He stopped short and reached for her as she approached him. They held their embrace and fell back together into a clean pile of snow.

"About that protector thing." He gazed into her eyes. "It sounds like a good idea to me. Maybe one day I could be more."

Jordanna melted at his words.

9

"I'M GOING DOWNSTAIRS TO STUDY AND DO LAUNDRY," said Beth as she searched the back of her closet. "Do you have anything you need washed?"

"No, I'm good, thanks." Jordanna looked up from a magazine. An O'Jay's song blared on the radio.

"I hope no one's down there. I really need to do some serious studying." Beth poked into the little pink box on her dresser that contained spare change.

"Why don't you just study in here?"

"Well, you've got the radio on and all..."

"Oh, I'm sorry. I don't need it on all the time." Jordanna reached over to turn it off.

"No, no, it's okay. I don't mind studying in the lounge." Beth lifted the overstuffed Xerox box—her makeshift laundry basket, now ripping at the corners. "I'll be back in a couple of hours."

*

Beth entered the laundry room and turned on the light. She unpacked and sorted her clothes before loading them into the empty machines. Farther down the hallway was the basement lounge. The room had a raw feeling, void of nuance. A worn plaid Ethan Allen sofa in brown and white sat on the far wall along with a couple of matching beat-up chairs. Against the other wall sat an old relic of an RCA television. If not for the cheery yellow color of the walls, the room would have been even more depressing under the harsh light.

She plopped into an overstuffed leather chair and sorted through her notes. The hissing of the overhead fluorescent light strips running along the ceiling along with the muffled chugging of the washing machines was just the right amount of dull background noise to help her study. She got up later to switch the clothes into the dryer. Coming back into the lounge, she settled once again into the chair, now warmed with her own body heat, and picked up her textbook.

After she'd read for an hour or so, eventually drowsiness overcame her. When the words began to dance on the page, she lost focus and nodded off.

It was close to dinnertime before she woke up and noticed the first stages of gray twilight at the window. She also noticed something she didn't expect to see: a face at the window.

*

Jordanna heard a knock at the door. When she opened it, upper classmen Bowden Wright and Laurel Clarke stood there grinning like two mischievous cats.

"Hey, Jordie," they chortled in unison.

"Hi, guys!" said Jordanna.

"We wanted to discuss something with you," Bowden said.

"May we come in?" Laurel asked.

"Sure." Jordanna pulled the door open wide and stepped back to let them pass.

"Well, we want you to know that we had you in mind for Entertainment Editor of the *Spotlight*," Laurel explained with an easygoing smile. "Since your freelance material has been so well received, we thought—"

Bowden broke in. "Your piece on the homeless situation in Philadelphia was great. Would you be interested?"

Jordanna hesitated but delighted inwardly at the invitation.

"You can think about it if you want," Laurel said. "But we know you'd do a great job."

"It's a bi-weekly paper as you know," added Bowden, handing her a copy of the newspaper.

"This is such an honor!" Jordanna took the paper, feeling her face flush.

"We thought you'd be perfect for it." Laurel chewed on a pencil. "And Dr. Morgan and Dr. Bradley both recommended you."

"Really? I'm so flattered!"

"So what do you think?"asked Laurel.

Jordanna beamed. "I think it's great. Sure, why not?"

"We thought you'd be a perfect fit for the job," Bowden said. "We're having a meeting next Monday night in Walden. At seven."

"We usually meet about once a month or so…just the immediate staff," Laurel said. "You know Bill Sorrello and Rich Capito, right?"

"Oh, sure."

"Great." Bowden looked at Laurel. "I guess that's all, right?"

Laurel nodded as they moved to the door.

"Monday night at seven," Bowden reminded.

"Okay, I'll be there. And thanks!"

Downstairs in the basement lounge, Beth sat stunned. While blood rushed to her ears, she pretended not to notice the strange face staring at her through the window and looked back down at her textbook.

God, what do I do?

She could no longer concentrate. The black text blurred and dissolved as she attempted to focus on the words. She wondered how long he'd been looking at her and wished it were her imagination. Stifling an urge to scream or call attention to her fear, she casually picked up her books and nonchalantly left the lounge. At the stairwell, she raced up the stairs, hurtling them two at a time.

She banged her shin on the last step, and her papers scattered over the landing. "Ouch," she uttered, swiftly retrieving the papers before stumbling up the rest of the stairs. Bursting into her room, she slammed the door and locked it.

Jordanna frowned. "What's wrong?"

"A man...I saw a—a man...he—he was looking in the window, the lounge window," Beth managed. "I think it was the Peeping Tom...the one they were talking about over at Guffing Hall."

"A man? What did he look like?"

"Dark hair. Really creepy."

*

Jordanna grew uneasy as she recalled her own eerie encounter last year in the clearing behind Cott Hall.

"Any facial hair?"

"A fuzzy kind of beard. He had a lewd expression."

"Dark hair?

"Uh, huh."

"I'll go call security." Jordanna slowly opened the door and looked both ways before running for the campus phone. She got a sick feeling in the pit of her stomach.

10

WALDEN HALL'S STUDENT UNION STOOD STATELY among the tall evergreens. Like a sleeping lion, the mansion commanded the crest of Walden Hill while its reflection shimmered on the pond below. As a child, Jordanna pictured herself as the matriarch of the whole estate while in the backseat of her uncle's car as it rounded the hill on the smooth, winding macadam.

The grip of winter, which had once settled over the campus, began to ease. The air crackled with impending warmth as lifeblood slowly seeped back into the frozen landscape. Lofty firs—their boughs gently coated with melting snow—glowed in the distant shadows while inklings of new life sprouted up along the fields and stretched toward the surrounding hills like the first breath of spring.

"Hey, I've been meaning to check out something in Walden—on the third floor. You mind going with me?" Jordanna said to Beth as they headed for the Student Union.

"When?"

"After lunch, maybe?"

"The third floor?" Beth winced at the suggestion. "Why? What's up there?"

"Well, I guess just some old furniture and stuff," said Jordanna. "You know, artifacts, stuff like that. I thought I'd do some research for an article for the *Spotlight*."

"On what?"

"The Colton family."

"Oh, like a retrospective or something?"

"Yeah, I guess. Frankly, I'd like to set the record straight about the story."

"What story?"

"Susie Colton. How she died and all," Jordanna said squarely.

"They say she committed suicide."

Her matter-of-fact manner annoyed Jordanna. "They? Who's they?"

"Everyone. Haven't you heard the rumor?"

"If it's just a rumor, Beth, how does anyone know how she really died? Why would they presume to know if they weren't there?" Her voice escalated as a thread of anger rose from deep inside her.

46

"Okay, you don't have to get so defensive." Beth's eyes flashed.

"I'm sorry. I'm just tired of hearing people like Kingsley Willoughby and his ilk trying to make the girl look like a freak or something. Doesn't he have anything else to talk about?"

"You've heard about Walden, haven't you?"

"What? Like there's a supposed ghost up there?" Jordanna said with a hint of derision.

"Yeah, I heard Kingsley and a bunch of them talking about it. Someone said one of the freshmen got so frightened that she transferred to another college."

"Because of a stupid story like ghosts up in Walden?"

"I guess."

"That's ridiculous." Jordanna eyed her. "I don't believe in stuff like that, do you?"

"Not really," she said with a shrug. "But some people around here do."

Beth and Jordanna entered the Student Union and went upstairs after checking their mail. The lunch line was so long, it wrapped all the way around the cafeteria. At a quarter past twelve, the line was barely moving.

"It's not usually this crowded," Jordanna said. "What are they serving, Chateaubriand?"

"Today's special is London Broil." Beth pointed to the posted menu.

"Ah, close enough. No wonder. I guess we should come back later. This line is barely moving. Why don't we go upstairs and check out the third floor and then come back?"

"Now?"

"Sure, why not?"

"I'm starving." Beth held her stomach.

"It won't take long. Besides, we're wasting our time standing in this stupid line."

A group of fraternity guys entered the lunch line led by Kingsley Willoughby, whose voice was so loud it could easily rise above the sea of voices at a fully packed football stadium.

"Hey, girls!" said Kingsley as he and his buddies sauntered past some of the cheerleaders in line by the coat rack. They hung their coats and turned to chat with them.

"Hey, Kingsley!" Debbie Hale greeted him with her trademark smile.

"Kingsley thinks he's God's gift," Jordanna said as they passed the swaggering trio. "Always with his entourage."

"Oh, he's all right," Beth said. "His buddies Dave and Kenny are okay."

"You're kidding. You think Kingsley's all right? He's a jerk. Besides, he talks through his hat, telling people that stupid rumor. It's really getting old."

"The rumor about Susie Colton, that she's alive and well and living—"

"Yes, Beth, that one," Jordanna sounded snappish even to herself.

"But what about Sarge? He's said the same thing."

"Oh, I don't believe that!"

"You sound perturbed, Jordie. Is something else bugging you?"

"No, why?" Her words belied the curtness obvious to both of them.

"I don't know. Just a thought," said Beth, trying to assuage the escalation.

"There's just a look in his eye that kind of sees right through me," Jordanna said under her breath.

"What?"

"Something in his eye disturbs me. Maybe it's just my imagination."

"Who, Kingsley? He just wants to be liked, Jordie," Beth said as they left the dining hall.

As they ascended the stairs, the voices in the cafeteria below dwindled into a soft murmur before dissolving altogether. By the third floor, Jordanna's anger had simmered, but she had not forgotten her mission to prove Kingsley and the rest of the college wrong about Susie Colton.

"I always feel like I'm in an old Shelly Winters movie when I'm up here," Beth said in a hushed tone as they made their way along the long, thin corridor.

Jordanna felt the same way. Walden didn't seem as frightening to her with the beat of everyday life drumming in the rooms and hallways, rising up through the stairwell. But once the silence took over, the ambiance changed. The walls on the third floor seemed thick with secrets that wanted to come out. As much as Jordanna was afraid to be alone in the mansion, she found herself drawn nevertheless, almost helplessly, as the pull from within would not let up. Jordanna led the way down the hallway. As they approached the last door at the end of the hall, Beth stopped short.

"What is it?" Jordanna said.

"I don't know," Beth whispered. "I'm not sure about this."

"It's nothing. It's just an old room. What's there to be frightened of?"

As they stood in front of the door, Beth's eyes grew large. "We're going *in* there?"

"It's okay. We can just look from here. We don't have to go in if you don't want to." Jordanna turned the knob. With a long creak, the door opened into darkness, and the familiar cool, dank odor drifted by.

"I can't!" Beth cowered toward the wall.

48

"Oh, come on, Beth, I'm right here with you."

"I'm sorry, Jordie, I'm spooked. I guess it's a case of mind over matter, but I keep thinking about the rumor."

Still holding the doorknob, a sense of dread came over Jordanna, and she promptly shut the door.

"I heard that someone was up in one of the top floor rooms walking around and saw something that he won't even talk about," Beth said.

"Yeah? Like what?"

"He says he can't talk about it because what he saw was so disturbing. He was really spooked by it, they say."

"Who won't talk about it?" asked Jordanna.

"Sarge."

11

ENGLISH PROFESSOR EUGENE BRADLEY'S OFFICE DOOR STOOD AJAR. His burly body hunched over his roll-top desk while he feverishly worked his pen across a yellow writing tablet. Jordanna hovered outside the door, hesitant to interrupt him even though she had an appointment. She checked her hair in the reflection of a picture frame in the hallway.

A moment later, he gestured with the formality of a doorman. "Jordanna, come in and have a seat." He returned to his desk.

The small spindled chair in front of the bookcase sat in the same place it had been the last time she'd visited. Had no one else sat in it since? She knew other female students—Laurel Clarke and Bowden Wright—and how they flocked to his office like honeybees. Of course, they had to meet with him as he was the proctor for the college's *Spotlight*. But Jordanna felt special sitting in his office with only personal issues at stake and that she'd been invited to share them. She was sure there were others who might have wished to receive his wisdom, but she coveted the idea that it was a special, almost exclusive thing, to be given a portion of his time.

Her eyes panned the room like a paintbrush moving over his pictures, books, and plaques on the walls with tiny engraved writing too small to make out. With respect for his privacy, she never let her eyes settle on anything for too long for fear of seeming intrusive—wishing more for a photographic mind so as to capture everything quickly and set it to memory to retrieve later, away from his notice.

She strained to see the face in the big frame on his desk. The woman had long dark hair and a faint smile like the Mona Lisa. Jordanna tried to match the lady's relationship to him. Wife…daughter…? She let her eyes linger as long as she could before becoming too obviously interested. *Who is she?* It would seem like such a superficial comment, one that a child would ask. Unless she used the word *paramour. Is that your…paramour?* But she could never be that familiar with him and would rather be kept guessing than show any signs of impropriety.

She studied it as long as she could before she averted her eyes in an effort to feign disinterest, letting them casually drift somewhere else to maintain her propriety.

A large wooden bookcase stacked to the ceiling bulged to overflowing with books. Had he read them all? The room grew still. His dark eyes peered through his thick glasses like tiny beads.

"So how are you?" he asked in a serious tone. He leaned back in his large black leather chair and positioned both arms squarely on the armrests.

"I'm fine, thanks." She mustered a coolness she didn't really own. Aware of his introspective stare, she wondered what he really thought of her.

"So what's on your mind? Anything you'd like to discuss stays right here, Jordanna, you know that, right?" He had the voice of God.

She nodded with assurance. Eugene Bradley's face was covered for the most part with hair. Eyes, nose, and lips filled in the gaps where the hair left off. His thick beard reminded her of steel wool. It made his round pink lips more so by comparison. Pink and gray were known to complement each other, she'd learned in art class. But she'd heard that a man with a full beard is probably hiding something. He had the kind of face that commanded attention, and she strained to see behind the so-called mask.

"You mentioned a boy before in our last session, a student...Jeff, was it?"

"Yes."

"I'm assuming you're serious with this fellow?"

"I am...yes." She nodded with a smile.

"I don't know him personally, but he seems like a very solid individual."

"I think so, too," she said. "And that's why I'm here."

His keen eyes turned soft and rounded behind his thick glasses.

"Well, first of all, Dr. B, I just want to thank you for your sessions over the past several months, and, well, since I don't have a father, I was wondering if I could ask you a favor?"

His dark jacket lent a priestly impression. She pictured him delivering his lectures, a divine counselor, his voice reverberating over the congregation.

"What is it?"

"I'd like to know if I could have your blessing?"

"My blessing?" He sounded perplexed.

"Yes, I'd like your blessing on my marriage. Jeff and I plan to be married."

She knew she could leave her heart on his big roll-top desk and it would be safe there. He looked at her intently. His eyes held hers and, in the moment, she felt the penetration of his stare, as though his eyes themselves had the power to lift her heart out of her own chest.

"Jeff's asked you to marry him?" He rubbed his mouth.

"Well, no, not yet, but our relationship is serious. I can see it in his eyes."

"You know by just his eyes?" He shifted in his chair, leaning further back.

"Well." She laughed nervously. "I guess you could call it a sixth sense. You know what I mean, don't you?"

His face stiffened as he placed his hands behind his head. "Jordanna, please understand something." He straightened and looked up at the ceiling while searching for the words. "Oh, dear, how do I begin…" His gaze dropped to the floor. After a moment, he met her eyes. "Jordanna, I like you, and I think you're a warm, sensitive, young woman. I do. But what I'm about to tell you may seem harsh, and I don't want to hurt you."

"What do you mean, Dr. B?" Her heart began to race as though he were a doctor about to tell her that she was sterile or had cancer.

"Jordanna, I can't give you my blessing." He leaned toward her. His eyes shrunk behind his glasses.

"Why not?"

"Frankly, I don't think you're ready for marriage."

"What do you mean? I'm not good enough to be someone's wife?" Blood rushed to her face. "You don't think Jeff is suited to me?"

"No, Jordanna, it's not that at all."

"Then what is it?"

He squirmed in his chair. Moments later, he leaned toward her again. He placed his hands on his thighs and spoke low. "The truth is that you don't love yourself, Jordanna."

Love myself? What is he talking about? Her muscles tensed as he explained his thoughts.

"It comes from a place of maturity and growth. You're still a child."

"I'm an adult. I'm almost 21." She spoke with surety.

"I'm not talking about age. Age has little or nothing to do with it. You can be 50 and still not love yourself."

She mentally retreated from him. *He doesn't know what he's talking about,* she thought. *Love myself? What kind of foolish talk is this?*

"You have to learn how to love and accept yourself first, before you can be married." His eyes were imploring, his voice soft and almost fatherly.

She could feel his sincerity. He wanted to take away the pain of the truth as quickly as it stung her, as any loving father would. She thought his wisdom would help her, but for now, his words tasted like bitter wine. "How will I know when I'm ready?"

"Just wait, Jordanna. You need to wait." He sat back and rubbed his hands on the arms of his leather chair as though they'd grown cold. His eyes bounced over her face, imperative that she understand. "You're covering up your hatred of yourself by putting on someone else's love for you. You suck it up too quickly. That's a mark that something is empty inside. You need to do it by yourself. You need to learn to love yourself."

She pictured the dry, yellow sponge in the kitchenette right off the downstairs lounge in Key Hall. It sat above the grimy sink next to the cleanser. She chafed at the comparison. "I love myself! How can you say that I don't? I love myself as much as anybody else. Laurel, Bowden? Am I so different from them?"

"I think you want to love yourself, Jordanna. I think you're desperate to do so."

"How do I do it?"

"That's between you and God. But right now, something's holding you back."

12

Early spring, 1981

BETH BRISCO UNWOUND THE TOWEL she'd wrapped turban-style around her head and picked up a thick black comb. "What time are we supposed to be at Rich's house?" she asked as she drew it through her shiny black hair.

"I guess around nine or so." Jordanna bent toward the mirror to inspect her face.

"What are you wearing?"

"I'm still deciding. I guess the turquoise angora."

"I love that sweater. Makes your eyes stand out." Beth plugged in her hair dryer.

Jordanna stepped away from the mirror and stood in front of her open closet. Her clothes hung neat and organized, with every blouse, skirt, and sweater in separate sections, arranged according to season. A knock sounded at the door.

"Jordie, phone," came the voice.

The scent of lavender drifted in as Jordanna opened the door. "Thanks, Julie." She hurried to take the call and closed the door behind her.

"Jeff said you and Dan can ride with us," Jordanna said on her way back in.

"Good. Dan's car is on the fritz." She swiveled, her body generous with curves. "Do these pants look too tight?"

"No, not really." Jordanna shook her head.

Beth seemed unconvinced as Jordanna slipped on her jeans. "I wish I had your figure," Beth said. "How do you stay so slim?"

"It's genetic. My dad was tall and thin," Jordanna explained, trying to deflect her pride onto just dumb luck.

"My parents are both short and Italian. Our family celebrates everything with pasta and meatballs." Beth rolled her eyes. "Are you *sure* these aren't tight?"

"Well, you don't look poured into them, if that's what you mean. You look great...really. Your curves are generous, but they're all in the right places, Bethy."

"Thanks for your honesty, Jordie. You're one of the few people I can really trust."

"Besides, Dan's smitten with you. You don't have to impress him anymore, right?" Jordanna grinned. "I'm still working on my relationship."

"Oh, come on now. Jeff is so in love with you, it's not even funny." Beth buttoned her blouse. "His feeling for you couldn't be more obvious."

Jordanna's heart leapt at her words.

*

Rich Capito's parents were out of town, leaving him with free reign of the residence for the weekend. At a quarter after ten, 280 Spring Lake Road changed from a quiet dwelling to a thrumming house party sizzling with sparks of young love and loud music. Most of Rich's friends from the Delta fraternity were there along with a dozen or so from their sister sorority, Alpha Pi Sigma. They spread themselves in clusters, migrating from room to room, in typical party fashion like they owned the place. Hamburgers, hot dogs, chips, and soda were plentiful. It was hard to tell if hard liquor was in the punchbowl. Only time would tell.

Some danced or gathered by the pool table downstairs. Some just mingled with their drinks in hand, enjoying the social scene or hoping to be seen. Kingsley sat in the living room with his arm draped along the back of the Capito's lizard green couch. He nestled against Debbie Hale, his prey for the evening. A Tiffany lamp on the nearby table bathed them both in a pale pinkish light. Debbie wore a painted smile as Kingsley grazed his face close to her ear. He looked ready to pounce—a ready lion and only minutes away from turning the light off. Poor Debbie.

Jordanna scanned the noisy crowd spread throughout the great room and enclosed patio, trying to find Jeff, who'd wandered off. In the far corner, Beth and Dan cuddled across from the punch bowl. She drifted over to one of the tables where cheese cubes, crackers, and crudités along with pretzels, potato chips, and dips sat in bright ceramic bowls. She scoured the tables for something healthy, settling for some carrot sticks and a pretzel.

"You wanna drink, Jordanna?" Rich asked from behind the bar where a television was tuned to *Saturday Night Live.*

"Oh, no, thanks. I'm fine, Rich," she said with a smile. "Have you seen Jeff?"

"Uh…actually, I haven't." He rubbed his finger under his nose while walking away.

One of the frat brothers, Kenny Fairchild, saddled up to her, hung his arm around her neck, and breathed into her ear. "Hi, Jordanna!"

She tried to ease away from his hot, alcohol-laden breath without making a scene. "Hi, Ken, what's going on?" She rubbed the salt from the pretzel and wished he'd remove his arm.

"Enjoying the party?" He looked at her hungrily. His glazed eyes grew big as he let them roam over her.

"Hey, have you seen Jeff?" she said, slowly moving away from him.

"Jeff? Oh, yeah, awhile ago. He was outside."

"Oh, so that's why I couldn't find him. Thanks, Ken."

He grabbed a handful of pretzels. As Jordanna stepped away, he grabbed her arm. "Jordanna," he said, still crunching.

She turned back around.

"You know he's still in a relationship with his old girlfriend?"

Suddenly, the music stopped and the room turned dark. As though on stage with a bad case of stage fright, she began to stammer. "M-maryanne?"

"Yeah." He grinned. "He went back home to Sicklerville to see her last weekend when you were away."

"Where'd you hear that, Ken?"

Her knees felt rubbery as the blood rushed to her face. Bits of pretzel crumbs stuck to his bottom lip. She cringed when he smiled. Even in the dim party lights, she noticed pretzel caked between his teeth.

With a smug smile he said, "Oh, I heard Kingsley mention it, I think." He reached for another pretzel and popped it into his mouth.

Kingsley. Of course, her own personal pariah. Now she disdained him even more. What was it about him that rubbed her the wrong way? Jordanna's insides roiled at Ken's words. This didn't sound like Jeff. The way he looked at her. The way he spoke to her. He seemed so genuine. His blue eyes so sincere. Now it appeared she was mistaken. He'd embarrassed her.

How had she been so wrong? But she'd only brought it on herself, she thought, jumping for the first person who paid her any attention at Colton as though she were desperate for it...sucking it in as though a baby at her mother's breast. She'd always been this way. It had been no different at Sarah Lawrence or in high school. She always wanted someone by her side. Her choice of boyfriends had always been wrong.

Dr. Bradley was right. How silly she felt now. The blood spread from her face down to her core and back into her limbs, rendering her weak and shaky, yet energized with her own outrage. She wanted to confront Jeff and went through the motions of the scene in her head, how she would approach him.

Then she thought how ridiculous it would look and mentally played out her tack, preferring a more subtle way to deal with her hurt. She did not believe in overcoming evil with evil; that would be wrong. But she deserved better. She deserved to know the truth about his feelings for her. Why did the truth always elude her?

Hoping the low lights of the room were dim enough not to give away her crushed feelings, and without a word to anyone, she exited the house.

13

CRISP LEAVES SCRAPED THE SIDEWALK as the night wind stirred. The thin angora sweater did little to keep her warm. The cold night air had no sentiment. Jordanna chided herself for not having the foresight to bring a jacket. She steeled her body to the swiftly dropping temperature, which cut through to her core, and stuffed her hands into her pockets before breaking into a jog. The cold stab of air didn't compare to the emotional blow she'd already received at the party when she'd heard about Jeff going back to an old flame.

The wind cut sharply as she turned from Spring Lake onto West Avenue, where somber, sleeping houses retired under a sliver of moonlight. In the commercial district, farther up the street, bold light intruded from the 24-hour convenience store onto the quiet street, spreading itself without apology. Next door to it, the health food store she often frequented looked different by night. Without its butter-yellow walls and curtains visible, the storefront looked plain, like any other. Appearances could be deceiving, that was for sure.

The Waynesboro train station stood stark and brooding on the hill. The last train must have pulled out hours ago. At the corner of West Avenue and Waynesboro Street, a lone car sat at the light. A man was at the wheel. She couldn't pull her eyes away fast enough before his face turned toward her. Like the touch of a hot stove, she cringed at the contact, regretting her curiosity, and continued her stride, hoping she hadn't given off a desperate vibe. She sensed he was needy, and she, obviously was vulnerable. She moved past the car, turned left, and followed the sidewalk that led to a tunnel under the train tracks.

In the darkness of the tunnel, she guided her way along by tapping her finger against the wall, detesting the imagined sooty grime packed into the cinder blocks. Moments later, the car engine revved. Headlights flashed against the tunnel walls, exposing her for a brief moment. The car slowed through the tunnel and passed by, leaving her walking in darkness alone once more with just the echo of her steps. It had to be close to midnight.

Just beyond the end of the tunnel, the streetlights appeared, casting enough light to see the sidewalk. The white circles of light, like stage spotlights, would lead the way safely back to the college. She kept her eye on the car and found it odd that the driver was now pulling up in front of the neighborhood deli about 100 feet ahead. The storefront was dark and had a *Closed* sign on the door. Why would he choose to park in front of a closed store at this hour? Her body stiffened. Paranoia gripped at the thought of him getting out of his car, possibly to follow her on foot. Each step in the direction of her destination felt wrong. She did an abrupt 180 and ran back into the dark tunnel.

The once intrusive lights of the 24-hour convenience store around the corner now spread out like a welcome mat. The warm scent of roasting meat lingered near the hot dog rotisserie as several hot dogs rotated inside the machine, even at this late hour. She moved away from the window and stood at the end of the counter with the pretense of buying something. Without any money with her, how long could she could pull off the charade? She turned down the first aisle, eyeing the stocked shelves.

Eventually, a group of loud, older kids came into the store as she came back to the front. She got a sense they didn't go to Colton or were perhaps drunk. A brawny guy who wore a leather jacket bought cigarettes while the others stood by the stacks of newspapers. A tall, redheaded girl sucked a bright green lollipop. Jordanna hoped to catch someone's eye so she could ask them for a ride back to campus. Would the redhead empathize with her situation? A lone female…out late at night.

She tried to get a read on her. The girl looked old enough to have tasted disappointment. She flirted with one of the guys as he ogled her. Jordanna wished she could have been part of it, part of their group, and longed to make a connection. But there was no place for her there, and the redhead never noticed Jordanna. No one did.

While she was disappointed to watch them leave, it felt right to let them go. She'd rather be alone in the convenience store than with four strangers who may have been drunk, or worse—drugged. She warmed her hands on the hot pretzel machine. How was she going to make it back to the campus? She had no intention of walking back alone, not now.

After a silent prayer, she stepped outside onto the brightly lit sidewalk. Concerned, but not desperate, she paced and prayed in the cool night air. A few cars passed. Then a hush came over the street when the night drew in for good.

It reminded her of midnight on New Year's Eve when she was 12 and had gone outside and heard the noise of revelers celebrating the New Year. The sounds of horns and banging pots came from somewhere down the street. She'd hung in the doorway, as cold as it was, and stared into the black night

59

sky until the reveling stopped and silence descended. It didn't feel any different. Just another midnight.

Across the street, the hair salon she frequented had a light on. How odd that anyone would be there at this time of night. A minute later, the light went off and the door opened. Vince, the owner, came out and locked the door behind him.

"Vince!" she shouted.

He looked up as he approached the car parked in front of the store.

She dashed across the street. "Could you give me a ride back to my campus?" she asked, jogging toward him.

"Jordanna? What are you doing out here at this hour?"

"Oh, I was at a party and decided to leave."

"Sure, hop in." He unlocked the car.

She opened the door and settled on the cold leather seat.

"You shouldn't be walking around alone." He started the engine.

She felt awkward sitting in his big black Cadillac but relieved and safe as he started the engine and pulled into the street. He approached the intersection where she'd made eye contact earlier with the man in the car. As Vince drove through the tunnel and out again, she looked over at the deli where the man had parked his car not long before.

The car was gone.

14

JORDANNA AWOKE DEPRESSED THE FOLLOWING MORNING. Before opening her eyes from a restive sleep, she remembered the lewdness of Kenny Fairchild at the party. His stare. The words that broke her spirit. The thought of Jeff lying to her about his former girlfriend hit like a Mack truck all over again. She wished it had been just another bad dream. Truth had been so important to her. She thought Jeff had been better than that. But apparently, he was no different from all the others.

Beth's bed lay empty. She vaguely remembered Beth asking if she wanted to go to church or something like that earlier, but she must have been half asleep.

Her alarm clock flashed 9:58 in green neon. She could make the campus Chapel service in Walden if she got up now. Although more content to curl up and feel sorry for herself, she threw back the covers. If anyone had ever turned her down, it wouldn't be God, although she hadn't paid much attention to her spiritual life lately. Her eyes sunk beneath a red, puffy outline in the bathroom mirror. Grief from the night before still clung like a vice. She silently let out more tears under the spray of the hot shower.

*

A late winter chill gripped the morning air. The faint chirp of a lone bird that had come back from its warm winter habitat, possibly too soon, pierced the silence. After chapel services on campus, she walked back to the dorm, taking the route that led past the gymnasium. Nearing the security office, she stepped up to peer through the window on the door. Sarge lay reclined in his chair watching television. After knocking gently on the glass, he turned and gestured her in.

"What's up?" he said, rising.

"Oh, nothing, really...just thought I'd stop by and say hi. Hope I'm not bothering you."

"Nope, not at all. Just watching an old movie." He sat back and folded his hands together, placing them on his waist like a belt.

She surveyed the room. Not much had changed since the first time she'd entered this room. It had been a year ago—last summer—while working as a lifeguard at the college's swim club....

*

The sun had dipped low in the sky and resembled a blood orange when she eyed Sarge over by the fence near the shallow end of the pool. As she sat on duty in the lifeguard chair, a heavy-set lady in a chartreuse bathing suit did her laps like an old steamboat chugging up and down the Mississippi. Sarge rested both hands on the fence as he focused on something. When the lady finished her swim and climbed out of the water, Jordanna came down from the stand and began to straighten the lounge chairs near to where he stood.

"Hi, Sarge!" she said. "What's going on?"

"Not much."

"The sunset is gorgeous, isn't it?"

He nodded. His rugged bronze face glowed in the orange light. "Listen, I was wondering if you've had dinner yet?" he asked matter-of-factly.

"Actually, I'm starved and was about ready to head to the dining hall. Why?"

"Well, I have a t-bone steak over in my room that I can't finish...was wondering if you'd want to take the rest of it?"

"Steak, really?" she said. She couldn't believe this grouchy old man had any kindness in him. What did she do to deserve it? The serendipity of his gesture made her smile. She could feel his defenses slowly diminish and her own as well. Sarge nodded and headed over to his room. A few minutes later he came back with a China plate. On it was a good-sized portion of a t-bone steak wrapped in plastic wrap along with a stainless steel knife and fork.

"I kept the bone for Toby." He eyed the dog. "I hope you don't mind."

"Sarge, this is too kind of you. Thank you so much." She flashed him a smile, then studied the plate. "Why don't you want this? It looks delicious."

"Well, I can't digest it too well since my cancer. Truth is, I have a goat stomach."

"A goat stomach?" she asked, going along with him, thinking he was just teasing her.

"Actually, 75 percent of my stomach is goat. I had stomach cancer a few years ago, and they gave me a new stomach." He patted his midsection.

Jordanna had never heard of such a thing, but his expression was so sincere that she began to realize the truth in his words. "I'm so sorry," she said, her tone sympathetic.

"When I eat too much, I can't digest it, and then I'm back in the hospital. Had to give up booze, too. But I'm alive, and I really don't care about the booze anymore. It's great to be alive." Sarge regarded her with an awkward half smile, then tipped his cap at her. "Enjoy it...glad to give it to you."

The succulent steak oozed red juice over the white china. It resembled the beef from the red-pink roast beef slabs when her mother took her to their favorite cafeteria-style restaurant in Baltimore. The chef wore a tall white hat and stood behind the large hunks of hot beef in the manner of a father proud of his toddlers.

*

Now, a year later, she stood inside the room again. The cramped office glowed overly bright for its size, magnifying every blemish on the pocked walls and scuffed woodwork. Crammed inside the room were a metal desk, cot, a small grill, sink, small white refrigerator, leather chair, and a 12-inch television, all of which could easily fill up a room twice its size. Around the corner, an old mahogany bookcase was stuffed with paperbacks. A row of grainy sepia prints hung on the wall; a layer of dust coated the tops of the frames. A solitary black and white picture hung by itself on the opposite corner—a curly haired toddler and a little dog. She wondered how lonely Sarge must have been living alone after hearing he'd lost his wife a long time ago.

"So this is your hideaway, huh?" She'd always had an inkling this room was his permanent residence, but her tongue always felt heavy when the topic of his personal life came up.

"Got all the comforts of home." He took a thick black mug to the sink and poured out the dregs, then turned off the television. "So how's college life treating you?" he asked, putting on his cap.

"It's good...classes are going pretty well this semester compared to last. It was rough there for a while—you know, getting adjusted to the pace. Not at all like it was in high school."

"I took a few college courses once but eventually dropped out...later enrolled in the service," he said with a wistful smile.

She took note of the pictures again. She focused on one of a group of men in military uniform standing in front of an airplane. "Where'd you serve?"

"Air Force."

"Is that you here?" She pointed to the picture of the B-29.

"Yep, me and my crew."

She paused at each picture, lending a rightful respect for the subject matter. She hated military photos—they all looked alike: grim faces that bore the same, solemn expressions.

"I'm going on my rounds in a minute…need a ride anywhere?" he said, adjusting his cap.

"No, thanks."

"You sure?" He picked up his keys.

"Yeah, I'm good."

An awkward silence hung between them as they stood alone in the room. She was grateful that he broke the quiet moment with the necessity to go back to work. She wanted to ask him about all of the pictures on his wall—who were the people and when were the pictures taken—but her curiosity was somehow usurped by shyness. One picture that captured her attention was of the little girl and her dog. The beautiful child looked to be about two or three years old.

Even more so, she wanted to ask him about Walden Hall and what he may or may not have seen up in the attic. Was Beth correct? Did he pretend that he saw something to play on the minds of the impressionable freshman as part of a hazing, pay-your-dues kind of initiation? Or was there something more?

15

ESSENCE OF WARM CHICORY WAFTED BY as Jordanna entered the dark café where Dr. Morgan sat alone by the window. "Hi!" Jordanna slipped into the black leather booth across from her professor.

"Hey, there. How are you?"

"Okay."

"You don't sound it." The professor's eyes crinkled in a discerning glance.

"Oh, it's nothing. Hey, this was a good idea." Jordanna changed the subject.

"Sometimes I need to get off campus once in a while," Dr. Morgan said. "Besides, I love the coffee here."

"Me, too. I love walking into town, especially on days like today. Hope I didn't keep you waiting too long."

"Not at all. I just got here."

"I love your sweater." Jordanna gestured toward the thick cable knit. "It looks so cozy."

"Thank you. It's my mother's."

"How is she?"

"She's doing wonderfully. Actually, she's taking a course right now, believe it or not!"

"You're kidding…another course? Your mother is so amazing!"

A waitress stepped up to the table holding two menus.

"I'll take a cup of chamomile," said Jordanna.

"Coffee for me, thanks," said Dr. Morgan. She leaned toward Jordanna. "So how do you like the student teaching?" She propped herself up on her elbows as a concerned look drew itself into her eyes and mouth.

"I was a little nervous at first, but I'm getting used to it. I just try to mirror you for the most part."

"It's not so hard once you establish an upfront relationship with the class. Let them know you're comfortable working with them. That allows them to open up."

"I guess it'll get easier with time."

"You're doing fine. I've noticed your improvement. You're getting more involved each week." Dr. Morgan nodded quickly like a bobble-head doll.

"What should I prepare for next week's class?"

"I was thinking we'll go over the essays on poverty and pick out the three best ones to use as examples. We'll divide the class into small groups."

"I thought Linda's story on the sharecroppers was wonderful," said Jordanna.

"Oh, yes, I agree. And Joe's story about his brother and the fire was also a good one. Except for all of the sentence fragments."

"You sound like Dr. Bradley!"

Dr. Morgan rolled her eyes.

"You know, how he's always talking about how fragmented society is and all," said Jordanna.

"Ah, those fragment scoundrels," Dr. Morgan mused. "They're everywhere."

Jordanna drew her finger over the top of the table. The wood grain contained swirls of orange and brown and was etched with deep scratches. Others who sat there before her had carved their initials into the wood...*T.L. loves A.B.* Others had carved their names...*Debby loves Bobby.* She traced the etchings backwards and forwards.

"So how are you otherwise?" Dr. Morgan asked. "You don't seem yourself lately."

Jordanna looked into Dr. Morgan's floppy brown eyes. They held a kindness that drew her in. "Well, it's my love life. Troubles again. I can't seem to shake them." She hated the sound of her words.

"I'm listening." Dr. Morgan rested her chin on top of her clasped hands.

"I met with Dr. Bradley and was so excited to tell him about Jeff. Now I feel like such a fool. You know, for having such enthusiasm about him."

"What happened...if I may be so blunt?"

"Since my father's dead and all, I wanted Dr. Bradley's blessing—his approval about Jeff and I getting married. One day, that is."

"Jeff James?"

"Yes."

"What did he say?"

"He said I wasn't ready for marriage—that I didn't really know what love is."

"Ah, I've heard him mention that before."

"What's worse, he said I don't love myself! Really, what does that mean?"

"Ah, Jordanna, if I knew that..."

"Who doesn't love themselves? And how does this have anything to do with my future marriage?"

66

"Why do you feel the need to be married so soon?"

"Jeff and I...we have—or *used* to have—this special bond and...well, isn't that what the world does?"

"You're still so young, Jordanna. You need to see the world before you settle down and marry. What's the rush?"

"Well, when two people are in love, they're meant to be together."

"Yes, well...as far as love goes, you know there are different kinds of love."

"What do you mean? Like agape love...brotherly love?"

"Yes, there's that, but I mean more like being in love with love itself. You know, like the love songs talk about. People in love. It's a romantic feeling and it fades rather quickly. And then there's a kind of love where one enjoys *being* loved or enjoys *the act of* loving someone. But in either case, it doesn't necessarily come from a place of true love."

"I don't see anything wrong with that. I mean, who doesn't want to be loved or to love someone else? What's the harm in that?"

Dr. Morgan regarded her curiously.

"Well, it really doesn't matter now since Jeff and I have broken up. I've prayed about it, but I don't seem to be getting any answers from God lately."

"Oh, I'm sorry to hear that."

"I thought we had a great relationship, but now it seems like he's dating his old girlfriend."

"How do you know? Did he tell you?"

"No, someone else did. One of his friends said he'd gone back to see her one weekend when I was away."

"Have you spoken to him about it?"

"I haven't talked to him. I'm afraid to, really."

"What are you afraid of, Jordanna?"

Just then, the waitress came over and placed two mugs on the table along with a carafe of hot water and a basket of tea bags.

Jordanna welcomed the intrusion. She warmed her hands on the steaming cup, hoping for the steam to lift the answers from deep inside her. The answers she had never considered before. "I guess I'm afraid to lose him."

"Why do you suppose that is?"

"I guess I want to be loved?"

"You don't feel loved without a boyfriend?"

"I don't know. I hadn't thought much about it."

"Maybe that's what Dr. Bradley was talking about when he said that you don't love yourself," said Dr. Morgan while putting her coffee cup down.

"What do you mean?"

"You need someone else to do it for you."

"Love myself?"

"Yes. When did your father die?"

"When I was five, why?"

"Well, I'm no psychologist, and I'm not for sure, but..."

"But what, Dr. Morgan?"

"It seems to me that you miss your father. I think you're looking for him in Jeff and in the others. When they don't measure up, you dump them. Or run away."

"I guess."

"Have you tried to work things out with these boyfriends or with Jeff?"

"Of course, that's all I've ever done. I've begged and pleaded with some of them, but the more I push, they more *they* run away from me."

"Perhaps you're trying too hard. People know when you're desperate."

"I know. That's why I don't want to talk to Jeff. I'm afraid he'll run away, too, like all of the others."

Dr. Morgan took a sip of her coffee. Her soft brown eyes turned serious. "Give yourself time. There's no rush. Let things progress naturally and don't try to manipulate them. Life's a process. Do your part and let God take care of the rest."

Jordanna let her words soak in. Pressing her hands around the cup, she raised it to her cheek to warm her face and hands and thought about her long-deceased father, whom she barely knew.

16

THROUGH THE OVERCAST SKY, the afternoon sun struggled to break free. *The angels are fighting the devils*, Jordanna's mother had always remarked when the weather didn't know which way to go. Jordanna sat restless in the last remaining minutes of her medieval history class watching the rain through the speckled gray-lit windows. In the far distance, Walden Hall loomed in the misty shadows.

The morning downpour now tapered to a fine mist as Jordanna pushed open the side door of Maginess Hall and headed straight for the Student Union. As she turned to enter Walden, she spotted Sarge coming in from the opposite direction.

"Hey, Sarge!"

He looked up and gave her an upward nod.

"I was wondering something…" She hesitated. "Would it be possible for you to do me a favor?"

"Like what?" He cocked his head.

"Could you go with me to the attic in Walden?"

"The attic? What for?" he said quizzically.

"I'm doing a project."

He lifted his eyes to somewhere over her head in the direction of Walden, then looked back down at her. "I guess so."

"If you have the time," she added.

"I was just going up to the snack bar. Come on, I'm buying."

Over hot cups of cocoa, Jordanna and Sarge shared a table in a corner of the student lounge. In the filtered half-light streaming from the skylight, she noticed the intensity of his eyes. Deep blue and penetrating, like the color of children's marbles, the icy edge they once held had softened. He took a bite of a doughnut and some of the powder scattered onto his chin.

"You know, that doughnut's going to kill you," she said with a grimace.

"Hey, we're all going to die of something." He took another bite.

"It's your life," she said with jovial sarcasm, feeling the stirrings of a father-daughter budding relationship.

When he finished his doughnut, he wiped his mouth. "Okay, you ready?"

"Yep." She took one last sip of her cocoa, now lukewarm.

They left the lounge and climbed the stairs to the third floor. Jordanna led the way down the corridor. As they neared Susie's old room, Jordanna's stomach twisted with excitement.

"Sarge, can we check out this room first?" She pointed to Susie's door.

He pulled out a huge key ring.

"Funny thing, the other day when I came by, the door wasn't locked," she said.

"Really? Don't know how that could be."

"You mean, you didn't unlock it for me?"

"Now why would I do that?" he said, trying one key after another.

"I don't know." She laughed nervously. "Weird, I guess."

"The door should remain locked." He firmly inserted a third key and turned the knob. The dry hinges rubbed together as the door opened.

Taking a step into the room, she tried to contain her emotions. Clusters of spider webs dangled along the ceiling. On the large wall was the countryside mural, just as she remembered. Her heart grew so light it lifted. She walked farther inside and realized she stood alone.

"Aren't you coming in?" she said, turning toward him.

Sarge lingered by the door, leaning up against the threshold with his arms crossed protectively across his chest. "See anything interesting?" He took a step while looking around as though walking into enemy territory. "Looks like just a bunch of old furniture is all." His eyes skimmed the room.

"It's old, but it's beautiful. This chest of drawers and the poster bed..." She wandered toward the window overlooking the pond.

The last time she saw the green water below, it was through the jagged glass of a broken window that had been partially obscured by a curtain rod, which hung precariously on the sill. Now the window was intact and by its appearance, did not look at all damaged the way it had been on that fated August morning years ago when her cousin fell to her death.

Jordanna remembered that day as if it were yesterday....

*

"Mommy, Mommy what happened?" Jordanna cried, running into her mother's arms.

"There's been an accident," Sarah said, holding Jordanna tightly.

"Where's Susie?"

Her mother stooped down, picked up her daughter, and whispered soothing words to calm her.

70

"What happened, Mommy?"

"It'll be all right, Jordie...it'll be all right," Sarah said. "One day it will be all right...."

*

Jordanna snapped back into the present. Sarge stood opposite her at the other end of the window. He peered out, his face somber in the shrouded light. The windowpane—glazed from years of wind and rainstorms—was still semi-transparent through the crust and smudges. She recognized the view. The only change was the trees that had grown taller. Their leaves and branches now gathered just above the window like the heads of curious children wanting to reach inside. Walden Pond sat below, its sparkling water bathed in sunlight while mallards rested along its banks. She took it all in with Sarge at her side and, for a moment, she forgot to breathe.

"It's so peaceful, isn't it?" She spoke a bit above a whisper. "Like nothing bad should ever happen here." She spoke her thoughts out loud and then turned toward the mural on the wall. The aesthetic scene of a make-believe countryside drew her in, it always had—a town of storybook character where evil did not know its way inside, or so it appeared. Tudors and Victorians sprouted jewel-like on floating hills once the color of pure emeralds while bounties of pines and maples rooted with pride along a slender blue creek. Cobwebs had stretched their own handiwork across the faded colors like lines upon an aging princess. Yet the beauty of the bucolic setting still shone through.

This had always been her favorite room in the house. She spent long hours in the make-believe town painted on the wall, gazing and dreaming of her place in it. She stepped over the dusty floorboards and fondled the smooth wood of the poster-bed frame in the corner where she slept soundly and dreamt her little girl dreams. It was hard to believe the furniture was still in such good shape. Time stood still for a moment.

Sarge slowly pulled himself away from the window and moved toward the door. Sensing he wanted to leave, she turned to follow. "I wonder what the attic looks like?" she said at his heels.

He looked at his watch.

"Is it okay to see one more room?"

"I guess. I have a few more minutes."

The attic stairs creaked under their weight. The familiar odor of dusty pine was just as pungent now as the days when she and Susie ran up and down the stairs, racing to be first. The stairway seemed even narrower now as though it had shrunk with age.

Sarge led the way inside and flicked on the light. A single, unadorned light bulb cast a weak circle of light on the dusty floor. He aimed the flashlight onto the floorboards, then onto the back wall where an old Georgian armoire stood half open, revealing a crackled mirror. The ruffle of a burgundy gown poked out at the bottom. Although crinkled and dusty, Jordanna thought it possibly the same gown she'd seen in a picture of her Aunt Adelaide at a cotillion or some formal affair as a young girl. Two more formals hung next to it in faded jewel tones.

Next to the armoire was a scroll-top desk. She recognized it as the same one as in her aunt and uncle's room, where a crystal decanter once sat on top of it along with a quill fountain pen bearing a big chartreuse feather. Jordanna liked to watch the big feather bounce as her aunt wrote, finding it comical. She wondered if it tickled her hand. In another corner, large stacks of books and boxes lay strewn in a jumbled heap on the floor.

"Look at all of this stuff! And all these books…" Jordanna mused.

Sarge aimed his flashlight into a corner of the room. Behind the piles of books, several watercolors and oil paintings were stacked against the wall. One picture formerly hung above the fountain in the downstairs foyer—a great blue heron on the water in a thick ornamental frame. Nearby sat a wrought-iron bust of someone's head.

She gasped. "Yikes, that's scary! I wonder who *that* is?"

Sarge didn't speak.

On the other side of the room, a few more large pieces of furniture sat clumped together, covered partly in sheets. As she walked back around, the pile of books she initially noticed drew her attention again. She paused to examine some of them up close—volumes of classic literature…Voltaire, Keats, Shelley. Surely, these must have belonged to her Aunt Adelaide while some others, like the Law Review books and journals, most likely belonged to her Uncle John.

Sarge stood by the door. She hoped she wasn't detaining him too much from his duties. He didn't appear at all hampered by her foray and was now patiently leaning at the threshold. He gave the impression that he was mesmerized by something.

"Sarge," she called from across the room.

He appeared deep in thought.

"Sarge? I hope I'm not keeping you from anything important."

"It's fine, Jordanna."

She turned back toward the books. Spotting an interesting one, she bent to pick it up. Wiping the dust off, she opened it. It was a poetry book with an inscription on the inside cover: *To Addie, with love, Paul.*

She held onto it and moved back to the armoire to rummage through the clothes again. In one of the larger drawers, a gold lamé clutch bag glimmered through a thick layer of dust. She remained drawn to the old armoire. At first, the dusty formals had intrigued her, but now something else drew her curiosity.

Below the dresses were three little drawers with tiny knobs. Kneeling on the floor, she opened the top drawer and looked inside. Finding it empty, she moved onto the second drawer, which was empty as well, but the third yielded something deep in the back, stuck to the drawer bottom. She pried out a small, brown leather book with gold embossing on the edges.

"Look at this," she said, amazed. "It's someone's diary!" She rooted around the bottom of the drawer. "Maybe there's a key somewhere," she said as she reached back and forth under some clothing and checked each of the drawers again. She clutched the mildewed book of poetry and the old soft leather diary like ill-fated prizes. "Well, no key here, but I'll find a way to open it."

Sarge glanced at his watch.

"Is it getting late?" she said, sensing his distraction.

"I'd better get back now."

"Oh," she said, taken aback. "Sorry to have kept you, Sarge." She scanned the room once more. She wasn't ready to go. The shadowed walls were dark and barren, but just beyond, something thrummed from within.

They left the attic and descended the narrow staircase back into the corridor. The kitchen crew had already begun the dinner preparations for later that evening as the essence of simmering stew permeated the hall. Once outside, Sarge turned toward Maginess Hall.

"Let me know if you find anything good—you know, in there." He pointed to the diary.

"Will do," she said with a wave.

Sarge gave a resigned smile. His face was still grave.

17

"BETH, YOU WON'T BELIEVE WHAT WE SAW in Walden Hall today!" Jordanna said as she burst into the room. "Oops, sorry to interrupt your workout."

"Who's we?" Beth looked up from her yoga pose.

"Sarge and I."

"You went up there?"

"Yeah, Sarge took me."

"What was it like? Did you see or hear anything weird—like a ghost or voices or—"

"No, Beth. No voices, no ghosts," she said flatly. "Actually, there was this statue thing of some guy's head, which scared me to death, but other than that, only furniture and stuff. We found all of these old books and clothes, and I found the coolest thing buried deep inside an old armoire—a diary!"

Jordanna grabbed a pair of scissors and sliced open the little piece of leather attached to the lock. The pages had yellowed, but the ink was still clear and legible. Under the flickering desk lamp, they sat reading the words...

March 23, 1943
We arrived back in the States after a long plane ride. Father has found us a nice house on a beautiful tree-lined, brick road in San Romero. I finally get my own room. I love it! It's so big and bright, and there's a veranda right off of my bedroom. I can smell the honeysuckle drifting up into my window. I love Florida!

July 17, 1944
Went to the beach and had a great time with Grace and Dolly and the gang. Tomorrow is Lena's party.

"Look at this!" Jordanna skimmed the pages.

May 23, 1945
I will marry tomorrow! I am so very, very happy. Mother has outdone herself orchestrating the whole event. John and I will be married at St. Paul's at 4 o'clock and then off to the cricket club for our reception. Dining and dancing...it will be a glorious event!

September 11, 1946
Our new home is like a dream house—big, stone and sprawling! I don't
know how I'll be able to maintain it by myself. I feel like a princess!

Jordanna and Beth sat transfixed while skimming through the diary. The
flowery scripted handwriting filled page after page. They sucked in the words
as though reading a romance novel for the first time.

"Wow!" said Beth. "She must have had an exciting life."

"I know. It's unbelievable." Jordanna fanned the pages.

"It's like a fairy tale life. I wonder who the diary belongs to."

The desk lamp began to flicker.

"You need a brighter light. I can barely read the words," said Beth.

In the middle of the diary there was a loosely folded page tucked inside.
At the bottom of the letter was a signature—*Always, Paul.*

Jordanna frowned. "Where's the rest of the letter? This can't be all there
is…just a closing, *Always, Paul.*"

Beth shrugged. "Maybe it's back in Walden, in the attic."

"This guy gave her a book, too." Jordanna opened the front flap of the
poetry book. She pointed to the inscription. "Look at this."

"Hmmm. Sounds romantic." Beth stood and wiped her face on the towel
around her neck. "Sorry, I can't stick around to read more…have a psyche
test." She picked up her notebook and headed for the door. "Be back later. Let
me know what you find."

"Okay and good luck," Jordanna said as the door closed.

Sitting alone with the diary, it didn't take long before Jordanna surmised
the owner of the diary. She was certain that it had to belong to her aunt,
Adelaide Colton. She flushed at the recollection as she skimmed through the
delicate pages, careful not to tear them. She wondered about the letter. Just
who was this person, Paul? Page after page in the same grandiose flourishes,
Adelaide described in long accolades the special times and events of her life.

The desk lamp flickered again, and finally it went out all together.
Jordanna made a mental note to ask Fuzz for another light bulb.

She put the diary away in her drawer and sat down to study. She tried to
get her head into the words of her textbook, but swirling thoughts left her
unable to focus. What remained foremost in her mind was not only the letter
she'd found, but Jeff. He hounded her every waking thought, and her feelings
for him would not wane. But the more she tried to put him out of her mind,
the more he lingered.

Eventually, Beth would be coming back to the room. Would it be wise to share with her roommate her relationship to the Coltons, especially her Aunt Adelaide, now that she knew about the diary? Jordanna had kept the story to herself for so long and had grown comfortable with her secret. It felt safe to hide behind the knowledge. But she didn't know how long she'd be able to keep her secret to herself.

18

LONG SHADOWS STRETCHED OVER WALDEN POND. The last bits of sunlight filtered across the horizon as the campus blushed to gold. Jordanna found solace as she passed by the pond on the way to Walden Hall. The crickets sang a gentle chorus. By now, the task of investigating the third floor of the old mansion would prove not as daunting as it once had. Her fears about being alone had not so much waned but were usurped by a more ardent need to find information about her family, particularly Susie, as well as the rest of Paul's letter. Urgency pressed in on her, coupled with a growing nostalgia. Its power seemed unrelenting, as though the fulcrum by which her energy fused. Her desire to set the record straight about her cousin weighed more than any irrational fears about the ghosts or other strangers.

As she neared the gym, the squeaks of rubber-soled feet and the *thwack* of a basketball inside left her anxious that Jeff might be around. She went inside to check out who was on the court. Of course, if he were there, she'd be struck dumbfounded, not knowing what to do or say, despite the scenarios she'd played out in her head where running into him and feigning disinterest were her first order. She'd want to play it cool, the same way she'd practiced in her imagination. Or pretend even not to notice him. That would be even more daring.

Despite her pretenses, she couldn't fool herself. She longed for him to approach her, to beg her to speak with him. She wanted to be his girl, his only love. But for what...another lie? Two-timer. She should have known her relationship with him wouldn't have lasted long. He was too good-looking to have kept to just one woman.

Derek McNeil and Rich Capito were on the court while a couple of other Delta frat guys lingered by the bleachers, seeming eager to get their turn. Her heart sank. She hoped he'd catch a glimpse of her...if only to show him her heart had not splintered into a thousand pieces.

She left the gym and headed for the Student Union. A frog hopped across the path in front of her on its way back to the pond, landing in the water with a soft plop. On the surface, everything seemed in order, yet something didn't feel right. She hated the dreaded churn of uneasiness—especially on campus, where it was supposedly safe. This was St. David's, not North Philadelphia.

The townspeople didn't even lock their doors at night. Her imagination rose, revealing scenarios of the past. News stories, tall tales, bad dreams all surfaced, giving her chills in the warm night air. There was no one around, yet the uncomfortable feeling of being watched clung like a vice.

The brook gurgled under the footbridge. Its gentle rushing captured her attention, and she felt small against the unknown forces of nature. The path seemed interminable. Like in a deep sleep, her feet kept pedaling her body along, but she felt more stationary than in motion. The lights of Walden Hall, like fireflies, flitted between the trees, and the movement of people inside the student lounge came into focus. It wouldn't be long before she'd be ascending the stairs. She raced up the hill and hit the worn marble steps two at a time. Dashing toward the door, the night pressed in on her from behind, almost pulling her backward. She stepped inside, closing the door to the night.

The lounge hummed with student life. Some engaged in clusters of small talk. Others sat alone, their heads buried deep in their studies. Adjacent to the lounge was a tiny chapel. She peeked inside before entering.

The chapel held the silence like a pristine glove. She always found this room to be enchanting and otherworldly, with the feeling the hand of God resided somewhere in the pews. There was so much on her mind that she didn't know where to begin. Did God really hear her prayers and pleas? She had often waited for some kind of reinforcing nod or signal but never received any tangible sign.

Of course he was a benevolent spirit, the father of Messiah Jesus, and his compassion rested on the whole world. She'd believed this since childhood Sunday school, when her teachers gave out prizes for reciting the 66 books of the Bible from memory. She sat in the back row next to the wall map of Israel and Egypt waiting for her turn while the teacher, Mrs. Gentily, took her pointer to the chalkboard, tapping it crisply on the slate. But there were so many children in the classroom, so many others who'd gotten the teacher's attention. They'd raised their hands often and always seemed to know the answers. She often felt guilty for not knowing what the others knew. She listened to the Sunday school lessons but let the words drift, feeling drawn to the map on the wall, into the desert where Jesus once walked. She dreamed of walking the sands of Jerusalem and swimming in the salty Dead Sea where they said people could float.

But now Jordanna had big girl issues and many doubts. She didn't know if the answers to her problems were anywhere inside the 66 books of the Bible.

She walked up to the front of the chapel and sat in the first pew. Above the altar hung the stained-glass configuration of Jesus at the Garden of

78

Gethsemane. Hands folded upon the rock, he looked up toward a stream of light coming down from heaven. Jesus. He looked so composed for being only hours away from being hung. She never understood the strength he had to allow himself the fate he so graciously endured. Death on a cross. It didn't get any more horrible than that slow, torturous struggle of trying to grasp one more fading breath and thinking it may be the last. Tears came to her eyes at the thought of him hanging—bruised and bloodied—at the hand of his enemies. The sufferings of Christ. Who could muster that kind of love?

She started to pray. Her emotions stirred within her like shards of hot glass. The urgency of her cries surprised her as her prayers rose from the deepest part of her, siphoning their way through the grit and mire that had wedged somewhere inside her heart. She'd never spoken to God with such a sense of necessity. From where had it come? She hoped no one would enter the chapel at this moment to see her crying, to witness her vulnerability. That was something she'd kept in check. Had God heard? Did he care?

After a while, the avalanche of grief slowed and silence resumed. The burden she'd been carrying was still there but now lighter. She left the chapel and stopped at the dining hall, hoping they'd still be serving dinner. Jordanna spotted Beth at a corner table with her head bowed into her textbook.

"Hey, there." Jordanna placed her tray down across from her roommate. "Still studying?"

"This is as good a place as any." Beth scooped up the last of her potatoes. "How about you? Y'okay?"

Jordanna knew she meant Jeff. She shrugged.

"How's Jeff? Are you guys back together?" Beth's shiny black bob swung as she spoke.

Jordanna shook her head.

"Have you even spoken to him at all?"

"No. And I don't want to talk to him."

"I'm sorry." She inspected Jordanna's tray. "Is that all you're eating?"

"I'll be fine." Jordanna picked off pieces of crust from a French roll.

"I think they're still serving," Beth said with concern. "You should eat more than that."

"Nothing looked good. Just greasy. And the vegetables looked spent. Besides, I'm really not all that hungry."

"Are you still not taking his calls?"

Jordanna shook her head again.

"Sorry." Beth looked down at her books, as if trying to search for a way to help in the very pages of the psychology book she held in her lap. "I overheard him talking to Scott Zane in the lounge earlier today. I just caught the tail end, but he sounded angry. I heard Kenny Fairchild's name come up, too. Maybe Kenny made up that story, Jordie."

"What would be the point?" Jordanna spread butter on the roll.

"Maybe Kenny likes you. Maybe he'd like to fill Jeff's shoes."

"Beth, come on. There has to be some truth to his comment. People don't come up with stuff like that on the spot. It had to be true."

"Is it so hard to believe that another guy is interested in you?" Beth said with a smile.

"Oh, Beth, please."

"Well, I know he's not exactly in Jeff's league but listen, Jordie, you need to have a talk with him at the very least. You guys make a nice couple."

"*Made* a nice couple, you mean."

Jordanna took in Beth's words and let them settle over her. She hoped they would lend a glimpse of the future with Jeff in some sort of clairvoyant sense. Perhaps friends could see something she herself couldn't. She missed Jeff but didn't care to risk her pride just to have a relationship. Not this time. She'd done that enough. Perhaps this was what Dr. Bradley had been talking about. His words rang in her ears as she recalled what he'd said to her in confidence in his office.

"Have you ever heard of not liking yourself?" Jordanna took a sip of tea.

"Huh?"

"Oh, nothing. Just thinking out loud."

She saved herself from spilling her heart. While she wanted the comfort, she didn't want the shame. Yet it surprised her that Beth didn't know what the expression meant. Then again, perhaps she did and played dumb. After pushing down the last bite of her roll, Jordanna cleaned up her crumbs.

"I better go," she told Beth. "I've got some stuff to do. I'll see you back at the dorm."

"Some more sleuthing, no doubt?" Beth looked up with a smile.

"Something like that."

"Hang in there, Jordie. It'll all work out."

As the warmth of the bread and tea settled, she began to feel better. She offered a wave and turned to go. Down the hall, there was the familiar jingle of rattling keys, and as she rounded the corner to go down the steps, Sarge was standing there in front of one of the conference room doors.

"You're just the man I want to see!" she said as he stood searching through his stack of keys.

"What's up?" he asked.

80

"Do you remember the diary I found the other day up in the attic?"

He nodded.

"My roommate and I opened it and read through it. It was incredible! All these entries about their parties, cotillions and, well, everything. Then there was this letter in the back from a lover or admirer that we found. I'm pretty sure it was written for my Aunt Adelaide!" Her words poured out so fast she barely took a breath.

Sarge stopped short. "Your who?"

Jordanna stood stunned. Blood rushed to her cheeks as she realized her mistake. His eyes bored into hers like lasers. Embarrassed at revealing so much, Jordanna fumbled for the right words.

"My aunt was...Adelaide Colton." She felt the tension of his gaze. "I guess I never told you that. Actually, I've never told anyone about my relatives."

"This is something," he said, clearly taken aback. "So you're related to the Coltons?"

She nodded. "She was my mother's sister. But no one should know of this, Sarge. I haven't told anyone since coming to this school. Please..."

Resignation came over him, and a chasm of silence took over, cutting the space between them. She'd just placed her heart on the edge, and she wondered if she'd ever get it back.

"Please don't say anything about it to anyone," she pleaded. "I mean, it would be so awkward—you know, how everyone talks about her ghost and all that. I'd rather it remain between the two of us, if that's all right with you?" She struggled to fill the gap, attempting to read his face. "Is it...I mean...would it be all right for us to keep it a secret?"

His face softened as he studied her. "Of course, Jordanna. I understand," he said in a tone she'd never heard from him.

With relief, she gave him a hug, shocking herself at the touch of the unexpected intimacy. "It's weird, though. I found this letter...well, one page of it anyway. I was hoping to go back upstairs and see if the rest of it could be up there. Maybe stuck in a book, or somewhere."

"I'm still in the middle of my rounds. I've got to finish up across campus," he said, adjusting his cap. "But I guess I can let you in."

"Thanks, Sarge. That would be great. There's still a lot of stuff I'd like to sift through."

They went to the third floor and then climbed the narrow stairway up to the attic.

"Here, you'll need this flashlight. I won't need it." He handed it to her at the attic door. "I've got another one in the car."

He turned to go. "Hey, you okay up here alone?"

"Of course."

"You sure?"

"Yes, I'm sure. I'll be fine, Sarge, really." She sensed his hesitancy. There was something else on his mind. "Sarge, about the ghost stories…" She paused, unsure how to continue. The pain of her cousin's long-buried death suddenly surfaced even stronger. Billowing grief rushed through her chest.

"Jordanna, what is it?" He bent his head closer to hers.

"Oh, it's nothing…" She broke into a muffled sob.

He put his arm around her.

"It's…it's the rumors about my cousin that bother me." She wiped her tears quickly.

Sarge's expression softened. "Susie?"

"They say she jumped out the window and committed suicide. I don't believe that. Not for a minute!"

He pulled his arm away. "It's been a rumor around here for a long time," he said, his jaw clenched.

"Where'd it come from?"

"Townspeople, students…it's common knowledge." He loosened his tie.

"Do you believe in ghosts?"

He stiffened. "No. Not really," he said dismissively. "But Gettysburg, now that's another story."

"What about Gettysburg?"

"You've never heard about the ghosts there?"

"No."

"Well, because of all the battles and skirmishes, a lot of soldiers died. According to their stories, the men who were killed in the war came back."

"You mean their ghosts?"

He nodded. "There were many souls lost there. Thousands of them. Word is, ghosts come back to revisit when there is an especially violent death, or so they say."

"Well, I know I won't see or hear of my cousin's ghost, because she didn't die a violent death."

He sat down on the bottom step. His eyes engaged hers.

"I know, because I was there."

The room grew still once more.

"My mother and I were visiting for the summer. We visited every summer for years until we eventually moved in permanently—for a while," she said, her voice low. "After my father died, Aunt Adelaide and Uncle John

82

both encouraged us to stay with them. They didn't want us living down in Baltimore alone."

"Tell me what happened the day Susie died." Sarge's voice was tender.

Jordanna looked down at the floor and up again, finding it hard to begin.

Her grief brimmed. "It's such a sensitive subject. I've kept it buried for so long—that day, I mean. I don't remember exactly what happened, and no one would ever tell me. Protecting me, I guess. But I was right there with her minutes before. I remember leaving the room, and by the time I got back, my Aunt Adelaide was screaming. My mother grabbed me and held me so tight, as if she were afraid of someone prying me from her hands."

"So, you say you were with her but...you don't know how she died—exactly?"

"No, I really don't know. No one does. At least, no one I know. We don't talk much about it. We never have. Now it seems it's all I've been hearing since coming to Colton. They talk about it more than our family ever did."

His eyes popped like small blue lights, and his lips spread into a weak, reserved smile. "I guess it's hard," he began," with all that goes on around here with the rumor about her."

"It is. Especially because, deep down, I feel responsible for it."

"What do you feel responsible for? The rumor?"

"No, her death."

"Her death?"

She nodded.

"How old were you?"

"Almost six. About a year younger than her."

"How could you have been responsible?"

"It was my idea to play the game."

"The game? What game?"

His beeper pierced the quiet of the hallway. He glanced down at his watch. His eyes flashed as he noticed the time. A moment later, he turned back to her. "Listen, I have to finish my rounds, but I'll be back. I have something to tell you." He turned to leave.

"What is it?"

He glanced back at her from the top of the steps. "It's a long story, Jordanna."

19

THE RAFTERS STRETCHED ABOVE HER. Frail wooden arms about to descend through the darkness. A flick of the light switch lent a feeble light, sending shadows across the room. The dark cherry armoire where she'd first found the diary drew her eye once more. It stood by itself against the longest wall, commanding attention. After years of neglect, the beauty of the craftsman's design was still evident. From the high arched top to the ribbon carved crest and finials, it must have been worth a fortune.

She recalled an old news story about an elderly lady who hid some prized paintings behind the panel in the back of an armoire, so Jordanna felt around the sides and back for any secret compartments or removable partitions. Rummaging through the dresses, she searched for possible hidden pockets and along the lining as well, where a letter may have been secretly stashed. Noting nothing unusual, she stepped away and scanned the room. It would be difficult to find anything as small as a piece of paper from amid the collection of books and artifacts that lay strewn along the attic floor. The odds of finding anything would be slim, but Jordanna was not so much patient as she was determined to find what she was looking for.

She laid the flashlight on top of a small table. Books of poetry, essays, and biographies filled with yellow, crusty pages reeked of mold and mildew. She picked up the smaller, lighter books first and skimmed them for any loose papers. One by one, she fanned them open, coughing at the whirling dust.

Eventually, she came to the heavier volumes. She sorted through dozens of books. A sweat broke on her brow. She'd been searching for hours, yet none of the books yielded anything in the form of a love letter.

Near the foot of the armoire, things began to look hopeful when an old family Bible appeared. Inside were newspaper clippings of the Colton family's parties and outings—pictures of Jennings by the ocean in Cape May when he was small and also one of Susie standing with Adelaide and John in front of a lemon tree in a *Tampa Tribune* press piece. Several stories about the Coltons' galas and fund-raising projects were headlined in the society section with pictures of them dancing together in their finery. The stories were all about the Coltons, but Jordanna found it odd that there was no mention of Susie's death. Where was the obituary? The death certificate? It began to look futile.

The hush in the room broke when she heard the creaking of the attic steps. Sarge said he'd be back to tell her something. When she turned, though, she was shocked to see Jeff standing in the doorway.

"What are you doing here?" She spoke with curtness, although her tongue felt like it had to push the words out. Her heart beat so fast it nearly popped out of her chest. "You frightened me, Jeff." Saying his name aloud sounded strange to her.

"You said you weren't afraid of ghosts," he said with a shy grin.

"I'm not. I thought you were afraid of the dark," she said smartly.

He took a step into the room.

"How did you know I was here?"

"I saw Sarge on the way over. He told me."

She turned away and went back to the books, attempting to ignore him. Good ol' Sarge. Yes, it would make sense that he thought they were still an item. She'd rather have heard that he followed her to the attic. The idea that he'd be that forward or desperate appealed to her.

A few moments later, his sneakers appeared in her peripheral vision. "Jordie, I need to speak with you." His voice cracked on her name. "Why have you been avoiding me?" His words hung in the air.

She stiffened. While she longed to hear him speak to her, all she could remember was the voice of his friend, Ken, and his words at the party. The way he'd said, "Maryanne," as if she were some precious queen. Maryanne, the saint from Sicklerville. Jeff's love. The words had hit with the power of a sledgehammer.

"Jordie, it's been months now. We need to talk. When you're through, may I walk you back to the dorm?"

His voice cracked again. The words sounded thin, like old parchment, and crumbled the moment they left his mouth—sucked up in the cavern of the room.

"I've got a lot of stuff to search through here. I don't know when I'll be going back," she said in a manner of dismissing him.

"Why are they of such interest?"

"I'm just looking through them. It's a pet project," she said tersely.

"Looks like you could be here for days."

He began to walk around the room, stalling for time and feigning interest she knew he didn't have. "There has to be over 200 books in here."

He picked up *The Woman in White* from one of the piles she'd already gone through. After glancing at it, he tossed it back and shoved his hands into his sweatshirt pockets. With Jeff in the room, it was hard to concentrate on her task. Her hands started to quiver. She'd grown tired, yet didn't want to leave. Simultaneously attracted and repelled by his presence, she didn't know what to do. This was the first time she'd been alone with him in months. She sat still, aware of her own breathing—and her pulse quickening.

"How much longer will you be?" he asked.

"I don't know. Why do you ask?"

With his hands in his pockets, Jeff shifted his weight and drew a circle with his foot on the dusty floorboards like a guilty child accused of stealing. She pretended not to notice.

"Jordie, what's going on? What happened with us?"

The words sounded small in the cavern of space surrounding them. She repeated them silently to herself, holding on to the pattern of his voice.

"I don't know, Jeff. Why don't you tell me?" she said with all the boldness she could muster. Her voice quivered. She'd be more careful not to do that again. She wanted to feel in control.

"I've been trying to, but you won't give me the time of day." His face looked crestfallen.

She held her breath for a moment, not knowing how to respond, yet she felt the balance of power shift in her direction. "I just need a break, Jeff. I think we need to be apart right now."

The words felt strong. No quiver this time in her voice. A keen smugness set in, and she busied herself with the book she was holding, lending the impression his presence was a distraction.

"Jordie, I miss you. I want to be with you." His voice was sharp with emotion.

Jordanna melted at his words. A part of her wanted to get up and rush forward to hold him, though the better part forced her to remain seated. Blood rushed within her and emboldened her spirit. She felt stronger inside than she ever had. A panacea for the mind and heart, love worked better than any medication.

She caught a quick glimpse. He looked even more handsome than before, with his dark wavy hair spilling out from under his red cap. She longed to tuck it back in, to rub her fingers through the thick tendrils and feel his breath on her neck. Something electric moved inside her, and she braced herself as if on a steep precipice. "No, Jeff," she said, her eyes meeting his. Although her body trembled within, she felt something lift from her core. "I don't think it's a good idea for us to be together."

Her words rang hollow to her and she wondered how they could have come from her mouth. They didn't seem like her words at all, as though someone else spoke them through her.

He looked like a wounded animal. She felt his pain. It was the same as hers. It singed like fire. *You will endure,* she told herself. *You will endure the fire. Press on through the pain.* Tears grew in her eyes. She waited for them to drop onto her cheeks, but they clung instead, forming a thick watery lens.

As he moved toward the door and down the stairs, a remarkable detachment set in. It felt similar to a movie set. Surreal. The sting in her eyes eased, and the tears dissolved as though on cue, floating back into her body. She felt on the edge of giddy as the pain subsided, and while he left the room and descended the steps, a sense of relief swept into her. Had she been here before, watching this scene? It felt so familiar—a slow death of sorts with nothing to stop it. *Things driven too far turn into their opposite. Dry ice is so cold that it's hot...laughter at funerals....*

Dr. Bradley's words came to mind. A desire to run after him suddenly welled up, a frantic need to tell him that she didn't mean what she'd said. Missing him desperately and lonely for his touch, she needed to be loved. Even if he had lied to her and hurt her, she felt that whatever he could offer would be better than no love at all. She'd been tired of looking for the right kind of love. Where would that be?

Her father had been the right kind of love, but he died. Where would she find another? There would be no one who could fill his place nor be as loving as her own daddy. *You don't like yourself, Jordanna. Why do you reach for tinsel instead of gold?* Dr. Bradley's words resounded in her head. His thick lips swelled in her mind's eye. It was then that she realized just how much she wanted the tinsel...she'd always grabbed for it. Somehow, the tinsel had been all she felt she deserved.

Jordanna attempted to go back to the books but felt drained after only a few minutes. While stretching to get circulation flowing when footsteps advanced on the stairway again, she felt adrenaline surge through her veins. He'd come back! She didn't know if she could stand up to him again. It would be too easy to accept him back into her life, like a drug fix. But the stronger side of her felt better to remain in control. If honesty were not a part of Jeff James's makeup, she wanted no part of him. She held that thought like a neon sign, blinking on and off in her mind. Like Dr. Bradley told her, she needed to love herself first, and she would. Yes, she definitely would.

When she got up, her left foot surged with pins and needles from sitting on it so long. As the footsteps grew louder, she braced to confront Jeff a second time. She was aghast when she pivoted to see the figure standing at the door.

20

BOWDEN WRIGHT AND LAUREL CLARKE SAT AT THE LARGE OAK DESK in the newspaper office preparing for their monthly staff meeting.

"Bill said he'd be late." Bowden looked at her watch while holding a pencil between her teeth

"Jordanna said she'd be here, but what about Elaine?" Laurel sorted through a stack of photos.

"I'm not sure. She told me she'd gotten three ads this month, so things are improving. Did you see these new pictures of the soccer team?" She fanned out the black and white photos across the desktop.

"Great shots." Laurel picked one up. "I think this one should go on the front page. It's perfect. Joe did a nice job with these."

Bowden took out her composition journal. "I'm almost through with my editorial."

"What's it on?"

"The student-exchange program and the importance of cross-cultural relationships."

"Sounds good to me." Laurel reached for her mug of tea. "When Bill gets here, I think I should give him the student council story and then we should brainstorm. We haven't had a good one in a while. Hopefully, Jordanna will be able to—"

"Knock, knock." Bill Sorrello entered the room. "Ladies, how goes it?" He took off his denim jacket and took a seat. "Sorry I'm late. Car trouble again."

"Oh, Bill, again? You're going to have to get rid of that old clunker." Bowden pushed up the sleeves of her yellow cardigan.

"How old is that thing?" Laurel asked.

"I know it's not new, but it gets me from here to there," Bill said. "Don't make fun of it."

"We're not making fun. We're just hoping the engine doesn't fall out of it while you're on the Schuylkill expressway is all." Laurel gave him a generous smile.

"Hey, it's old, but that's its charm," Bill defended.

"Do we have any more of those little chocolate biscuits? I saw some in the drawer before," said Laurel.

Bowden shook her head. "Sorry, I already checked. Nothing but the crumbs." She pushed the empty container across the desk.

"Aw, I love those things," Laurel said.

"Sorry. I'll try to pick some up for our next meeting." Checking her watch, Bowden queried, "Hey, I wonder where Jordanna is? It's almost 7:30."

"Bill, we talked to Jordanna about the position on the paper. She's on board with it." Laurel leaned back in her chair.

"Sounds fine to me. So what are we brainstorming tonight?"

"Oh, I don't know. We need ideas for the holiday issue, and Dr. Bradley suggested that someone cover the Business department's Free Enterprise contest," Bowden said. "I'm pretty sure it'll be in Atlantic City this year."

"I can take that one," Bill said. "I don't mind driving."

"Are you sure?" Laurel sat grinning in the overstuffed chair by the fireplace. "It's a long way to Atlantic City."

He eyed her. "Hey, I might have a new car by then. You never know."

"I'll believe it when I see it, Sorrello," she teased him.

Bowden suddenly sat up straight in her chair and picked up a pen. "Oh, before I forget, we have to cover Dr. Campoli's trip to Nicaragua last month. Also the Alvin Ailey Dance company review. I guess we can let Jordanna cover that."

"Alvin Ailey? I've seen them. All they did was run around in a circle. That'll be a tough first assignment, don't you think?" Bill said wryly. "Where is she anyway? Did she say she was coming tonight?"

"I'm pretty sure I saw her walking over to Walden earlier," Laurel said, putting her tea cup aside. "In the meantime, let's jot down some ideas we might have to spice up the next couple of issues."

Over the next hour, they worked in silence.

Finally, Bill yawned. "Phew, I'm spent. I don't think I have any more ideas. How about you guys?"

"I'm done, too," said Laurel.

"Okay, let's call it a night. We'll reconvene in two weeks. Hopefully, everyone will be able to attend."

As they opened the door to leave, a rush of cold air blew by them.

*

Kingsley Willoughby towered in the attic doorway. His six-foot-plus presence loomed in the dimness. Jordanna's stomach lurched as foreboding filled the room.

"Hello, Jordanna," he said.

"Kingsley, what are you doing here?" she asked, taken aback.

"Why wouldn't I be here, Jordanna? I go to Colton." His eyes pierced through the faint light while his hands untied the bandana around his head.

"I mean, what are you doing up here?" she said, trying to maintain her composure. Her pulse quickened as he took a step into the room.

"I heard something up here and noticed the light in the stairway as I was walking past the registrar's office." He ran a hand over his freshly shaved head as he stepped toward her. In his other hand, he held the bandana. "I had to drop off my check. Just wondering who'd be upstairs at this hour."

"Well, I'm nearly on my way out now. I was just looking for a book..."

"The library has plenty of them," he said smartly.

Jordanna wished he would go. His presence often unnerved her and now, alone in the attic, she felt even more uneasy. As fear rose in her chest, she wished she hadn't sent Jeff away so quickly.

"I'm interested in history, and there are a lot of historical books up here. You know, artifacts," she said tensely.

The intensity of his gaze bore down on her. "This place is eerie, don't you think?"

She let his remark pass and closed the Bible. She hoped he wouldn't mention anything about Susie. That would be the last straw, prompting her to have to lay into him then. She got up from the floor at the sound of more footsteps coming up the stairs again. Sarge couldn't have come back at a better time. She was relieved he'd come back so quickly to tell her the long story he'd mentioned.

"Kingsley, what's going on?"

It was Jeff's voice, from the top of the steps.

"Jeff—" began Kingsley.

"What are you doing here?" Jeff said tersely.

"Not much. I saw a light on and wondered who was up here."

Jordanna reached for her coat. "I was just leaving." She put it on and picked up the flashlight.

"What are you guys, some kind of ghost hunters?" Kingsley grinned.

"No one's looking for ghosts." Jordanna turned off the light and aimed the flashlight in front of her while descending the steps.

21

THE FOLLOWING MORNING, Jordanna sat at her desk prepping for her English exam. Piles of notes lay in neat piles on the desktop and floor. While Jordanna was deep in thought, Beth rushed in the door.

"Did you hear about Sarge?"

"No, what about him?"

"He's in the hospital."

"What! What happened?"

"I don't know, but they took him to the emergency room last night. Fuzz was talking to some of the guys about it upstairs."

"Do you know what hospital he's in?"

"I think Bryn Mawr."

Jordanna had wondered what happened to Sarge when he didn't come back to Walden and recalled the strange look in his eyes while they were up in the attic.

She went back to her book and attempted to study. The English Lit test was in a few hours. But her efforts were usurped by thoughts of Jeff—and now, Sarge. She stared at the pages where the black letters of words lay like leaden particles. He had cancer, he told her once. She hoped that it was nothing as serious as that.

After a quick shower and coming back to her room, she found a note under her door. She didn't recognize the last name. Scrawled on the paper was the name *Perkins* and a phone number. Curious about the caller, she immediately called the number.

A man answered. His voice sounded thin.

"Hello, this is Jordanna Bronson. I had a message to call this number," she said.

"Hello, Jordanna. It's Sarge."

"Sarge! I heard this morning you were taken to the hospital. How are you?" she said with a worried tone.

"Oh, it's nothing to worry about, I'll be all right."

"What's wrong?"

"It's probably just my ulcer. It's been acting up again. I hope to get out of here in a day or so."

"That's good. How do you feel?"

"Not bad...just waiting for some test results. The doctor should be here sometime today."

"I'm so sorry you have to be there," she said sympathetically.

"I'm calling because I wanted you to know something. It's about what you were looking for up in Walden the other night."

"Yes, I was hoping you'd come back. What? Wait a minute...."

From behind someone's open door, loud music poured into the hallway.

"I'm sorry, Sarge, what did you say?"

"The letter you were looking for...I have some information about it that you might be interested in," he said in a tinny voice.

"About the letter? You mean my Aunt Adelaide's letter?"

She wished her dorm mate would shut the door and was tempted to do it herself, but it wasn't within reach.

"Can you hear me?" he said.

"Yes, barely."

"I have something to tell you, but if this isn't a good time, perhaps it should wait until I get back to the campus," Sarge said.

"Hey, could you please shut the door?" Jordanna called out while cupping the phone. "I'm sorry, Sarge, someone's stereo is blasting."

With her curiosity peaking, she pressed the phone up to her ear, straining to hear him over the music.

Through a strangled voice, Sarge told Jordanna something that she could not believe she was hearing. Did she hear him correctly?

After letting the words sink in, the impact was too jarring for her just to sit. She had to move. She had to tell someone. She wanted to run to Sarge to have him repeat what he said because she may have misunderstood. Could what he said really have been true? She had to find out.

*

When Jordanna arrived at Bryn Mawr Hospital, she hastened to the information desk, where a pleasant senior citizen gave her directions and pointed to the row of elevators at the end of the corridor. She pressed the button for the third floor. Passing the nurse's station, she arrived at Sarge's room and knocked gently before entering.

"Hi, Sarge," she said, her voice barely a whisper. She approached the bed with the trepidation of walking up to a sleeping animal. She stood at the foot of his bed, buzzing with anticipation of what to say first.

"Listen, if you want attention, you should just ask for it. No need to be so dramatic by checking into a hospital," she said with a grin.

"I guess I overreacted again. I'll do better next time," he replied, keeping in step with her. A dull sparkle lit in his eyes.

"Sarge, I had to come down to see you in person because what you told me was so incredible, it's hard to comprehend, you know? I can't believe you actually knew my Aunt Adelaide!"

"Yes, I hesitated to call, realizing it would come as a jolt to you, but something in me said I should do it," he said.

"I'm so glad you did. This is unbelievable!"

"Everyone calls me Sarge, but my real name is Paul Perkins. I'm the Paul in the letter you are looking for." He smiled reticently.

Jordanna had heard these words over the phone but seeing him in person, the man who had loved her Aunt Adelaide once, the words became all the more real. She stood watching him intently, almost not believing the serendipity of it all. Paul Perkins, the landscape gardener those many years ago.

"How did you know her?" she asked.

"Addie and I went to school together. I fell in love with her—love from afar, of course, because she was in a different social class. I knew she could never be mine, but that didn't stop my feelings for her." His voice began to break up, and he reached for a sip of water. "I remember the first time I saw her eyes up close. They were as green as the leaves we were studying in botany class."

Welling up at his candid revelations, she moved closer to his bedside.

"They mesmerized me...her eyes. They caught my attention one morning, and I never let them go after that. She was a beauty." Sarge smiled to himself and took another sip of water. "I can still see her," he murmured, gazing at the ceiling for a moment. "Your eyes remind me of hers."

Jordanna blushed.

"Well, after meeting Adelaide, all of the other girls paled in comparison, I guess." He chuckled softly. "But when the likes of John Colton came courting her, I knew I'd never have a chance."

"So you were just friends?"

He nodded. "I wanted it to be more, but.... Later, I heard that she'd gotten engaged to him and that was the last I'd seen of her. Then one day, many years later—oh, it must have been a good 20 years when she called me out of the blue. I was in shock, I tell you!" He smiled tenderly. "She'd seen my name on a truck while in town one day."

"And that's when she called?"

"Yep. We talked for the longest time—like two friends just picking up where we left off," he said wistfully. "We laughed and cried together that day she called. She'd been through so much and, frankly, I was shocked to hear of her troubles. And then she asked the most unbelievable thing—if I'd like to do some work around the estate. I had a landscaping business—moved it up north many years ago from Florida—and plenty of work, but it was all so sporadic, you know, and there was always room for more business. But that wasn't why I took the job." He paused and looked up at her.

"Why, Sarge?"

"I just wanted to be close to her," he said after a moment.

Jordanna soaked in his words. "I still can't believe this. It's so unreal!"

"And I stayed there a good many years before...well, before I moved on."

"What made you leave?"

"It wasn't my idea. It was Addie's. And it's something I could never figure out." He looked over to the window as though searching for the answer. "I had my own idea, but it was strange...very strange what happened on my last day there." He shook his head. "I was tending the wisteria. I'd been tending it for hours. It was the largest vine on the whole estate...huge, this vine. Addie loved purple flowers, as you may well know yourself. Anyway, while I was trimming it, she came out through the patio, walked over to me, and said in a very calm, collected manner that I should leave. I said, 'What are you talking about?' and she just repeated that she didn't think it was right for me to continue working for her under the circumstances."

"Circumstances? What circumstances was she talking about?"

Sarge closed his eyes. The silence between them rose until he finally uttered a faint reply. "It was after my child died..."

"Your child?"

"Yes, I once had a child. A little girl," he said with a resigned smile. "Her name was Susie."

"Susie?"

"Yes, Jordanna. This may come as a shock to you, but your cousin Susie was my daughter."

22

WITH A SHIVER, JORDANNA FELT THE ROOM SHIFT. She wondered if Sarge possibly had been delirious from his medication and not thinking clearly. Surely something was intruding on his reasoning ability for this couldn't possibly be true. Susie was his daughter? She wanted to believe him but found it so incredible because she had never been told this before now.

"Your daughter? How can this be?"

"It's a long story." He shifted his weight against the pillows.

"Let me help you." She pulled the pillow from behind his back and reshaped it before placing it back. "Better?" She poured him a cup of water, feeling much like the nurse she once wanted to be. She wanted to make sure he was perfectly comfortable, so there wouldn't be any interruptions, however dubious his story seemed.

Jordanna waited while he drank, wishing he'd hurry. Her anxiety mounted. Was this another bad dream? To distract herself, she scanned the room. The bulletin board on the wall listed the hospital's day-to-day activities: bingo, flower arranging, pinochle. A plainly drawn sunflower design was placed at the top of it as a child might have created the design. It belonged in a kindergarten, yet she understood the way time somehow inverted things. The young grow old and the old regress into youth—of sorts—once more.

Just outside the door was the pressing energy of doctors and nurses immersed in serious medical issues and ethics so far beyond their reach. Tests scheduled...operations performed...diagnoses determined. The outcomes reviewed in dark private rooms while people's fate and very lives determined the day's drama. Yet, through all of it, someone took the time to draw a happy face inside a sunflower. She didn't know whether to smile or cry. She hated seeing him in this helpless position. She longed to see him back at work, strutting in his dress blues, protecting the students at Colton. He did not belong here.

Sarge shifted again. His eyes looked gaunt and yellowed. He cleared his throat while placing the cup back on the tray.

"You were saying, Susie was your daughter." The words sounded odd.

"Yes," he said with a sigh.

"I'm listening." She sat on the side of his bed.

"Not long after I began working on the estate, my wife became pregnant. It was shortly after Addie and John were having problems, as she was trying to conceive. It was a rough time for both of them, John and Addie, and my heart ached for her after her miscarriage."

Jordanna sat transfixed by his words, feeling the moment too surreal to be true.

"So I asked her if there was anything I could do—what one would usually say to someone who'd just buried their child. But out of my deep feelings for her, I meant it. I would have done anything for that woman." His voice quivered. "I loved her."

"Really, Sarge, this is all too incredible for me to comprehend."

"Yes, I really believe I did." His face reddened as he developed another coughing spell.

"Sarge? Are you okay?" She thrust the cup of water at him, hoping it would ease the situation. "Finish it, Sarge. There's plenty more right here."

He took a sip and leaned back against the pillow. His skin looked gangrenous against the white of the bedsheet that clung to his body, rendering him more like a sack of old bones.

"You look really tired." She noticed the purplish crescents that hung beneath his eyes.

"Oh, I'm alright. I'll be fine, Jordanna. I've been in bed all day, so how tired can I possibly be?"

Her heart felt heavy as she forced a smile.

With a shaky hand, he placed the cup of water back on the portable bed table. "I'm okay," he said in a thin voice.

Just then a nurse appeared at the doorway and stuck her head inside the room. "Closing time," she announced in a clipped tone and hurried away.

Jordanna sighed at the nurse's sharp interruption. She wasn't ready to leave! There was so much more to the story, and he'd only begun. She would have stayed all night to hear the rest of it and to be absorbed in every detail he was only too willing to tell. She ached to know more and wished for a way to stay.

"Sarge, I'm sorry, but they want the visitors to go now," she said with a frown.

His face seemed to shrivel on the pillow like an old peach. "It's okay. I'm starting to feel a little peaked anyway." He closed his eyes.

Until now, Jordanna thought she was the only one who had a secret. The story of Sarge and her aunt left her dumbstruck. It was unbelievable that while she was a little girl visiting her relatives all those summers on the estate,

Sarge had been on the Colton estate, too. She could recall seeing someone mowing the lawn and planting trees from time to time, but it was always from far away—the figure of a man in overalls with a cap pulled down. He had brown hair and not silver, like Sarge's, and she never heard him speak.

So he had been the one who toiled in the estate's magnificent gardens. Every inch of ground came to life through his hand. He must have been the one who planted the Japanese flowering cherry trees on the hillock above Walden Pond and the dozens of deep purple crocuses that sprung up like a carpet in late winter. The rose beds and ivy draped arbors and pergolas mirrored scenes from the magazine pages of *Better Homes and Gardens*.

Her mind raced. She had so many questions for Sarge and tried to fill in the blanks with her own imaginings. If John Colton wasn't Susie's biological father, did Susie know her real one? Had she met him? Jordanna thought about the reality of the situation and weighed the facts. Sarge would have no need to lie about such things. It's not surprising that he or any man would have found her aunt attractive. Her Aunt Adelaide was beautiful. No wonder Jordanna felt such a connection to Sarge. He was really more like her uncle than just the campus security guard.

"I'll be back first thing in the morning," she said softly in his ear as she moved closer to him.

He nodded slowly without opening his eyes. She touched his hand before leaving the room.

23

"Morning," said Beth, munching on a banana.

"Is it morning already?" Jordanna asked, sleep still thick in her voice. "I'm still tired."

"You didn't have any nightmares keeping you up last night, did you?"

"I don't think so," she said with a yawn.

"How's Sarge?"

"I guess he'll be okay."

"Do they know what's wrong with him?"

"He thinks it's his ulcer, or something stomach related. He looked kind of pale, but he wasn't in pain."

"That's good," said Beth. "My mother has an ulcer. She was hospitalized for it once a few years ago, but she's okay now."

"I'm going to see him again today." Jordanna threw back the sheets and looked at the clock. "I hope Julie can lend me her car again."

"Want some company?" Beth said.

"No, that's okay. I'd rather go alone. I have some things I need to sort out. But thanks, just the same."

*

Peace swept over her as the hospital elevator quietly rose to the third floor. Jordanna said a quick prayer before stepping off and proceeding down the corridor where the familiar smell of ammonia and rubber gloves hung as though an invisible fixture. Nurses with sympathetic eyes hastened from room to room, juggling charts and trays. Their jobs were difficult, yet they made their efforts appear more in the spirit of just a daily walk in the park. As she passed each patient's room, she couldn't help but glance in. Her spirit ached at the sight of the bedridden. Thin, pale faces hovered above mounds of white pillows. Were they asleep? Or dead?

She offered up silent prayers for all of them—that God would heal their fragile bodies, cringing at the sight of tubes and machines aiding and assisting within their own sterile functions. Some of the rooms had two occupants while others had more private accommodations. She didn't know which she'd prefer for herself. Would it be better to be alone to cry in private? Or would a roommate lend an opportunity to commiserate...share stories? Misery loves company, they said.

Jordanna turned the corner and spotted his name on the little plaque at the entrance to his room. *Paul Perkins.* She liked the alliteration and decided that she preferred his real name to that of his nickname. Though calling him *Paul* would take some getting used to.

Upon entering the room, his bed was empty. She checked the bathroom. Two nurses were talking, and she heard one of them mention that someone had been just taken out for a test, yet she didn't catch the name through the controlled chaos of the nurses' station. It was probably Sarge, so she turned for the waiting room.

Stark white walls held several serene landscape paintings and lithographs. A portrait of the hospital's founder took up the wall between two windows. One painting drew her attention: a picture of a blonde-haired girl walking in a field of poppies. She went over each brushstroke the painter had given the girl's dress, the poppies, the sky. The child didn't look happy or sad, as though the painter wasn't sure what emotion to give the child.

On the tables lay several worn magazines, and a bookshelf contained a dog-eared copy of *To Kill a Mockingbird.* The view from the window was obstructed by another wing in the hospital. To the left, a lone skinny tree grew by itself, its branches thin and bare on a strip of hill above the parking lot. A large rain cloud had grown dark and gradually took the sun's place as the sky gave way to a sullen gray cast. A damp chill filled the room from an overzealous air conditioner, and Jordanna crossed her arms over her chest. She got up and paced a bit before walking back into Sarge's room.

A few minutes later, a nurse stood at the threshold.

"I'm just waiting for my friend to come back from his test," Jordanna said, looking up. "I'm Jordanna Bronson."

The nurse stopped short. "Your friend?"

"Yes, Sarge—I mean Paul. Paul Perkins."

She took a step into the room. With a soft voice, she said, "I'm sorry, but Mr. Perkins passed away early this morning."

*

Black stormc louds rumbled overhead as Jordanna left the hospital. She quickened her pace as the rain began to pour. If only it could wash out the grief that singed her chest. Another father, of sorts, was now gone. Her emotions churned and swelled, fueling her own personal storm within. She pulled out of the parking lot as tears clouded her vision. The rain began to pummel the car, further obscuring her sight. As the windshield wipers slapped back and forth to fight back the cascading water, even at the highest speed, the rain kept one step ahead. She clenched her hands on the wheel until the pressure seared her palms.

When she got to the dorm, she ran to her room and locked the door behind her. Her sadness gripped with the tightness of scalding chains across her chest. The pressure continued to build until she felt her heart would burst. The intensity subsisted and for a moment, petrified her, stealing her breath until she cried herself into a shallow, restless sleep.

Later, when she awoke, the ache of knowing she'd never see her friend Sarge again cut like a dull blade. It seemed everyone she grew close to died or left their imprint in her soul before they left her. First, her father, followed by every boyfriend she'd ever clung to, and now Sarge. The pain of losing someone was something she'd learned early, although the experience would never prepare her for the next loss.

*

She never understood death, how it called on the young and innocent, too soon, sometimes. Its clutches came when you least expected them. When her father had died, she watched her mother cry at the dining room table the night he'd taken a turn for the worst in the hospital. The sight of her mother's grief cut too much into Jordanna's own fragile core as she saw her mother's body shake under the weight of her pain. She'd never seen her mother cry so hard and ached for her to stop. She watched at a distance—frightened at the rawness—while unknowingly giving her mother a respectable privacy to shed her grief as she buried her head in her arms on the table. The wrenching cries induced Jordanna's own quiet tears.

Her mother looked up from the table, her eyes red. "You can cry, Jordie, if you want to," she'd said, then lay her head back down, not even noticing Jordanna's tears had already fallen.

She remembered the days and nights with just her mother after her father's funeral...those first desperate hours when the loneliness soaked through to her bones. The first holiday after he'd passed away, Jordanna and her mother ate Thanksgiving dinner by themselves at a local Howard Johnson's restaurant. A waitress in a beige uniform hovered over the table. Sarah made an attempt to be jovial and smiled throughout the meal, but the

100

only light in her eyes came from the candle's reflection at the edge of the table. The booth felt cold under her thighs even through her thick corduroy pants.

Jordanna watched car headlights pass busily on the highway outside the window. Everyone seemed to have a place to go, people to visit. Jordanna could tell her mother was trying to make the best of the holiday for her. With only the two of them, it didn't feel quite enough as they sat across from each other in the quiet restaurant. Neither admitted that the turkey tasted like notepaper.

Soon afterward, nights came when she'd creep down the hall to check on her mother, to see if she were still breathing. She would stand outside her door, watching across the room the silhouette of her mother's body lying in bed. The bright orange glow of the illuminated alarm clock shone behind her like a setting sun.

One night, her mother's body didn't move. Fear set in as Jordanna's eyes bored into the room. She stood frozen while straining to will her mother's body into movement, wondering why it wasn't going up and down as it had before when they slept together. Those lonesome nights when her mother said it was all right. "Just for tonight," she'd say.

Jordanna held her breath. She locked her eyes on the horizon of her mother's body tucked under the sheet and blanket. Her feet adhered to the hardwood floor like suction cups. She stared so long and hard, her eye muscles began to strain. Then she saw movement. Ever so slightly. Was it her imagination? She waited until she saw it again rather than fool herself. Yes, her mother was alive! The anxious pounding in Jordanna's heart slowed to normal as she slithered joyously back down the hall to her own room, content that her mother had not died. But her paranoia over being left behind by her one remaining parent still clung, even years later.

One late summer evening, about 8:30, she came home after playing outside. By then, the sun had long left the horizon, and the atmosphere blurred to gray. She rang the doorbell to their second-floor apartment, but there was no answer. Her mother always answered the bell. Her cheerful voice behind it assured whoever stood outside that she was coming.

Jordanna rang the bell again and again. There was no cheerful voice. Where was she?

In a panic, she ran outside to look for her mother's light blue Rambler in the place where she usually parked—in the middle of the parking lot by the large evergreen tree. Not seeing it, she ran around to the back parking lot on the other side of the building, hoping her mother had parked the car in a different spot. The grip of fear ripped further into her bowels as she stood alone by the dumpster in the empty lot, her eyes fixed to each set of headlights traveling down Queen's Chapel Road in the murky twilight.

One by one her hopes deferred as cars by the dozen swept by. She couldn't stop pacing. Her breath came faster, and then the fear sent her body to shaking. When her mother's powder blue Rambler eventually turned into the parking lot, it wasn't soon enough.

Jordanna's world had stopped for a while.

*

"When are you coming to St. David's?" Adelaide asked by telephone one evening. "When you stay with us for the holidays, why don't you consider moving in...live here—with us? There's so much room in our house, Sarah. We'd love to have you."

"Oh, Addie, thanks but...we're okay, really."

"Sarah, your family is here," Adelaide said firmly.

"Addie, I appreciate the offer, but Jordie has her friends, and I don't want to uproot her. We'll be okay, really," Sarah said, not wanting to be a burden to anyone.

"You both need to be with us. We're your family," Adelaide insisted. "She needs a father figure, Sarah. With Jordan gone, what's holding you from coming up here? Susie and Jordanna are like bookends. They adore each other and should be together."

"All right, I'll think about it." Sarah acquiesced to her older sister.

"Sarah, please. I want you to move up here by the spring," Adelaide said firmly.

"We'll see, Addie, we'll see."

*

A new world opened for Sarah and Jordanna when they moved north to live with John and Adelaide the following year. Weekend trips were sometimes long, country drives up to Sugarloaf Mountain or to Cape May on the New Jersey shore. Jordanna found it cool that she could see her reflection in the patina of her Uncle John's Lincoln Continental and loved to feel the breeze in her face while sitting between her mother and cousin in the back seat. Uncle John sat tall as he drove over rolling hills and farm country, one arm draped outside the window. They always stopped at the same ramshackle-looking restaurant right off the highway on the way back from their mountain sightseeing. Her uncle said the Peacock Inn had the best food. It was there that she first tasted spumoni ice cream and learned how to tie a Windsor knot.

The restaurant had an adjoining farm, and after the meal, Uncle John walked her and Susie across the parking lot to see the peacocks. Jordanna stood close to her uncle and startled whenever one suddenly displayed its opulent feathers. While she reached out to hold his hand, Jordanna pretended it was her father's hand, not just her uncle's that she was holding, especially when others were around. *Yes, I have a father.* Her uncle's dark coloring was a direct contrast to her father's sandy hair and sea-blue eyes, but that was fine with her. It was everything to have a father. It didn't matter what he looked like.

Her mother appeared happy living with the Coltons. Her cherry-lipped smile and sultry voice had a lightness Jordanna hadn't known in a while. But up close, Jordanna sensed something was wrong. Her mother's smile always looked strained. Yet they both tried to find a place for themselves even in the shadows of the great Colton mansion.

24

THREE MICROFICHE MACHINES SAT AGAINST THE FAR WALL of the campus library adjacent to the magazine racks. Jordanna threaded the first of two thick spools of film the librarian had given her into the machine. Dozens of headlines from 1966 spun past as she cranked the handle. She slowed down long enough to catch the Colton name or any semblance of a headline title that may have involved them. *Coltons Host Prime Minister* caught her attention, and another one, dated several months later, featured her aunt and uncle at a benefit party they hosted at the estate. A third showed them at the Academy of Music along with a tow-headed little boy.

After exhausting the first spool, she placed the second one into the machine. After nearly an hour of searching, her eyes felt heavy. It seemed that in all of the publicity that her aunt and uncle received, very little had included their daughter, Susie. Discouraged, she left the library and headed to Walden Hall.

The air grew thick as sauna heat as she climbed the stairs to the third floor attic. Sunrays pierced the room through the vent slats, casting white streaks across the dusty floor. Something caught her eye in the corner. An old black trunk. How had she missed it before? What could be inside? Old coins? Rare gems? Her only recollection of old trunks was that they belonged to pirates and inevitably contained a secret map revealing a hidden treasure. She chuckled to herself thinking she could be that lucky.

A stale cedar scent rose up as she lifted the heavy lid. Piled inside were what appeared to be stacks of clothing and blankets covered in clear plastic garment bags. Reaching below, she grazed something near the bottom and pulled out a frayed black scrapbook containing black and white photos.

On the first page she recognized her aunt in a picture with some others on a tennis court. Everyone wore white. Her aunt held a tennis racket over her shoulder. On the back of the photo were the names *Betty Arnold* and *Grace Spencer* written in pencil. There were other pictures of Aunt Adelaide and Uncle John and a few of a little boy who must have been Cousin Jennings when he was a toddler. On the last page, she found a picture of her mother wearing a turquoise bathing suit while she stood between Adelaide and John on the boardwalk in Ocean City, New Jersey. The photographer had snapped the picture just as a giant wave had risen high behind their heads as though ready to descend on top of them.

She looked inside the chest again, hoping to find more pictures. Where was Susie? How come there weren't any pictures of the child? No information or details about her life. No birth or death certificate. Nothing. It was as though she didn't exist.

Disgruntled, Jordanna put the pictures back in the trunk. All except one. Sweat formed at her temples and brow. She searched the chest again, hoping she'd overlooked something. Weariness beset her like a cloak. She felt the room close in. The heat was finally getting to her. If she didn't leave now, she may pass out.

After a quick stop in the dining hall to get some lemonade and a sandwich, she went back to her dorm. In the near distance, the local train ground along its tracks announcing its arrival. She thought about Mr. Upland and his progress at the nursing home, and guilt for not visiting him lately pressed in. At the fork in the path were the gymnasium and Sarge's old security office. Toby's blue dog dish lay at the foot of the door. Sweet Toby. Who was taking care of the dog now? She knew the front door would most likely be locked, so she went around to the back entrance, inside the gym.

Sarge's office was halfway down, past the second row of bleachers. The gym was quiet. The bleachers empty. It felt odd to her, like watching a silent stage. Yet the sights and sounds of gym life—games, cheers, dances—echoed in her mind. When she'd tried out for the cheerleading squad her first semester on campus, she'd sat on the bleachers near the door to his office. She longed to make the squad, if only to wear the cool maroon and white cheerleader's uniform.

The only light that came into the empty gym was through the small window high above one of the basketball hoops. As she made her way to the security office, a shadow floated by from somewhere across the room behind her. Her heart quickened. She didn't turn around but steeled herself to keep walking. A moment later, her tensions eased as the nasal squawking of a gaggle of geese passed over the building. Their shadows flitted by as they passed the sun.

She approached the door to the security office and her instincts proved right. The door was open. Once inside, the room appeared different than she remembered, as though she were looking at it for the first time. The black leather chair where Sage used to sit looked lifeless. It felt cold and unyielding when she sat on it, trying to find some familiarity, sitting where he used to sit. It was as close as she could get to him now. Scanning the room, her gaze fell upon his old black and white Zenith television, his empty Viking's cup on the side of the sink, the black phone on the wall. In the still of the moment, she imagined how it must have felt to spend time alone in the room as he had all the years he'd been at Colton. She took a deep breath, hoping to somehow get closer to him by sharing the air that he at one time breathed himself.

The refrigerator held three packages of coffee creamer and a bottle of dark brown ale. The desk drawers didn't have much in them other than security logs and a few pencil stubs. Glancing at the pictures on the wall, she spotted the one of the little child with the beach ball. She attempted to remove it from its frame, curious to see if there were any markings on the back. Pulling the picture out, she cut herself on one of the metal barbs used to keep the backing intact. There was no name on the back, just a date: 1962. The child looked to be about two or three years old. Susie was born in 1959. This must have been her! *Susie. Sarge's daughter.*

Jordanna studied the picture, peering intently at the background figures to see if any looked familiar. A woman's hand rested on the child's shoulder. A couple of small children were blurred in the background. He'd been so close-mouthed at first, never volunteering who the child was or her name. Jordanna was sure he'd noticed her curiosity that day in his office when she visited. At least she thought so. Now she understood his reticence. It all came into focus why didn't he talk about his daughter.

Jordanna still had questions. She knew her mother was probably the only one still alive who might know the answers.

25

JORDANNA PLUCKED A LONELY RED ROSE from the bush outside her mother's house and held it to her nose, breathing in the sweet intoxication. She stood by the fence, watching from a distance while her mother passed by the front bay window. Through the prism of glass, Sarah Bronson looked matronly—decades past her real age as she grasped the wooden cane.

The sight halted Jordanna in her tracks. When did her mother become so old? Jordanna wished she had the power to adjust the scene to a less formidable one—one that could capture time at its most captivating, relegating the subject in the lens more subjective, more perfect. As with any instrument of viewing, there were options. Soft focus lenses, fast and slow shutter speeds, aperture settings. If only life came with built-in cameras to parse just the best of times. To slow the speed of life down before it spun out of control.

Sarah moved slower than Jordanna would have expected for a woman only in her late fifties. With her palsy, even simple home tasks seemed monumental. But she maintained her independence and stubbornly kept pace with her neighbors, not wanting to be a burden to anyone. Jordanna always worried about her mother but lately even more so. What if she fell, or couldn't call for help? Jordanna had heard the stories....

A girl she had known in her eighth-grade class once walked into her house after school and found her father lying dead by the stove in the kitchen. He was barely 50. Jordanna feared this would happen to her one day. At Jordanna's prompting, Sarah acquiesced and accepted her neighbor's Siamese kitten from the new litter last spring, pleasing both Jordanna and Mrs. Higgins. Jordanna wasn't sure how a Siamese cat from Mrs. Higgins would be able to help, should her mother need it, but at least she wouldn't be alone.

Jordanna stepped up to the front door. She knocked, rather than use her own key, making her visit more of a pleasant surprise than a misconstrued break-in.

"Hello, sweetheart," said Sarah with a gracious smile as she opened the door. Upon closer inspection after a warm embrace, Jordanna was happily surprised her mother didn't at all resemble the same woman spied from across the lawn. Her eyes were quick, her skin taut and smooth. Her face retained a radiant blush even as she neared her sixth decade. Appearances were deceiving, indeed. Her mother's house always smelled the same...a sweet blend of warm fruit and laundry soap.

"Something smells good," said Jordanna.

"I'm making a roast. Are you hungry?"

"I'm starved!"

"Dinner will be ready soon." Sarah entered the kitchen, and Jordanna followed.

Her mother puttered in a red-and-white-checked apron, a line of sweat gathered on her forehead as she basted the hot roast in the oven. It took a lot for Sarah to attempt to make anything in the kitchen. Jordanna admired her mother's perseverance, despite the fact that Sarah had been convinced she'd never acquired the necessary cooking skills to arrange a proper meal.

Jordanna glanced around the room. The dark walnut furniture, draped in sentimental doilies, shined in lemon wax. The collection of photographs atop the credenza grew denser with every visit. What once had been a smattering of headshots now resembled more of a gallery. And those photos for which she couldn't find a frame were placed up against other pictures, formally displayed in silver or brass, alongside the bric-a-brac. Jordanna wouldn't be surprised if the photos of her mother's long-time friends—and their children's children—would end up somewhere on the walls one day.

Treasured knickknacks lined the tops of tables and elsewhere, spilling out to just about any place there was room. Jordanna cringed at the clutter. An orgy of memorabilia. She longed to wipe the surfaces clean, to put away all of the junky souvenirs her mother had acquired over the years. There were tiny dolls, china figurines, bottles, bells, shells, pins, and ornamental glass objects. They seemed to multiply with each visit, like the photographs. But she realized that asking her mother to get rid of her collection would be like asking her to take away a part of herself. It would hurt her mother as much as asking her to cut off her own finger. Over the years, she'd come to respect her mother's memorabilia, even though it chafed her sensibilities of order and simplicity.

In the warm light of the dining room, Sarah had set the table with the special china, etched with pastel pink rosebuds, and crystal glasses. Two lit candles shimmered in the center on either side of the centerpiece garland. Two more burned brightly on the fireplace mantle. The scent of warm cranberry permeated the air. As the sun tucked itself into the horizon,

Jordanna and her mother sat down to dinner. Sarah opened a bottle of sherry. A warm salty breeze filtered through the window.

"Everything looks delicious, Mom." Jordanna reached for a piece of crusty bread. Sarah's sense of aesthetics lent much to the dining experience. However, Jordanna wondered why her mother insisted she couldn't cook, when most everything she cooked was delicious. If her mother thought she couldn't cook, at least she knew how to make the meal memorable.

"I'm glad you like it. Eat up. I've got plenty." Sarah took a sip of sherry and began to carve the roast. "So what is this great news you have? You've kept me wondering for so long."

A sweet ardency grew in Jordanna's stomach. "Well, you'll never believe what's happened over the past few weeks!"

"What is it, dear?"

Jordanna put her fork down and began to share the story of her friend, Sarge, and all that she'd discovered in Walden Hall. "I've wanted to tell you sooner, but with you being away and all, I thought it best to tell you in person."

She began at the beginning, taking her mother on a step-by-step, vicarious journey of how she met him and what happened. "...and then I found Aunt Adelaide's old diary, too," she continued with excitement. "Isn't that amazing?"

Sarah's face bore an edge as though she were preoccupied. She sat stiffly in her chair, her gaze hovering somewhere in the distance in the next room. Jordanna turned in the direction of her mother's gaze to see what the distraction might be. Finding nothing out of the ordinary, she turned back around to prattle on about her discoveries.

"...and behind the diary, I found this old love letter! Well, at least the last page of it. I'm sure there's more, but that's only the half of it. I actually met Paul Perkins! You know, Aunt Adelaide's landscape caretaker. We call him Sarge on campus. He's been a security guard at Colton for years!" she gushed. "Isn't that neat?" She continued to chatter, effusing more about what she'd discovered. "You know, Aunt Adelaide's paramour! Did you know she had a lover? Can you believe it?" She got up to get her purse and groped inside to find the letter with Paul's signature. "And wait 'til you see this!"

She chatted merrily until she realized her mother didn't seem to share the same enthusiasm. Distracted, Sarah continued to fix her attention on something in the living room. Jordanna turned around again to see Pudding walking on the mantle, her tail near the flame of the burning candle. Suddenly, the cat yelped as it flew down off the mantle. The blazing candle tumbled behind her. As the candle rolled over the hearth, it landed inside the nearby brass magazine holder stuffed with newspapers.

"No!" said Sarah, struggling to get out of her chair. "The candle!"

A corner piece of a newspaper turned orange, and the flames quickly devoured the paper as smoke rose. Sarah headed for the kitchen, where she rummaged inside the pantry, Jordanna right on her heels before flying past her, almost tripping over her mother's cane.

"Where's the fire extinguisher? I know I've got it in here somewhere. Oh, there! There it is, behind those bottles on the right. Jordie, can you please reach in there for me?"

Jordanna bent down and grabbed the extinguisher. Fumbling with it for a time, she became exasperated. "Oh, come on," she said in frustration, struggling with the nozzle. "How does this stupid thing work?"

Sarah reached over to try her hand at it, and after a few moments, shot a spray onto the kitchen floor. "There it is," she said, and they proceeded back to the living room, where the smoke had turned the contents of the magazine holder into an all-consuming fire, sending up charred bits that dropped and curled on the oriental rug. As the blaze ensued, the threat of the nearby drapes catching fire wasn't far behind.

"Mom, we can't do this ourselves. I'm going to call the fire department!"

Minutes later, the shrill alarm of fire engines blared as they barreled up the street. One by one, three red trucks pulled to the curb. Jordanna was embarrassed by all the fuss, thinking that one truck would have sufficed the needs of a tiny Cape Cod. The firemen jumped out and darted into the house, pulling a thick black hose behind them. Her stomach grew tight with fear that her mother would lose her home and prayed that it would be spared as smoke poured out of the living room window.

Neighbors trickled out of their homes to gawk in their driveways, their faces stony with fear. The newly married couple her mother mentioned earlier came over to ask if they could be of help and inquired how the fire got started. Too nervous to speak, Jordanna let her mother do the talking.

Jordanna's heart raced. The smoke curled up toward the frame. *Please, don't spread. Please!* She fought to remain calm for the sake of her mother. Then she remembered the fire on Queen's Chapel road. It had been at their apartment complex early one morning while awaiting the school bus. Flames lapped through the balcony door window of an apartment across the courtyard. The hungry flames hovered along the pink bricks, quickly turning them ashen gray. Although the fire had started in another building, she feared that somehow it would spread to the other buildings, possibly her own. Then she saw the school bus coming up the street. For the first time in her life, she didn't want to go to school. Her throat went dry. She ran back home to tell her mother.

Jordanna heard the neighbor's murmurings, their supportive words as they huddled together like a pack of frightened meerkats. Both Mr. and Mrs. Higgins had come outside and stood next to Sarah. Jordanna was sure that her mother wouldn't reveal the real cause of the fire. She wouldn't mention it had anything to do with Pudding, so as not to make the Higgins' feel even remotely responsible.

Jordanna kept her eyes on the house. The beautiful yellow Cape Cod.

*

When Jordanna awoke the next morning, she smelled the burnt embers even before getting out of bed. She came down the steps as her mother hung up the phone.

"Who were you talking to, Mom?" She rubbed her eyes.

"A contractor. I've already called Mr. Dollfus about the fire insurance."

"I hope it's covered." She plopped onto the loveseat.

"He said the damage should be insurable," said Sarah as she sadly perused the room.

"How long will this place smell so bad?"

"They said it'll be awhile before it completely subsides," said Sarah.

"It's horrible."

"It won't be long. We'll keep the windows open as much as possible."

Jordanna covered her nose with her pajama sleeve. "It's like living in an ashtray."

"We'll have to live with it for now. But look on the bright side. I figure since we have to get a new rug and wallpaper, I might as well get some new furniture, too. These living room chairs are nearly shot."

"I remember when we got these at O'Neill and Bishop," said Jordanna. "I loved that store."

"I did, too. But I think they went out of business."

"We're lucky the whole house didn't burn."

"Yes, we're very blessed."

"Mom, I'm sorry…about the fire."

Her mother sat back and rocked without saying anything for a moment. "It's not your fault, dear."

"If I hadn't suggested you get a cat, this never would have happened."

111

"Sweetheart, it's not your fault. I love having the cat. If I didn't want her, I wouldn't have accepted her when Mrs. Higgins offered."

Pudding purred under Jordanna's caress. She noticed tiny lines around her mother's eyes by the morning light of the bare window.

"Are you ready for breakfast?" said Sarah.

"Not really."

"How about some nice eggs?"

"No, not now. I'm really not that hungry, Mom."

"You need to eat something. You're whittling down to skin and bones." Sarah gave her a disconcerted look.

Jordanna balked deep inside at the possibility her mother thought she was anorexic…or worse, bulimic. "Mom? I need to ask you something."

"What is it?"

"I want to know something about Aunt Adelaide and Paul. Their relationship."

"What relationship?" her mother asked as her brow knit.

"They had a baby together. You know, Cousin Susie."

Her mother's features turned sharp. "Susie? You think Susie is a product of Adelaide and Paul Perkins?" Her mother's eyebrows rose in disbelief before she chuckled nervously. "No, Jordanna, that's ridiculous. That is absolutely not true!"

26

The Coltons
September 1946

"JOHN, THE HOME IS LOVELY." Adelaide gazed at the pristine landscape. The pond at the foot of the hill sat like a splashing green emerald as the wood ducks circled and dived along its perimeter. Everywhere she turned, the Colton estate bespoke a classic beauty, from the fresh-leaved greenery of the rhododendrons dappled in sunlight to the charm of the climbing white clematis along the wrought iron trellis. As John Colton drove the black Hudson along the long stretch of winding macadam, Adelaide rolled down the window.

"The air smells so sweet...like honey." She allowed the wind to drift over her face. "I can't believe how huge these grounds are...so rambling. Do we own all of it?"

"It's about 17 acres." He pulled the car around the circular driveway, parked under the shade of an oak tree, and turned off the engine.

"I can't believe all this will be ours." She took in the vastness of the Spanish-tiled mansion. "It's beautiful, John."

"I'm glad you like it, Addie, I thought you might think it a bit too much, a lot to maintain, but I assure you my grandmother's gift to us is...well...just *that*—a gift. So if you'd rather live in something more practical, please don't be afraid to tell me."

"John, it doesn't matter where we live. I'm sure I'll get used to the size. Although it does look a bit drafty."

"We could tear it down and rebuilt a smaller house if you want," he said, turning toward her.

"You're crazy, John Colton." She slapped his arm. "It will stay as it is. We'll just have to grow into it. I'll make sure I have enough sweaters in my chifforobe is all."

She smiled as he leaned in to kiss her. Surely this was the kind of home she'd always envisioned for herself. As the daughter of a traveling European diplomat, her roots had never been more than fleeting respites—London, Prague, wherever her father needed to be. So anywhere John Colton would choose to live with her would be good enough; however, she'd never imagined it would be this good.

They got out of the car and walked up to the front door. Arm in arm, they approached the threshold. After unlocking the door, John lifted Adelaide off her feet and carried her into their home.

*

On a warm, morning in July, close to a year of living at the estate, Adelaide felt ill shortly after arising. After the third day of excessive nausea, she became worried. What possible ailment could linger for so long? The fear of contracting virus or bacteria from a recent trip the Caribbean was her first thought. Although she'd received the proper shots, the chance of encountering something from the water or vegetation was always a possibility.

When the nausea let up, she drove directly to the doctor's office. A call came later the next day from the doctor himself. He had the results of her blood test. Adelaide was pregnant.

"What color should we paint the nursery—pastel blue or green?" Adelaide asked in her seventh month of pregnancy. She stood in the alcove of their bedroom holding paint samples by the bedroom window.

Pulling on his suit jacket, John replied, "Doesn't matter to me, Addie…whatever suits you."

"I'm leaning toward yellow."

"I thought it was blue or green you were considering?"

"Oh, did I say that? Oops, I must be losing my mind a bit. I haven't slept soundly lately—twisting and turning most of the night—nor eaten so well either."

"Yes, but you look wonderful, darling." He kissed her on the nape of her neck. "I need to run now. It's late."

"Okay, see you this evening—oh…" She gasped, holding her stomach.

"What is it, Addie?"

"I just felt a sharp pain."

"Is it the baby?"

"It probably is nothing. I'll be okay, John."

John waited at the door.

"Go to the office, I'm fine." She waved at him.

"Well, if you need me, just call."

"I will."

John watched a moment at the doorway before leaving.

A few minutes later, another stab of pain sliced across her abdomen. The fear of miscarriage loomed. She got out of bed and crawled to the bathroom, where she managed to splash water on her face. The pains came on again as she writhed in agony on the cold marble floor.

"Mrs. Colton, are you alright?" said the maid with a gasp at the sight of Adelaide stretched out by the bathtub. "I'm going to call the doctor!"

An hour later, Dr. Porter, a stately man with a flashing white mustache and matching hair entered her bedroom. "I'm going to have to commit you to complete bed rest, Adelaide. Unless you want to harm the fetus, or worse, lose it, you'll have to do as I say," Dr. Porter said pointedly after examining her.

"Every day, all day?" she asked with exasperation.

"I'm afraid so."

Adelaide fell back onto the pillows and sighed. "All right, you're the doctor," she said, feeling helpless.

"I want you to get as much rest as possible." He packed up his bag. "If there's any more pain, have someone call me immediately."

Adelaide gave him a slight nod. At 23, she questioned her maturity for such things like having a baby. There would be no tennis or activities she'd grown used to enjoying, along with the burgeoning sense of belonging she'd come to know through her new friends at the country club. She knew that soon all of her social life around St. David's would come to halt, at least for a while. Was bringing a child into the world the best situation for her right now?

Though glimmers of doubt gave her pause, deep in her spirit, she relished the fact that a miracle of God was weaving inside her and she would soon have someone to nurture—a gift. If only she could remain healthy until the baby was ready to be born.

*

"Good morning, Mrs. Colton. How are you feeling today?" asked Hilda.

"Besides bloated and uncomfortable?"

"Well, this should help you get your mind off of things," said Hilda, handing her the breakfast tray.

"It looks wonderful, Hilda, but I don't think I'm in the mood for all *this*." She winced at the shiny yellow omelet and crusty brown bacon.

"I'm sorry, Mrs. Colton, I should have asked if you wanted eggs. I just assumed—"

"Well, it's too late, now. I'll just nibble this piece of toast."

The maid excused herself and slowly backed away just as John was coming through the door.

"What's this I hear about eggs?" he asked with a smile. "I'll take those eggs. They look exquisite, Hilda." He gave her a wink.

"Oh, Mr. Colton," Hilda said with a blush. "I expected you'd have your breakfast downstairs, sir, as usual."

John took a forkful of the omelet on Adelaide's plate. "Excellent, Hilda," he said while helping himself to another bite.

"All right, Mr. Colton, but if you want your own breakfast, you know where to find me," she said, moving toward the door.

"I'm so terribly bored," Adelaide said with a whine while struggling to sit up and readjust the covers. In her seventh month, she'd been bedridden for over three weeks.

"I can bring you some more magazines or the morning paper, Mrs. Colton. I—"

"Please nothing more to read, Hilda. I think I've had enough of current events."

"Addie, I'm sorry," said John. "I wish I could make things better for you."

"It's not your fault, John." She picked up the glass of tomato juice.

"It won't be long now before the baby is born. Just try to focus on that."

"I am focusing on it. I wish it—I mean little Jennings or Carolyn—would come soon." She ran her fingers over her abdomen.

"You'll be all right, Addie." He kissed her forehead.

"Are you going to work now?"

"Unless you want me to stay with you."

"Absolutely not!"

"Alright, I'll see you tonight."

*

Several weeks later, heavy contractions woke Adelaide in the middle of the night, and she was taken by ambulance to the hospital. On February 26, 1947, at 1:03 in the morning, she gave birth to a son. They named him Jennings Walden Colton.

27

Four years later

ON A COLD, GRAY MORNING, as she headed back from her morning errands in Philadelphia with Jennings in tow, something piqued Adelaide's interest. A green truck parked along a side street had a familiar name imprinted on the side. *Paul Perkins' Landscaping.* She wondered if it could be the same Paul from her school days in Florida. They were both enrolled at the local university in Tampa where her family had settled after coming back to the States.

"What are you looking at, Mommy?" asked Jennings.

"See the big green truck over there?" Adelaide pointed to the truck parked on the other side of the street. She craned her neck but couldn't tell if there was a figure inside the dark interior of the truck's cab.

Jennings pressed his nose up against the car window, leaving a circle of fog on the glass.

"It says, *Paul Perkins' Landscaping.*"

"What's that?" he asked.

"Landscaping? It's the tending of land and gardens," she lovingly explained. "Like Mommy's roses in the flower garden."

As they sat in the car waiting for the light to change, Adelaide studied the truck's gold insignia, approving of its color combination against the hunter green background. What would the odds be that it was her friend Paul's landscaping business? The last place she'd seen him was thousands of miles away. The connection would be slim, she concluded. The thought lingered until the traffic light turned green. Jennings wiped his red mitten on the foggy glass, leaving a streak in the vapor as she turned for home.

The following morning, the frozen pond at the bottom of hill looked starkly white.

"Do you think the pond is ready for ice skating?" Adelaide asked John while looking out the bay window in the dining room.

"Well, it's certainly been cold enough. It's near 35 degrees right now according to the thermometer," John replied, "and it's been below freezing for over a week now. I would think it would be."

"Actually, I guess what I'm asking is…is Jennings ready?" she said.

John crossed his arms over his chest. "For skating?

"Well, you and I love to skate…maybe it's in his genes. He's been asking about it all winter."

"I'd love to take him. The sun's out, so it shouldn't be too terribly cold for him," John said.

"I'm going to look for those skates Althea gave us last year. They were her son's first pair." Adelaide went upstairs to Jennings' room, where he sat on the floor engrossed in his train set. "Jen Jen, do you want to go outside today? To go ice skating with Daddy?"

His head jerked up, and his eyes grew big. "Skate!"

"Come here, sweetheart." She gave him a hug and rocked him gently in her arms.

He quickly pulled away and began to hop up and down.

"Where did we put your ice skates, Jen?" she asked, moving to the closet.

"Skate, skate," he sang jubilantly.

She stretched up on her toes as she searched the back of the top shelf.

"I think I found them." She reached for a chair. She pulled the boxes down and opened them, taking the skates from one box and his snowsuit from the other. She bundled Jennings in the fur-lined parka and matching nylon pants that dragged on the floor as he walked.

"Little ice monkey," she said with a grin. "Let's go! Daddy will put your skates on outside at the pond."

*

The crisp air held a stimulating mix of frost, wet woodlands, and chimney smoke as John and Jennings walked down to the pond with their ice skates. Jennings took to the sport quickly for a boy a little over four years of age. He half-skated, half-stumbled, as he made his way out to the middle of the pond with John right behind him.

"Look, Daddy!" Jennings pointed to something across the pond.

"What is it, little man?" John replied.

Some older children were sledding down the hill on the other side of the pond by Chaminoux Road.

"Daddy…sled!"

"That's a toboggan, Jen," he said while bending to make sure Jennings' hood was tight.

As they skated, John stood behind him while holding both of his hands—

ready and waiting for him to stumble. Slowly making their way across the ice, they were soon joined by some of the neighborhood children who were putting on their skates by the stone pavilion. As John and Jennings edged toward the center of the pond, the unmistakable sound of ice in the first stages of cracking pierced the air. Oblivious to the danger and with his eyes on the toboggan, Jennings managed to squirm and break free from John's hold. He began sliding over to a point near the cracking sound.

"Jennings, no!" cried John.

Watching the child step toward the dark ice, John darted toward him. Inches from the crack, John strained to reach out and push him away from the danger spot. Jennings fell and immediately cried.

"Jennings, I'm sorry, little man. I didn't mean to hurt you," he said, picking him up, wincing at inflicting any pain on his son. "Jen-Jen, look over there," he said to distract him while dusting snow from his pants.

John held Jennings tightly, still reeling from the impact of the incident. The child's cheeks were cherry red, as bright as his scarf and mittens. John brushed the fresh tears from his face as two of the children came toward them on the ice.

"Is Jennings all right, Mr. Colton?" asked one of the girls.

As she neared, John recognized her as the little girl who sometimes babysat for Jennings. She wore a pink wool hat and matching scarf.

"Just a little shaken is all, Wendy," he said. "But there's a hole in the ice forming right over there. I think you'd better go back. The pond isn't safe right now."

"A hole...yikes! Bye, Mr. Colton!"

The girls scampered back to the hill.

With Jennings in his arms, John skated back across the lake.

28

Seven years later...

"JOHN, WE'VE BEEN INVITED to the Smiths' shore house in Stone Harbor next weekend," Adelaide said from the top of the stairs as he came into the foyer.

"Oh, Addie, again?" he said while sorting through the mail.

"John, they're lovely people. I don't know what you have against them. Besides, Stone Harbor is so lovely." She headed swiftly down the hall to the bedroom.

John followed her up the stairs. "It's not the Smiths, Addie. It's just that I have so much work to go over." He entered the bedroom, stripping off his tie. "These briefs are stacking up by the minute."

"But John, we haven't done much of anything lately, and since we've been invited, I'd hate to—

"Hate to what? Say no to another social engagement?" He unfastened his belt. "Heaven forbid you should stay home. You'd think I wasn't enough for you sometimes."

"Oh, John, I don't know what you're talking about," she said from the dressing table while brushing her hair.

He sat on the bed to remove his shoes before carrying them into the closet. The walk-in brimmed with clothes—shirts, sweaters, and dark suits in every hue of black, gray, and navy hung atop a row of shiny shoes the color of black and oxblood. On the opposite side, Adelaide's wardrobe of colorful satin gowns and crisp linen dresses, blouses, and suits lined three-quarters of the closet, mirroring a department store's inventory.

"I love you dearly, and you know it." She put down her hairbrush and walked over to him, putting her arms around his waist. "Okay, I'll cancel next weekend. But don't forget tomorrow."

"What's tomorrow?"

"The picnic."

"What picnic?"

"In Fairmount Park. You know, our annual outing with the country club. The Arnolds and Biddles will be there."

"Oh, no, I forgot all about that, Addie, I'm sorry."

120

"Oh, John, does that mean you're not going with us?" She pouted. "Please, John, please make time for us. Don't disappoint Jennings. Not again, John, please."

"Okay, okay, I'll go." He raised his hands in surrender.

*

"Jennings, we're getting ready to leave now," Adelaide called up the stairs.

"I'll be right there," he yelled down from his room.

"I hope the weather cooperates. We've had so much rain the past week," Adelaide said to John as she closed the cooler.

"What's in there?" John asked.

"We're in charge of the salads—we have chicken and tuna—and, of course, Hilda's scrumptious deviled eggs. Everything's on ice."

"Looks like the sun wants to come out," he said, standing at the door. "I'll bring the car around."

Jennings rushed down the stairway carrying his baseball glove.

"Okay, do we have everything?" she said to herself. "Let's see, we've got the cooler...the umbrella and chairs are already packed...oh, I forgot the sun lotion. Jennings, please take the cooler outside. Daddy is bringing the car around. I'll be right back."

Within the hour, the family was on the Schuylkill expressway en route to Fairmount Park. Adelaide glanced at John, knowing he would rather spend the day in his study working on law briefs than socialize with any of her friends. His chiseled features weren't perfect, but they still sent a warm feeling through her body. She turned to see Jennings, a mini-replica of John, in the backseat looking out the window.

"Are we almost there, Mom?"

"Yes, Jennings. It won't be long. Just a few more miles."

*

The park looked lush and inviting. Dozens of trees dotted the landscape and nestled in meandering clusters along the Schuylkill River.

"There they are!" Adelaide spotted the Arnolds and Biddles at a double picnic table as they pulled into the parking lot. "Hello, everyone!" she called as she hopped out of the car.

Franklin Biddle had already taken command of one of the grills, trying to light it. Stacks of food were laid out on top of one of the tables—hotdogs, hamburgers, potato salad, and a plate of blood red tomatoes. Bright yellow ears of corn looked freshly plucked straight from the fields of New Jersey just across the river.

"Hi, there!" said Althea. "So glad you could make it, John. We weren't sure about you coming."

John laid the cooler down on the picnic table. "Glad I could make it, too."

Adelaide gently poked him in the ribs from behind. "Liar," she whispered and kissed him on the cheek.

Betty Arnold wore a wide-brimmed hat and sunglasses and sat next to Althea Biddle, who nursed a tall drink.

"Honey, you remember Betty and Althea, right?" asked Adelaide.

John smiled at them. "Hello, ladies."

"And their husbands, Franklin and Joe," she added.

"Gentlemen, nice to see you again." John shook hands with them. "How's that fire coming, Franklin?"

"Finally got her lit," he said, putting on his chef's hat. "Now, folks, let me know what it'll be...medium, well, or rare."

"Addie, one of the boys brought a canoe. If Jennings wants to join them, he's welcome. Teddy is with them now," said Althea.

"Jennings, you remember Mrs. Biddle's son, Teddy, don't you?" asked Adelaide. "He's about your age."

"I think so. Can I go down there now, Mom?"

Adelaide looked toward the river. "I guess it'll be all right. But don't stay out too long. We'll be having lunch soon."

The sun and breeze gently relaxed them as they sat chatting and drinking under the shade trees. Teddy and Jennings, along with some of the other children, chased each other around the trees and picnic tables, occasionally stopping to pick at the food trays like hungry birds over a feast of roadkill.

"Anyone for another hamburger?" Franklin called from where he stood by the grill, his face sweaty. "I've got three more."

"I could go for one," said Joe.

"More lemonade?" asked Althea.

"I'm so full, I'm ready for a nap." Adelaide sat back on the chaise lounge.

In the near distance, she watched John and Betty play badminton in the open field.

Shortly after lunch, the wind began to pick up, and the sun slowly retreated behind a thick, menacing cloud—ominously turning blue and then black as it rolled over the river. Within minutes, rain began to fall—lightly, at first, and then heavier. Another big storm was on its way. The rain turned to

122

heavy pellets shortly before a rumbling of thunder. The sudden drenching scattered everyone to the safety of tents or umbrellas. Some ran under the trees with large canopies of leaves and branches while others stood with towels over their heads.

The summer shower picked up in intensity as thick droplets descended, pummeling the grass into muddy puddles and turning the nearby parking lot into a shallow pool. The river appeared dangerously high. Several inches of rain had fallen the previous week along the East Coast—a summertime nor'easter, the meteorologists were calling it—hitting the Delaware Valley particularly hard. Soon sparks of lightning flashed in the nearby trees. By now, it didn't seem the storm would be ending any time soon.

Suddenly, a muffled desperate shout came from the nearby pavilion where some people waited out the storm.

"Donny...Donny!" the woman shouted. "Donny, where are you?"

Two small children stood by her side, clutching her legs. She had a look of desperation as she paced back and forth while calling his name, a frantic edge to her voice. The children began to call, echoing her. Their tiny voices rang out, but the gurgling and clacking of the rain and thunder squelched all attempts for their words to carry more than a few feet.

"Mom, I think Donny's the boy we were playing with out on the canoe," Jennings said. "Maybe I should go down to the bank to see if I can find him."

In a matter of seconds, before Adelaide could process it, Jennings darted out from the pavilion and tore through the muddy landscape, racing toward the bank of the cresting river. At the sight of Jennings nearing the edge of the embankment, she felt her stomach twist. She desperately called for him to come back, but he kept running toward the river. She wanted to reach out and snatch him or send John out to bring him back, but she couldn't formulate the words. Besides, John had already headed back to retrieve the car to bring it closer to their spot on the picnic grounds.

The boy, in red swim trunks, appeared as a dot upstream. He had drifted under the aqueduct and hung onto an overhanging branch, trying to use it to pull himself onto a large boulder jutting out from the bank. Jennings climbed out to one of the boulders just barely above the surface and grabbed a loose limb, walking precariously across it as Adelaide watched in alarm. Seeing Jennings disappear below the edge of the bank, Adelaide became numb with fear. No doubt he had already entered the choppy water.

She raced out from under the umbrella and toward the river after him. Her frantic scream tore through her throat until she ruptured her vocal cords. The sounds of her own screaming plunged her further into hysteria until the day's colors morphed into a mottled gray, moments before she collapsed.

When she awoke, she was told the news. Fortunately, little Donny had made it to safety after the threat of being swallowed up by the raging river. But Jennings, not being so fortunate, had drowned.

*

Hundreds of people came to offer their support and condolences at his viewing. With a heavy heart, Adelaide stood next to John, barely propped up on his outstretched arm, at their son's casket as, one by one, the mourners drifted by, offering their sympathies.

"We're so sorry…"

"What a brave little boy…"

"He's in heaven now…"

But only snippets of their words caught in Adelaide's ears. Her acknowledgements became rote as she nodded in a half-smile through tear-stained cheeks. John stood erect beside the casket in the somber light of the torchiere; the pain in his countenance could not be hidden. The days and nights after the funeral ebbed slowly…so slowly that Adelaide wished her life would end.

29

A YEAR AFTER JENNINGS' DEATH, Adelaide found that time and space apart from her son had taken away something of her soul, as though a part of her still lingered somewhere out on the Schuylkill River where he'd drowned. While her spirit sagged, she bore the pain of losing Jennings as courageously as she could. To muster a smile took all the strength she had, as daunting a task as asking a statue to render any mirth. She eventually learned that putting up a brave front was nothing more than stepping out onto a large stage and casting herself into a heroic role. Tossing her emotions into the wings, the show must go on despite the pain. The pain seared until all that was left was numbness.

She and John strived to keep active in the community, hoping the swirl of activity would lend a panacea to their mending hearts. Yet even through their efforts, it seemed that nothing could dent the pain for long. It clawed with the desperation of a rapacious wolf. At the same time, she slowly began to find occasional respites from her grief, submerging herself into ladies' group functions at her church, or when she headed up charities. As she reflected on the 11 short years with Jennings, the precious memories gave her the strength to partake of life again, if only with half her heart engaged.

As she walked along Main Street one summer afternoon, she spotted a green truck similar to the one she had seen several years ago in Philadelphia. It was parked outside the diner in Waynesboro. Under the gold insignia of *Paul Perkins' Landscaping*, there was a phone number. Tears eased from her eyes in a bittersweet remembrance of the last time she saw the truck with Jennings beside her. Visions of his copper hair tucked loosely under his hat and his quick, green eyes flashed before her.

Suddenly, her heart grew heavy, and her spirit was sucked out of her. Grasping the nearby lamppost she tried to regain her composure. Her tears had caused momentary blindness and embarrassment as people passing her on the street witnessed her emotions, casting furtive glances while she pretended not to notice. She hated people seeing her in such a state of grief, the way her face crumpled and winced. After the moment passed, she fumbled for a pen and jotted the phone number down.

Weeks later, she came across the paper with the scrawled number in her purse.

"Hello…hello? Yes, this is Adelaide—Adelaide Walden, actually, Colton now…Adelaide Colton. May I speak to Paul Perkins, please?" Her voice quivered as the anxiety spread into her throat. "Is this you, Paul?"

Adelaide could feel the rhythm of her heart, and, if she didn't know better, it could have been beating on the outside of her chest.

Adelaide and Paul chatted for the better part of an hour, reliving their former schooldays together down south and quickly catching each other up on their lives over the past 20 years. Their nostalgic rendezvous was so natural that by the end of the hour, she offered him a job working at the Colton estate. When she hung up the phone, she felt the day couldn't have started off better.

*

The estate came alive in the hands of Paul's handiwork. Once beautiful, it became almost breathtaking now. One day, while hosting a women's auxiliary luncheon, Addie left the room for a moment. On her way back, she stopped and stood by the bay window in John's study overlooking the pond. The beds and borders popped in rainbow colors. Every inch of soil was tended so perfectly that it was no surprise the exquisite gardens and grounds garnered landscape awards by the local horticultural society. His designs reflected a deep love for his work as his talented handiwork shone everywhere— ambrosia for the senses in all four seasons. Just looking out on the estate lifted her spirits, but not for long. Since Jennings' drowning, Adelaide's grief still hung heavy. She continued to push past the pain as much as possible.

"Addie?" Althea's eyes narrowed with concern. "Are you alright? You haven't said one word in the past hour."

Adelaide startled at the invasion of privacy. She turned from the window toward her friend, Althea, standing in the doorway.

"I'm sorry, Al, I'm a bit unfocused today. I'm not sleeping too well lately, and my body seems to shut down at the most inopportune times, I guess," Adelaide said, trying to be gracious.

"I understand. I just hate it when you're depressed. Is the medication working for you?"

"Oh, I guess so," she said.

Althea had kind eyes behind her wire-rimmed glasses.

"Please don't worry, I'm all right," said Adelaide, trying to appear genuine, not having the heart to tell her the medication wasn't enough. In fact, the anti-depressants were not working for her as well as expected. She

126

wanted a higher dose and had gotten some from the doctor hours before the lunch meeting and hoped the pills would kick in soon. Adelaide was grateful to have such a friend as Althea, and usually talking out her problems had been something Adelaide could do with ease. But lately, Adelaide had become reclusive and wanting more time to herself. She sensed her friends and some of the townspeople had begun to gossip that she was no longer the same person. The vitality she had once now felt stunted and dry. Frankly, she didn't care.

"Al, can you excuse me? Please go on with the lunch meeting without me. Stay as long as you want. I'm going upstairs for a nap. I can't seem to keep my eyes open."

"Of course, Addie. We're nearly finished anyway. I'll let Hilda know that she can start clearing the plates now. I'll stay around to help her."

Adelaide gave a nod of approval and walked upstairs to her bedroom. Deeply moved by the death of her son, Adelaide found she was often not only depressed, but her self-esteem was impacted as well. She'd wanted to one day have another son, for John's sake so he'd have someone who could, one day, work beside him in the law firm.

But this was not to be. Adelaide couldn't become pregnant, and it became the fault line between them.

*

"Do you still love me, John?" Her voice broke as she called to him from the divan.

"How can you ask such a question, Addie?"

"Oh, John, I don't know how I'm going to go on without—"

He rushed to her side as she wept, wrapping his arms around her, a panacea she could always lean on. What would she do without her Jennings? Now they were alone...childless. Her fears welled up within her, threatening to snuff her out. She still had John. Her body clung to his as they wept together. But in her insecurity, she wondered for how long could she keep him happy?

On especially hard days, Adelaide was given to fits of exasperation, often at the expense of help around the house.

"I told you not to trim back the bushes so severely," she said crossly to Fernando, Paul Perkins' assistant, her hair whipping around her head as she pointed toward the row of conifers and azaleas that lined the back veranda. "And I despise ajuga. I don't want it planted over the stone wall. I told you that a month ago. It's such a nasty, invasive plant. Pull it out immediately."

The gardener looked shocked at her displeasure.

"What are these roses doing here? I didn't ask for these." Her petulance rose.

"But, Mrs. Colton, I—"

"I didn't want this color, Fernando," she said. It clashed with her interior furnishings and didn't match the color scheme she'd envisioned for the estate. She'd have removed the roses herself if she didn't have someone else to do it for her, not realizing that roses don't take well to being moved around a garden, even at the hands of an expert who believed that roses do their best blooming when planted only once. Adelaide didn't care about the habits of roses. It was *her* garden, and the roses would have to be the ones to acquiesce.

The assistant scratched the back of his head, trying to explain his reasoning for planting the roses in the perfect sunny patch of ground by the stone wall, but it didn't make any impression on her. After this, she turned on her heel and marched back into the house. She ran to look for John, whose caress could abate her wrath. At least for a moment, until it flared again if even a loose feather from a damask pillow danced uninvited in the room.

30

DURING NORA PERKINS'S LAST TRIMESTER, she had been plagued with pre-eclampsia. The doctors kept a close eye on her situation, but the dangers subsided and her health gradually improved. She eventually gave birth to a healthy baby girl.

"She's so beautiful, Paul," Nora said to her husband while she cradled the baby.

"She looks like you," Paul said with a smile. "Let me take her while you rest."

Paul Perkins and his wife were overjoyed as they began their life together with their new baby in the little cottage he had built on the outskirts of Berks County.

One morning, about six weeks later, Nora looked pale.

"What's wrong, Nora?" Paul asked her one morning.

"I don't know. I'm just...so weak. It's hard to breathe."

Paul took her to the hospital, where tests revealed a weakened heart. Nora's breath came in tiny bursts as she tried to explain that she was having trouble swallowing. Amidst the chaos of the emergency room, her husband paced the hallway, where he watched the doctors through the window in the doorway try to resuscitate her. His body tightened when the body language of doctors changed. He tried to read their eyes, searched for any glimmer that he could be wrong in his assumptions, but he wasn't. He knew it was bad news they would bring him. His beloved wife, Nora, lost consciousness and never revived.

The question of where his life would be without his wife was one that Paul Perkins had never pondered. Now that he was faced with it, he was overcome with not only his own loss but also the loss the child would have to bear as his daughter was now without a mother. Before she'd passed away, he'd often lay awake at night, turning to see her frame taking up the other side of their bed. Now he saw the vision of her body only in his mind as he imagined her amid the rumpled bed comforter and wondered if he'd ever get used to sleeping alone.

The shock of losing his wife, along with his new responsibilities in caring for his daughter, rendered him physically and emotionally frazzled. The only joy he could find was looking into his baby's eyes and seeing his beloved Nora in them. The more he looked at her, the more he saw in her tiny pink cheeks and clear gray eyes the tangible resemblance to his late wife. The innocent gaze as she looked at him was almost as though Nora was saying, "It's all right, Paul, I'm still here with you."

Paul spent nearly all of his time consumed with how he'd raise his baby girl alone without the assistance of the motherly hand of his wife to aid and guide the child. For now, her care and feeding was relatively easy. Warming bottles and changing diapers were simple tasks. But how would he know how to take care of her needs when more important matters would arise...where the sensibilities of a woman would be necessary?

Alone in the world now without Nora, his life would benefit by having someone to love and care for; however, he doubted his own abilities to provide a good home for his child The joy of his newborn child had touched him deeply—the softness of her face and hands, the smell of her hair, was like nothing else he'd experienced.

The bond between them had been instantaneous. He enjoyed his new life with his daughter, and the dimension it added was something that overwhelmed him, at times. Spending his days with her was so fleeting. The hours together seemed to slip by. He loved the sound of her sucking milk from a bottle, watching her cheeks puff and hearing her coo. He would have given her all the time in the world for the rest of his life, if only he had it. For now, it would be all right. A few weeks or months off from work would not impact his finances too drastically. But he wouldn't have the luxury of time to give her for long.

The emotional struggle tore at him and the strain it bore wore him down. Many times, the battle of what he should do brought him into the wee hours of the morning with the question still brazen and bare before him. *God, where do I go from here?* While holding her in his arms, the idea of sending her away became more and more an unwanted option. The thought of not being able to touch her skin or smell her sweet breath wrenched his insides.

But as he eventually made peace with the brutal realization that, one day, separation would come and things would be different for him and his daughter, he wondered which one of them would suffer the most. Other days, he thought how ridiculous it would be to give up his own flesh and blood. Having her raised by another family he didn't know, or worse, a family who may or may not appreciate her, grieved his heart. He had heard the stories and

130

couldn't bear to hear of the atrocities of some of them. Surely, adoptive homes could be a good thing, but the chance of one not being a perfect home for his daughter was more than he wished to consider. At an impasse, he became desperate to find an answer for what to do.

A devout man, he prayed day and night. Each day began on his knees, praying that God would reveal the right path to take. He was willing to do whatever was necessary to make it right for his daughter. After many hours of prayer, Paul's vision of what he should do remained an enigma, but one day, the fog began to lift. Although he received an answer to his prayer, he was still unsure if he had the fortitude to go through with it. Again, he spoke to God, asking for strength.

The following week he called Adelaide and asked if she'd meet him in town. It had been four months since he'd last been on the estate. In a quiet café on Main Street, he spoke the words he had practiced over and over until they didn't sound so strange in his ears.

"I've been thinking about you and want to ask you something, Addie. It's really not easy for me, so please…please pardon my—" His voice broke off as his emotions caught up with him. He quickly rubbed his eyes and then ran them through his hair before plopping them squarely on the table.

"Is everything all right, Paul?" she said with concern.

"Oh, everything's fine. The baby's healthy and I'm adjusting, I guess."

"I'm so sorry, Paul, you know…about Nora."

"It's all been like a bad dream, you know? All except the baby—she's wonderful."

"I'd love to see her," she said with a smile.

"Actually, that's what I wanted to talk to you about."

"Your baby?"

He took a moment to collect himself, to pose the question he had pondered for so long….

*

Adelaide was taken aback. "Adopt? Susie? I…I'm not sure. Paul, why would you want to give her up? I mean…well, she's your daughter!"

He took in her beauty—creamy skin set against thick auburn hair. Her eyes held the simmer of deep green coals, and he had found himself mesmerized by them more than once. He often lost a bit of his concentration if he lingered too long in her company. She had commanded his attention even as far back as his schooldays. While in class, she could glance over at him and the cast of the morning sunlight seemed to set her eyes aglow. It gave him a shiver, and he wondered if anyone else had noticed. He tried to keep his feelings for her in check.

Holding her gaze now for a second, he quickly averted his eyes. When he brought them back to her, his spirit swelled within him, and he knew the answer. For the first time since his prayers, he knew for sure that if he couldn't have his beloved Nora to raise Susie, the next choice would be his first love, Adelaide. The opportunity for her to be raised amid the love that only the rich are fortunate enough to give their offspring would be a blessing not only for Adelaide and John but also for himself, Paul thought. It could be a win-win situation for everyone if Adelaide would accept the offer. He would still be able to see his daughter, who would now have everything he couldn't give, plus he would be able to bring joy and love into the life of a woman he'd loved once from afar.

"Addie, I've been thinking about this night and day for months. It hasn't been easy for me. This is the hardest decision I've ever made. It's just that...well, it's so clear to me that I could never know what to do for her. Susie needs a mother, and there's no one else in my life."

"Paul, I'm...I'm just so...so, I don't know." She picked up her teacup.

"I don't want to give her up, but I don't see the alternative. Besides, I don't know how responsible I'd be, you know, as a father...a father on my own, a working father. She needs time and attention. How am I able to provide that and still work? How would I be able to take care of her without leaving her alone? I don't see how I can do it all."

Adelaide set her cup down. "Paul, I'm honored...so honored that you would even consider me to raise your daughter. I mean, it's so unexpected, really, I'm terribly flattered."

"Well, you're really just my extended family, in a way, I've known you for so long. I could never just give her up to an adoption agency. That would be completely out of the question."

"You have no other relatives? A sister, perhaps?"

"No, there's no one, Addie. My parents have passed away, and it's just me now."

They sat there for a while longer while he held out hope that she would accept his offer.

"I'll let you know, Paul, but I'll need some time. It's not something I can answer today. Can you understand?"

"Yes, Addie, it's fine. Take your time. I know it's a serious endeavor and however long you need to discuss it with John is fine with me. I want the best for my child. I want what's best for everyone."

Paul saw by her eyes that her feelings were pulling in all directions now. He knew she'd have the time, her own son Jennings now deceased, but did she have the will to raise his child?

*

Susie had dark hair and a sweet, pink countenance. The child was such a blessing and an unexpected gift that the ache in Adelaide's heart from the loss of her beloved Jennings slowly mended with the love she bore for Susie. At first, she was unsure that anything could bridge the pain of losing Jennings, yet her one close friend in whom she confided encouraged her to take the child, to love her as though she were her own, stressing that in time she'd grow to adore Susie much in the same way as Jennings. She wasn't so sure but tried to assuage herself with these thoughts.

"Let's take a trip, Addie," John suggested one morning. "I think it would do us both some good to get away." He put the newspaper down and focused on her response. His eyes bore the hope that his suggestion would lift her spirits.

"Where would we go?" she asked, placing Susie's bottle down.

"Anywhere you'd like."

"Would we take the baby?" She planted a kiss on Susie's forehead while the baby cooed.

"Of course!"

"Well...I don't know, really."

"I've been thinking about it, and I know of just the place."

*

A week later, the couple took their daughter down to Tampa to meet John's aunts, Louisa and Alma, older spinsters who lived together in adjoining yellow bungalows on a quiet brick-laid street.

"What a precious baby," Aunt Alma cooed while holding the child.

"She certainly has a sweet disposition," Louisa added. "And so beautiful."

Over the next few days in Florida, Adelaide grew to smile more. In the warmth of the sun and the company of John's sisters, she found her pensive mood lifting. But sometimes, she felt that the death of Jennings would embed a permanent scar on her psyche and that she would no longer have what she had before in the manner of a carefree personality. Not like before her son

Jennings' death or years before when, as a girl, she held nothing back. Her energy had a rhythm that anyone standing near her could feel.

But now her mood was tempered, weighed down by her new circumstances. There was something important that she should tell John but something inside her held it in.

She and John took a walk one morning. While strolling down the redbrick road, she reached for his hand. His face looked so content; her heart ached for what he didn't know. She longed to tell him what was on her mind. One day she would gather the strength to tell him the truth, she consoled herself. Yes, hopefully, one day he would know.

31

Seven years later
Summer of 1966

"LET'S SEE WHO CAN RUN TO THE WATERWHEEL FIRST!" said Susie to her friends, the neighborhood boys, Jimmy and Eaton Packett.

"Are you ready? On your marks, get set, go!"

In the early morning heat, the children flew past the pergola and the footbridge. Only seconds from the waterwheel, Susie turned mid-sprint to see how she fared in the race. *Whoosh.* Six-year-old Jimmy ran past her, almost knocking her down.

"I win!" he declared, raising his arms in victory.

Susie came up from behind, followed by little Eaton.

Not to be out done, Susie ran over to the apple tree by the creek and began to climb. "I bet you I can climb the highest!" Her agile arms and awkward legs found their own symmetry as she pulled herself up the tree. The limp she bore from a foot abnormality, metatarsus adductus, had slowed her pace but not her spirit. "Hey, there's apples up here!" She picked a bright red McIntosh and sat on one of the branches.

"I want one!" Jimmy said.

"Me, too," Eaton said. Skinny and frail, the little child clung to his big brother and mimicked his every move.

"Eaton, you're too small to climb up, so here's one for you." Susie tossed an apple down to him as Jimmy made his way up. "Heads up, Eaton," she said as the apple clunked on the ground below.

Later, they picked up their bikes and rode them down the driveway onto Chaminoux Road. Hot sun on their necks and a fresh breeze in their faces, the children pedaled along the tree-lined streets of St. David's. At the train station, they stopped to get a drink before heading farther into town.

"Hurry up, Eaton!" Jimmy called back to his brother, who lingered behind, trying to keep up, his little legs pumping and his face red from exertion.

They pedaled down West Avenue and slowed in front of the store windows. Under the shade of the Five and Dime store's awning, the children eyed the merchandise behind the glass. A mannequin posed in a yellow seersucker shirtdress was propped against the backdrop of a seascape mural. Bright boxes of laundry detergent sat in one corner with colorful beach balls and assorted merchandise on display in another.

"Let's go inside," said Susie, eyeing the dolls. She dropped her bike down on the sidewalk. The others followed suit.

A blast of cool air met them as they swung open the heavy glass door. Inside, the aroma of soft pretzels emanated from behind the counter. They scampered down the wide staircase leading to the ground floor, where the toy department beckoned. A carnival of balls and bats, games and candy, all wrapped in bright purple and orange and lime green beckoned invitingly as the children roamed down the aisles.

Within seconds, a matronly woman came over with pursed lips and glasses, staring down at them as if they were already in trouble just for being in the store. "May I help you?" she said in a firm tone.

"No, thanks, just looking," Susie said.

It didn't sound like the woman wanted to help them but rather to shoo them out the door. "Remember, you're not allowed to touch anything!" she emphasized, raising her index finger and holding it in the air a second longer than it needed to be. The clerk kept her eyes glued to them as though she was waiting for something to go wrong. Focusing on their every move, she came out from behind the counter, her stubby legs rubbing together, while following them up and down the aisles. Every time Susie turned the corner, she noticed the clerk staring at them from over the top of her glasses. They hung by a gold chain around her thick, rubbery neck, which also held a gaudy plastic beaded necklace that draped down to her chest. She obviously hadn't anything better to do.

"Let's get some bubble gum!" Susie eyed the blue and orange Bazooka display by the counter.

"Did you bring any money?" asked Jimmy.

Susie dug into her shorts pocket. "I have a nickel. How much do you have?"

"I don't have any money," he said. "Neither does he."

"It's okay," said Susie.

"They're a penny each. How many pieces would you like?" the clerk said.

"Five," said Susie while handing her the nickel.

The clerk put the gum in a tiny bag and placed it on the counter.

"Thanks, ma'am." Susie took the bubble gum and handed a piece to Jimmy as they walked back up the stairway. "Do you want a piece, Eaton?" she

136

asked, extending her hand as he eagerly grabbed it.

They left the store and gathered their hot bicycles that had been frying in the sun. Taking the same route as before, they pedaled back to the estate. Susie felt sweat trickle behind her ears and down her neck. Jimmy's face was bright pink, and little Eaton struggled to keep up, his hair matted down around his neck as though he'd been doggy paddling in the pool.

When they reached the estate, they threw down their bicycles at the foot of the waterwheel, where they stuck their heads under the cold spray, basking in the refreshment.

"Wanna stay for lunch?" said Susie.

"Sure," said Jimmy.

"Let's go."

*

"This watercress could be fresher," Adelaide said. She curled her nose while placing the half-eaten portion back on her plate.

"I don't know how anyone can fill up on watercress," said John with mock disapproval. "You should try the chicken salad, Addie. Mine was delicious."

"Do you want another sandwich, Jimmy? Eaton, dear, how about you?" Adelaide said, holding a silver tray in their direction.

The boys busily chugged their lemonade and stopped to nod.

"Yes, please," said Jimmy as he reached for the last remaining sandwich. "I'll split it with you, Eaton."

"Hilda, please bring some more sandwiches," said Adelaide.

"But not watercress!" John said with a smile.

"And more lemonade," said Adelaide.

"Daddy, when are Aunt Sarah and Cousin Jordanna coming?" asked Susie.

"Aunt Sarah and Cousin Jordanna are coming to town soon," John said, peeking out from behind his newspaper. "Tomorrow is it?"

Adelaide nodded.

"What time?"

"On the 5:17," said Adelaide.

"I'll pick them up," John offered.

"I can't wait!" Susie wiggled in her chair.

Hilda brought out a large carafe of lemonade and a tray of sandwiches.

"Hilda, I told you no watercress!" said Adelaide as she eyed the tray.

"Oh, so sorry, ma'am, I didn't hear you. I'm so terribly sorry—"

"It's alright, Hilda," John said soothingly.

Susie cringed when her mother began one of her tirades. Embarrassed by the sudden change in mood, she wished her friend Jimmy and his little brother weren't there to witness it. Her curtness cut like steel on butter. Why did her mother have to be so cross? With the prescience of someone twice her age, Susie felt it was best to let it pass. Defending the situation only made Adelaide more adamant.

Earlier that morning, Susie had passed her mother in the hallway, and she recognized the smell she had once too often met in the vicinity of her mother's presence. She had the "mommy smell." Although she was barely seven years old, the little girl's insights, once more, had given her the wisdom to adapt to her mother's shortcomings. When the mixture of L'Air du Temps met with alcohol, Susie knew that trouble could not be far behind.

"I need to take care of some things," said Adelaide as she abruptly stood. "I have so much to do before they get here."

"Okay, darling." A tiny line appeared between his eyes as she left the terrace and went into the house. He glanced at Susie. "And…your birthday party!" he said with a wink in Susie's direction. "That's what she really meant!" He smiled at her and went back to the newspaper.

Susie watched her mother leave the portico and disappear inside the mansion. Despite her father's words, she felt the sandwich she'd eaten twist in her stomach.

32

"I HOPE I GET A PONY!" Susie said.

"A pony! That would be neat!" said Jordanna.

"If I got one, you could ride it, too, Jordie!"

"Not now, Susie. Not this year. I've already told you that you're not ready for one," Adelaide said. "Just finish your breakfast, both of you, before your oatmeal gets cold." She set her coffee cup down, missing the saucer. "Oh, for Pete's sake," she said at the sight of coffee spilling onto the linen tablecloth.

"I'll get a rag, Mrs. Colton." Hilda promptly left the room.

"Why not, Mommy?" Susie asked.

"We've been over this before. You'll get a pony when your father and I feel you're responsible enough to handle one. Not before," she said with the crispness of a schoolmarm.

"Maybe next year, Susie." John donned his suit jacket.

"Don't gulp your milk, Susie," Adelaide said with a scowl as she got up to follow Hilda into the kitchen.

"Why do you want a pony so badly?" her Aunt Sarah quietly asked when Adelaide left the room.

"I love ponies. They're my favorite animal." Susie placed her glass of milk on the table.

"Well, I have another surprise for you for your birthday, which I think you'll like better than a pony," her aunt said with a smile.

"Really, Aunt Sarah...what is it?"

"You'll find out tomorrow. Now finish your breakfast, both of you. Your mother and I have a lot to do this morning," she said as she got up from the table.

Susie and Jordanna quickly scooped up the last remains of cold oatmeal clinging to their bowls.

"Let's go to the attic!" Susie scampered across the dining room to the stairway in the main hall. Jordanna followed close behind.

They bounded to the third floor, where they discovered a huge cedar closet containing an array of full-length gowns and a few dusty wigs. Prancing around, the girls stumbled in the stiff satin. Donning wigs and hats and beaded clutch bags, they preened and laughed when they caught sight of their reflections in an old Venetian mirror attached to the antique armoire. The Georgian lace bodices hung more to their hips than their waists, and the wigs and hats practically swallowed them.

"Look, Jordie, I'm you!" Susie said while trying on a brassy blonde wig that resembled her cousin's hair color. She tucked back her own dark locks and topped the wig with a ruby hat garnished with rhinestones.

They stared at each other in the mirror. Almost twins. The resemblance was uncanny.

*

They often rode their bikes along the walking paths, or hiked in the wooded hills by the pond. Sometimes they found it tempting to sneak food from the pantry, believing food tasted better outside. They once got pieces of cold fried chicken, and Hilda helped them wrap it up before they scurried off into the trees behind the estate, pretending to be on a picnic. When it rained, they used the upstairs hallway for makeshift games; the shiny oak floor was smooth and perfect for sliding. Their exuberance bordered on wildness—more tomboyish than lady-like—as they slipped on the stairs and bounced bottom first down to the second-floor landing, with occasional bumps and bruises to show for it.

The game they never tired of was hide-and-seek. In a 20-room mansion, the possibilities were endless of where to hide—the pantry, under the duvet-covered poster beds, behind the formal gowns in any number of Adelaide's closets. The children never ceased to enjoy rousting each other out of the hiding places of choice, giggling in unison in celebration of finding, as well as being found.

Rain or shine, they'd spend hours together in Susie's room. Washed in pastel pink with an eggshell wainscoting along the perimeter, as well as a pastoral mural that stretched along two of the walls, the room looked designed for a princess. Her canopied bed had a pink and white comforter and a top quilt of white satin. They used the oversized bay window for dancing, often transforming the windowsill into a Broadway stage where they'd sing and dance, or stretch to wherever their imaginations took them.

One day during their playtime, the girls engaged in a pillow fight, sending one of the crystal lamps crashing to the hardwood floor in Susie's room. The noise was loud enough to send Adelaide flying into the room with Sarah on her heels.

"What is going on here?" Adelaide said sternly.

"Mommy, Jordie broke the lamp!" Susie said. Her face color grew to match the pink in the pillow.

"Jordie, do you see what's happened here?" Sarah rushed to quell the situation, quickly casting the blame on her own child. "If you continue to behave this way, we won't be welcome in the house anymore."

Susie stood in shock at the sight of the broken shards of glass. She knew what the lamp meant to her mother...what everything meant to her. Breaking a lamp or anything was a big mistake.

Everyone stood motionless, afraid of what Adelaide would do. Susie was grateful that the others were there to help temper her mother's rage. They all watched Adelaide's anger rise, and her eyes appeared to be growing out of her head. It was nothing Susie hadn't seen before.

"No, she's the one who hit the lamp!" Jordanna said, coming back defensively.

"Jordie, I don't like that attitude," Sarah firmly replied.

"Sarah, let me handle it," Adelaide said. "Do you see what happens when you break the rules, girls?"

"But Mommy...," said Susie.

"I've told you both before not to play with the pillows. Now this lamp is broken."

Adelaide picked up the remains of the lamp. As she held it, shards of crystal fell to the floor. She waved it in the air. "Can you see what you've done?" Her auburn hair whipped and snapped with the same vehemence as her tone.

"I'm sorry, Mommy," Susie said while curled up in defense on the edge of the window seat, "but it was Jordie, she did it!" Susie inched closer to the window and leaned back on it. "She started throwing the pillows at me. It was her idea!" She pointed a finger at Jordanna.

"Be careful, Susie. Come back from the window. You could fall," warned Sarah.

"Alright, girls, let's settle down now. What's done is done. It's over. Let's not have any more excitement today. We're all busy getting ready for your birthday party tomorrow, and we don't need any more broken lamps," Adelaide said as she rubbed her temples.

Susie slowly exhaled the air she'd been holding back.

"I need another drink," Adelaide muttered to herself as she left the room. Sarah followed at her heels.

Things remained quiet for a while in the mansion, but in the time frame of a few hours, another interruption disturbed the peace. The sound of a scream broke through the otherwise quiet morning. In a short time, a screeching siren and flashing lights drew the attention of everyone at the estate. At a distance designated by the ambulance crew, they were told to stand back while two men in white shirts and dark pants rushed over to the child, who lay in a pool of blood on the slate patio. One worker tried to lift her onto a stretcher to bring her into the ambulance.

"No, wait! Don't move her yet," an attendant firmly demanded. "Check her neck."

"I'm trying to get a pulse," said another.

Apprehension and anxiety were in the air. Most notably, a high-pitched shrill scream could be heard above the commotion. Adelaide stumbled down the marble staircase, her hair flying in all directions as she frantically yelled her daughter's name. In strangled sobs, she screamed as she raced through the front door to the back of the house before slipping into a bed of azaleas. She picked herself out of the bed, ripping her mud-spattered silk pants. Out of breath, she rushed to the child's side.

"Susie, my Susie!"

The words poured out in throbbing, pathetic bursts. A blonde wig sat askew on her daughter's bleeding head.

33

Susie was taken to Bryn Mawr Hospital, where she lay in intensive care—a tiny pupa enclosed in an air-tight bubble hooked up to a ventilator. A jagged green line scratched across a black screen; its clinical message delivered with a sonorous beep. The doctors milled, huddling by themselves while they murmured in sober conversations. Adelaide sat at her daughter's bedside, holding her hand. The hours crept by. John paced the floor while Adelaide quietly prayed. One of the doctors eventually came into the room, his face tight with concern. Addie stood and grabbed John's hand.

"We don't have much hope for her, Mr. and Mrs. Colton, but there's still a chance she could come through. But I can't make any promises." He placed his arm lightly on Adelaide's back, but she was impervious to any sympathy.

Adelaide glanced at John before fresh tears erupted again. His countenance barely resembled the robust features of his days when they first met on the hot summer night at the ball. The lines around his eye and mouth seemed chiseled by a mad sculptor. His eyes, dim behind his horn-rimmed glasses, appeared much older than his 45 years.

"Addie, you need to come home." John placed his arms around her shoulders.

"No, John, I need to stay with her." She wept. "I just…need to be here for her. When she wakes up, it's me I want her to see. Do you understand? It's important that she sees me…that she knows I'm here." Her voice broke again.

"I understand, Addie, but you haven't eaten anything all day." He massaged her shoulders and placed a kiss on her cheek.

"I'm not hungry," she said.

"You need to replenish yourself somehow, Addie. Please reconsider and come home with me. Just for the night."

She shook her head.

"Well, I'm going to get you something to drink, at least."

*

Paul waited just outside the door. He watched from a distance as they stood together in front of the bed where his daughter lay. This was his child. Why did he feel so inhibited? Even more so, he wondered how this could have happened to his daughter. He wished he'd been there when the accident happened. His mind raced with the possible causes.

"Paul!" said John, taken aback as he approached Paul at the doorway.

"Hello, John. I heard about Susie. How is she?"

"Not so good, I'm afraid. She's in a coma." He looked resigned.

"How did it happen?" Paul's voice broke.

"She fell, Paul."

"Fell?"

"That's all I know. That she fell out the window. The window to her bedroom." Remorse etched his sullen features. "I was going to get Addie something to drink," he said, holding a cup. "May I get you something?"

Paul lent a weak smile, shook his head, and entered the room. Without a word, he walked directly to his daughter. "Susie," he said softly, his voice breaking, "Please wake up...we need you." His throat tightened, and he found it hard to swallow. He bent to whisper in her ear, "Susie, I love you."

Adelaide's muffled sobs, along with the metallic *plink* of his daughter's heart monitor machine, tore at his heart.

"Hello, Paul," she said through her tears.

"Addie...how are you?" Paul said soberly.

"I'm sorry, Paul." Her voice trembled. Even though her eyes were red and puffy, he saw her beauty.

Soon John came back into the room with a cup of water and held it out to her. "Addie, please reconsider coming home with me. You can come back first thing in the morning. You'll need your rest."

Her eyes remained fixed on Susie. She appeared barely aware of anything else in the room. She could only shake her head to her husband's pleas.

"Alright, I'll see you in the morning, Addie." He moved to the door. "Are you sure?"

"Yes, John, I'm sure." She wiped her eyes.

He came back and wrapped his arms around her. "I love you, Addie."

"I..." Her voice trailed as he slowly turned to leave. "...love you, John."

The ventilator droned in a sober rhythm, while Susie's body mirrored that of a miniature mummy, her chest lifting and dropping at the mercy of the machine.

The questions churned in Paul's mind as his body shifted sharply, feeling like it, too, had been crushed and bruised. His concerns would only be a natural extension of his love for his only daughter. The imminent one being, *How did this happen?* He felt the pressure build in the room, the silence

144

broken only by the beeps and hissing of the machines. Paul counted Susie's breaths, while Adelaide moved closer to her, to adjust and smooth the sheets.

"She fell from a window?" he asked her.

"Yes," She bent to open her purse.

"What window?"

Adelaide rummaged inside her purse as one stirring a thick stew. "Her bedroom window, of course," she said after a long pause. Her voice sounded strained. "They'd been playing."

"Who? Jordanna and Susie?"

Adelaide remained silent, then finally said, "Yes, the girls had been dancing by the open window...up on the cedar chest in front of it."

"But...how...?" Paul stopped himself short. "Did Jordanna push her out the window?" His voice rose.

"Oh, no, nothing like that! It was an accident." She flushed. "An accident. To explain an accident is...well, it's impossible."

She busied herself in her purse again. Adelaide's arm, now deep inside, continued to stir as she feigned an outward preoccupation. He watched her with a keen eye. The purse practically swallowed her arm. Then she bent her head down into the dark interior. What was she looking for? She sat curled in the chair, half buried in her purse. Had she wanted to crawl inside? It seemed she was avoiding something. Did she think she could divert him from making her talk, hoping he would not speak his mind while she was busy...engaged in something in her purse?

She seemed afraid of something. Was it about Susie? Was she afraid the child would die if she spoke about her for too long? Jinx her life? By not addressing the circumstances, did Adelaide think the situation might go away on its own...her dear daughter would sit up and pull the tubes from her body? Paul glanced at Susie beneath the plastic bubble and then back at Adelaide. Somehow she unwittingly telegraphed her own fears onto him. Fearful that the very questions would suck the last breath of life out of his dying daughter, he kept his thoughts to himself, though they burned to come out. He hoped the truth would come out eventually. He had enough to contend with in the presence of his dying daughter.

Paul lifted Susie's tiny palm, pressing it to his cheek. He brought it to his nose and breathed into it, hoping the very breath could find its way somehow into his daughter's lungs. "I love you, Susie. I love you, sweet girl. Please know that I love you, my precious one," he whispered into her ear.

34

THREE DAYS LATER, SUSIE COLTON WAS PRONOUNCED DEAD. She passed away at 11:32 on an August morning in 1966, just two days before her seventh birthday. She was buried alongside Jennings in the family's burial crypt not far from the estate. The cause of death was cited as an accidental fall.

A string of mourners extended all the way around the cathedral. The townspeople poured in to catch a final glimpse of the Coltons' child. The air shimmered in the morning heat. Their dark suits and dresses clung to their bodies as they waited in line.

Paul stood watching from the back of the chapel. Wafting through the cool air, the scent of roses permeated the room. But it wasn't the same rose aroma as in the gardens he often tended. There the roses evoked warmth— heady and sweet—with a scent that bespoke peace and solitude. Today, in the church, the rose scent cloyed and lingered like an uninvited guest. Like a slap on soft skin, it tinged his olfactory senses sharply. H wanted to regurgitate the odor as it was repugnant to him in this setting. He once loved roses and couldn't get his fill of the fragrance, but now the delight he once held in their presence had been sucked up by the coldness of the surroundings. *Roses shouldn't be here,* he thought. This was not their proper setting. The disparity was irksome. His daughter's funeral. His beloved Susie.

"Such a lovely child," Betty Arnold said to the man standing next to her. "It's just so awful, I can't even think about it."

"It's sad enough to lose a child, but the Coltons have lost two," Althea Biddle whispered to her husband, Franklin. "I can't fathom how they can take any more tragedy," she said, wiping her eyes. "There must be a curse to having old money...so sad it is."

Paul strained to hear their comments. His eyes swept over the people who had come to see his daughter for the last time. The gratitude he had for the faces he saw, those who had taken the time to honor her, welled up inside him. He wanted to shout, "That's my daughter! Isn't she beautiful? That's my baby!" All of these people, he pondered, had come to see his Susie. His child. He wanted to tap them on the shoulder or turn around and tell each of them that he was her father. He longed to run up to the casket and wave his hands and announce, "Listen everyone, I have an announcement. This is my little girl, and I still love her." But when his rational thoughts took hold, he realized that the choice he made many years ago would preclude any admissions like that. They would never know.

Many a day on the estate, he stood watching her surreptitiously from behind an evergreen, catching a glimpse of her curly hair shining in the sun as she ran through the fields or sat by the lake feeding the ducks. It took all of his strength not to approach her too closely. His fears of becoming too attached to her stood as a precipice between them. He loved his daughter but thought it proper not to invade her space. If he had gotten too close, who knows if he'd be able to separate himself from her again? Perhaps the tug of fatherly affection would pull him back to the nights when he rocked her to sleep and bathed her soft head, enamored by the sweetness of her skin and the sound of her breathing.

He stood before the tiny white casket, barely recognizing the resting body lying there. He cringed at the red velvet and satin interior, the image of a bed of blood. The pancake makeup clung to her skin like chalk, making her appear like a freakish doll. Her lips bulged on one side, appearing propped up from the inside. The chin looked crooked. With her eyes closed, the little girl in the casket could have been any little girl. The only thing that resembled his daughter the way he'd known her was the color of her hair, set in sausage curls, the way she'd sometimes worn it. The rest of it was hideous. The mauve colored sleeves came down to her elbows and the contrast with the white gloves looked like two peppermint candy sticks. He smelled formaldehyde. Surely this wasn't his Susie! Where had they placed her? The urge to scream brimmed inside him. *Where's my daughter? What have you done with my Susie?*

If only he could have been there to catch her, the day she'd fallen from the window. He pictured the form of a child falling downward in the form of a flailing rag doll in slow motion. Before she landed on the hard slate three stories below, he would have strained to reach out and catch her, cradling her in his arms. He knew he should keep the line moving, but he could not tear his eyes away from her.

Then she appeared to move. There was no mistaking the shift he witnessed. He refocused his gaze. Then the peppermint candy swirled into red, and all at once, he shuddered. His legs buckled, and he grabbed onto the casket. He swayed a bit before steadying himself, regaining his strength. An usher came to help him. Once more, his eyes caressed her from her hair down to her tiny gloved hands that held a rosary with a tiny gold cross. Longing to burn the image into his consciousness forever, he mentally photographed her features, closing and opening his eyes quickly several times. He fought to maintain his composure and knew that people were still waiting in line behind him. Would his lingering at the casket reveal him as being someone who truly loved this little girl? Did his hand tremor give him away? His tears? Could they see the resemblance in the dim yellow candlelight surrounding the coffin? Surely not, he figured, as the girl in the coffin didn't resemble him in the least. Not anymore.

He did not want to leave her side. He clutched the smooth side of the casket and reached in to feel the scarlet satin interior. His hands drew across it. Back and forth he moved his fingers, feeling the material drift under his touch. Seamless, it felt, like a flower petal. He envisioned the closed bottom end of the casket open up and his daughter's eyes slowly open. For this wasn't real. It couldn't be. He remained by her side until the usher came back and gently took him aside by his elbow. He took out a handkerchief and wiped his brow and forehead. John and Adelaide stood a few feet away.

"I'm sorry, John, Adelaide. She was a mighty special little girl. I'm sure God is taking good care of her now," Paul said as he extended a hand to them.

"Paul, thanks for coming." John patted him on the back.

Adelaide looked over at him and reached to shake his hand. "Hello, Paul," she said softly.

"Addie," he said. Her grip felt limp and as he hugged her, he felt the bones in her back pop through her dress. "How are you doing?"

"I'll be all right." Her face was wet with tears.

As his eyes swept over her, he realized that he still loved her. She had the same innocent expression as she did the day he met her at the coffee shop. He'd watched her squirm, not knowing whether she should accept the offer of his only child. She still hadn't fully recovered from the death of her son, this he knew. She'd pined for the child like a lonely lover. But her flashing eyes quelled his own doubt in her that she'd be a good mother to his daughter.

With disdain, he now questioned his original idea of giving up his precious girl. At the time, he thought it would be best for her. Best for them. But how can this be the best? His little girl didn't even make it to her seventh birthday. He didn't have enough faith in himself to raise her properly, yet even the ultimate sacrifice of giving her a new home didn't yield any better results. He wished he could trade places with her in the casket, grieving the day he had even considered placing her in someone else's hands and hating himself for it.

Even at this moment, the thought overwhelmed him. The fleeting thoughts of wanting to crush her for what she had possibly allowed to happen to Susie dissolved as quickly as they had surfaced. He could no more hurt Adelaide Walden Colton than himself. The very sight of her quenched his anger and soothed his spirit, albeit for a moment. When the reality that his daughter was gone hit him again, he not only felt sorry for himself but even more so for Adelaide. She wore her devastation like a veil. Yes, sadness was only natural. But there was something else in her eyes that he couldn't quite read. Her expression yielded not only that she was hurt, but something else he couldn't quite determine. He wanted her to know there was no reason to feel guilty. Certainly, he didn't hold her responsible.

But the words never came. He only hugged her and wished her well as he walked away into the arms of her sister, Sarah, nodding in the direction of little Jordanna, who was by her side.

"Hello, Paul," Sarah spoke with a weak smile. "How are you?"

He nodded. "Hello, Sarah, I'm…as well as can be expected. And you?"

"Oh, it's been so hard. But we'll get by."

Jordanna stood by her mother, not saying a word. She wore the shock of the event on her face like a stunned doe. Her eyes focused blindly. Paul nodded and gave her a hug before he walked away. He needed to get out of there. He wouldn't be able to sit through the entire service. His head throbbed. The vulgar scent of cold roses seemed now to taunt him, along with the mourners, who were once a blessing to him. It seemed their features turned right before his eyes. Their faces became caricatures, offbeat and oddly twisted.

A woman's witch-like laugh cut through the drone of murmuring. Her red lipstick smile grew into the grotesque grin of a circus clown. What could possibly be so funny? How they dared to laugh and smile. Giggling, smoking, talking…is that all they could do? What talk could possibly be of importance at a time like this? Unctuous morons. He needed to get away from all of them.

He opened the chapel door and walked out into the warm, summer air, breathing it in as though for the first time.

35

October, 1981

EVENING DREW IN, and Sarah got up to close the curtains.

"Paul must have really loved Aunt Adelaide," Jordanna said.

"Yes, I suppose he did," said Sarah reflectively. Her eyes looked strained. Strands of gray had woven in along her temples, and her shoulders arched under an invisible weight.

"That's amazing...about Susie," said Jordanna. "I never knew she was adopted."

"You were too young. I would have told you later, but..." Sarah shook her head. "She was such a lovely little girl, and she looked a bit like Adelaide. It was strange, really, as there was no blood between them."

"It must have been nearly impossible to give up his own daughter," said Jordanna. "I can't even imagine it."

"I'm sure it was. He was such a pleasant man and always so polite. Actually, I liked him myself," she said with a wistful smile and sat back in her chair.

"You did?"

"I don't know if it was because I just wanted something of Adelaide's or if it was genuinely something I wanted. But, in any case, I grew very fond of him, and I looked forward to seeing him." Sarah smiled. "I even paced myself so that he'd have to see me, you know, positioning myself where I knew he'd be...like in the rose garden or by the wisteria."

"Really, Mom?" Jordanna sat up on the loveseat and leaned in closer.

"The estate was so large, I had to work at figuring out the most innocent way to get his attention without looking like I was trying too hard. I just enjoyed his attention because after your father died...well, I was alone." Sarah took a sip of wine. "But I was so jealous of that love, I must say."

Jordanna cocked her head. "Jealous?"

"I found a letter he'd written to Adelaide. I was feeling so sorry for myself...you see, I had wanted the letter to be written to me."

"That must be the missing part of the letter I'd been looking for!" said Jordanna.

150

Sarah forced a smile. "She seemed to have it all. All of my life living with Adelaide, it seemed she got everything and all I got was the scraps. For once, I just wanted something—something special. And when I found out that she had lied to John about the baby's real parents at the adoption, I just felt—well, I wanted to punish her, I guess. I took the letter and threw it away. It just wasn't right. Can you understand that?"

Jordanna nodded outwardly, not wanting to upset her mother. Inside she couldn't believe her mother could be so bold.

"When Paul lost his wife, I felt so sorry for the man. I had wanted his attentions, but he seemed only to have an interest in Adelaide. At least, that's what it appeared. I used to watch her from my bedroom window. The way they'd talk and she'd smile—always asking him to plant things, her favorites and such. I'm surprised that John didn't notice. But with his traveling and all, I guess he'd overlooked it."

"But Mom... how did Susie really die?"

Sarah looked down at the coffee table. Her face drew sharp. In place of an answer, she stood, collected her plate and glass, and took them into the kitchen. Stacking them on the drain board, she took a deep breath and turned to Jordanna, who followed and now stood in the threshold.

With her hand resting on the sink ledge, Sarah formed her words slowly. "You know how she died, Jordie. She fell out of the window."

"Yes, Mom, but why?"

"I don't know, Jordanna. I really don't know exactly what happened. It's something Adelaide never spoke about."

"It always seemed like no one talked about it," Jordanna said.

"I know. It was Adelaide's wish not to. And John's, too."

"I never understood that. It was like some weird secret society after she died. Everything became so hush-hush. It was never the same," Jordanna said.

Sarah busied herself at the sink and then turned on the faucet. The water ran onto the dessert dishes as she rinsed away the crumbs. Sarah let the water run for longer than necessary.

"But I need to know!" Jordanna urged, the words louder than she intended. She hated raising her voice to her mother, but something inside snapped.

Her mother looked shocked, as though Jordanna were asking for her very soul.

Jordanna stepped closer and stood eye to eye with Sarah. "Mom, please. All these years, why won't anyone tell me how or why Susie died?" She placed her hand on top of her mother's.

Sarah pulled her hand away and put the dish down. Then she picked up the big sterling silver spoon, which sat on the drainboard.

"No one has ever talked about it, sweetheart," she said as she wiped the spoon until it shined, then moved to the drain board where she passed a terrycloth towel over every inch of the board in long, slow strokes. "When talk of the incident arose, someone always changed the subject. Either John or Addie, it didn't matter. No one seemed to want to talk about it."

Her words hung thick in the air—each syllable strained to find its way out and once out, awkwardly drifted until it disappeared. Sarah stopped reflectively and lent a small smile.

"I tried to ask Hilda, but it seemed neither she nor anyone knew much of the details, and if they did, no one desired to remain on the subject for very long. This was the only way we knew how to cope in moving forward, especially Adelaide. After all, it was no one's fault. At least, that was the drawn conclusion." She wiped something imaginary on the countertop. "Besides we've been over this before," she said with finality.

"I don't remember, Mom. I really don't."

"You don't remember? You don't remember the times we stayed up half the night?" Her eyes suddenly came to life with a blaze seemingly tempered with pity.

"No, Mom, I don't!" Jordanna said, crossing her arms across her chest.

"We discussed it for hours, Jordie." Her face constrained.

Jordanna tried to reach into her mind to pull out what her mother was saying. All that remained were fuzzy half-recollections that rose and fell at their own discretion. Her mind raced to catch up with them. It left her dizzy and perplexed. The stirring of her childhood memories floated airily—a carnival carousel with happy faces and swirling hobby horses bobbing and spinning in a blurry haze. Round and round the memories churned over the years. She could almost reach out to touch them before they disappeared from sight, only to return again and again...just close enough to catch a glimpse but never to hold for long.

"After it happened, your Uncle John said the topic was closed," her mother said. "And that no amount of dwelling on it would amount to anything worthwhile. It was an accident, and that was the end of it."

"Just like that?" Jordanna said. "How can that be the end of it?"

"It's the way they chose to handle it," Sarah explained. "Jordie, you don't think the question hasn't crossed my mind before? I've thought about it many a time."

"It's just so weird. Wasn't anyone else curious?"

"I don't know," said Sarah.

"I've searched everywhere and there's no mention of it," Jordanna said shaking her head, following right behind. "It's not even in any of the newspapers."

"You've researched it?" Sarah said with a knitted brow. Her eyes grew stern.

"Yes, I felt it my responsibility. The rumor on campus is that she jumped out of the window. I wanted to squelch it the best way I could. Find out for myself."

Sarah shook her head disbelievingly and spoke with the discipline of a schoolmaster. "Jordie, all I know is that on the last day of Susie's life, I heard Adelaide yelling in Susie's room. I was downstairs at the time, helping her look for her missing diamond bracelet. And then I heard a scream. I raced upstairs and saw Addie by the dresser. Then I saw you run into Susie's room. I was right behind you. And that's all I know. Don't you remember that?"

"It's all so cloudy to me. It's always been cloudy."

"Jordie, I've told you all that anyone knows, really," said Sarah with a beleaguered expression. "Why are you bringing this up now?"

"Did Aunt Adelaide murder her?" Jordanna's voice rose. "Was she jealous of her own daughter?"

"No, of course not!" Sarah's voice rose.

"People don't just fall out of windows. It's crazy!"

"She may have been playing there...or perhaps saw a bird at the window and reached out too far. I'm sorry, Jordie, no one really knows."

"Who was Aunt Adelaide yelling at?"

"I don't know, really. She was distraught over losing her bracelet. That much I know."

"I think someone does!" said Jordanna.

"I wish I did know!" Sarah said with exasperation.

"You know! You're just protecting me!" Jordanna's anger erupted. "You've always protected me! It's because I did it, isn't it? I killed my cousin! Is that what this is all about? All these years, the counselors, the hushed tones?"

Jordanna remembered the psychologist's words of long ago but never pieced it together. *She may not remember the incident in the years to come. This would be a good thing...."*

Sarah averted her eyes from Jordanna's gaze. Jordanna's fear rose, and she began to tremble. "Just tell me the truth! All I want to know is the truth!" She ran out of the kitchen.

"Jordie, Jordie, please, sweetheart, please don't do this to yourself," Sarah said, following after her.

Jordanna lay on the living room sofa, her face buried in the pillows. Sarah sat beside her and ran a hand lightly over her daughter's back. Jordanna always loved the touch of her mother's fingernails through her hair and the along the back of her spine. Right now, though, she didn't feel a thing.

"We've been over this before. You did not kill Susie!" Sarah said softly. "You were only a little girl...a child. Jordie, please." She moved her hand in a circular swirl into the small of her back, the way she'd done countless times before when Jordanna was a little girl. "Yes, it's true, Jordie, that I've protected you. Of course, I have. You were all I had. But it was out of love for you, not lying to you. But as far as you having anything to do with Susie's death, that's ridiculous."

Jordanna remained face down on the sofa, trying to sort out her feelings.

"I don't know exactly how Susie came to fall out the window, Jordanna, but you were not even in the room."

Jordanna didn't move.

"Jordanna, do you understand what I'm saying to you? I saw you run back inside after the scream. You ran back *after* the scream, not before. I heard the scream from the hallway and saw you run into the room. Why do you hold this...this guilt inside you?" Gently gathering her daughter's long mane with her free hand, she raked it with her fingers. "Jordie, why do you feel responsible when you didn't have anything to do with it?"

Jordanna slowly turned over to face her mother, her vision obscured by her tears. "Are you sure? How can you be so sure, Mother?"

Jordanna's words sounded puerile, an echo of when she was a child, uttering the same words to her mother...when she'd already begun the process to mend her own wound and push the pain so far down that no one could reach it.

And now, after all these years, it seemed the wound resurfaced. Jordanna longed to assuage every ounce of the memory of that day, wishing to wring out the ache like dirty water from a sponge. She felt trapped by the guilt of that awful incident. It pressed upon her as a coiling snake wrapped around her psyche. It squeezed by its own will.

Little by little, over time, the snake lost its strength with the help of her psychologist, who showed the frightened girl how not to feed it. Its lack of feeding caused it slowly to die, and gradually she came out of her depression. Her progress came along like a textbook case, at first, the doctors thought.

But, unbeknownst to all of them, the snake was merely hibernating. The past had dredged itself up again. Slithering up through the mire, it yearned to take another breath of air. Long buried in the turbid matter of her subconscious, Jordanna still had a way to go before she'd be completely free of the lurking demon that threatened her own peace of mind and her ability to accept herself. The unconscionable thoughts held on like a piece of wounded flesh.

Sarah spoke softly. "Jordie, I don't claim to know the heart of a killer, but the Bible says everyone's heart is desperately wicked. Who can know the depths of the human heart? But if I thought you'd killed or had any part in killing your cousin, I think we'd have told you by now. You'd know, Jordie. You'd know." She stopped to assess her reaction. "I don't know how Cousin Susie came to die. It's a mystery. Aunt Adelaide never told a soul. That day she turned into a different person. Even before then, something changed within her."

"What change? I don't recall any change in her," Jordanna said.

"You were much too young to notice."

"I do recall her smell, though."

"Smell?"

"Susie called it the 'Mommy smell.' It smelled like sour perfume."

Sarah pulled a handkerchief from her apron and wiped her daughter's tears. "Yes, I suppose I remember that scent well. It was probably the Scotch. She drank a lot of it. Not at first, though. It started off slowly, just as a social thing as I recall. Then, after the children died, it became her panacea. I tried to shield you from it. Sometimes her outbursts were deafening. I couldn't take it."

"Is that when we moved to Mullica Hill?"

"Yes, I couldn't bear it any longer. She even fired one of the maid staff for buying the wrong brand of early young spring peas. Even the townspeople had caught wind of her state of mind. There were murmurings and gossip that Uncle John was thinking about putting her away in Byberry. The state mental facility was looking more the ideal spot for her—if there ever could be an ideal."

"That is so sad, Mom."

"Her tantrums became so hard to live with that even the last maid on staff had quit. I looked in on her from time to time, but I had taken you away from the situation because the tension between her and John became too much for me to bear. It tore me up." She took a sip of wine.

"Is that when she fired Paul?"

"Probably."

"Paul said he'd always wondered why. He said she just blew up one day out of the blue and fired him," said Jordanna.

"I can imagine her doing it. Alcohol changes people. Perhaps he'd lied to her. I know she never liked being lied to. Not that anyone does, but she took it so seriously. She'd snap and curse the ground before she'd let someone lie to her again."

"Did Uncle John have her committed?"

"No, he never did. He spoke to me about it and asked my opinion, but I told him it was his choice. I would support him in any way I could. But I couldn't make such a decision."

"Do you think she pushed Susie out of the window for lying about the lamp?"

"No, Jordie! She loved Susie."

Jordanna wiped her face and sat up.

"But as much as she loved Susie, there was still a void in Adelaide's heart from Jennings' death, something that Adelaide didn't want to admit, especially to herself. Everyone told her that in time she'd grow to adore Susie much in the same way as Jennings. She wasn't so sure at first. But I'm sure she did love the little girl. I know she did. No, Jordie, she couldn't have done that. But no one knows for sure. That was the thing about Adelaide. She kept things close to the vest."

"How do you mean?"

"She didn't let you see inside her. It was always the outside that was important to your aunt. The veneer. She kept it shiny. From her hair to her shoes, she was perfection, the epitome of grace. And she was a controlling person, too. The details mattered. Things had to be just so with her."

"I remember we weren't allowed to play in the living room."

"Oh, yes, her home was like a picture book, immaculate, nothing ever out of place."

"And she loved roses," Jordanna said.

"Yes, the roses. She loved her garden. I think it was the roses that kept her sane."

"I remember them. And the day she yelled about the color or something not being the right shade…"

Jordanna loved roses, too, and shivered at the comparison.

156

36

Spring, 1982

MERION HILL CRICKET CLUB SAT CLOISTERED BY TALL EVERGREENS, a commanding presence in Waynesboro. Sweet air swept through the trees as Jordanna approached the rambling main house on the expansive property. She stepped up to the porch and entered the main foyer where people gathered in dress attire, milling in pockets around the lobby. Their murmurs blended into the thick walls and carpets. A warm scent of meat in the browning stage drifted in from the nearby kitchen.

"May I help you?" a soft voice came from behind her. Standing at a cherry wood reception counter, a petite, gray-haired lady smiled brightly, wearing lipstick a shade too harsh for her sallow complexion.

"Yes, hi. My name is Jordanna Bronson."

"Welcome, Ms. Bronson, how may I help you?"

"Well, I'm looking for some information." Jordanna fished for the old black and white picture she'd found in the attic and drew it out of her purse. "The lady in the middle is my Aunt Adelaide Colton," she said, holding up the picture.

The lady reached out for the picture and held it close as she examined it.

"She was a member of the country club and is deceased now, but I was wondering about some of the women standing with her. I think I know their names and was wondering if they belonged to the club here?"

"My, this picture was taken some time ago, I see," the lady said.

"Yes, around 1956 or 1957," Jordanna said. "I'm pretty sure two of the ladies are Betty Arnold and Grace Spencer. I'm not certain as to who is who, but I think the brunette is Grace. I'm unsure of the fourth woman there on the end holding the racket. Is there a way to look up either Grace or Betty in an old register, or something? I'd love to talk with them."

The lady's face tightened. She quickly shook her head. "I'm sorry, Ms. Bronson. I'm not sure if I can be of any help to you." She pursed her lips.

"Oh, no," said Jordanna. "No way at all? I just wondered if you had any record of any one of them. Maybe I could speak to someone in your membership department?"

"Well, Beverly is not in today, and I am assuming her responsibilities. But, unfortunately, we are not allowed to give out the names of the members to the public—unless, of course, you are a member."

Jordanna hid her impertinence and tried not to raise her voice. "No, I'm not a member. But like I said before, my aunt and uncle were members many years ago. You may have heard of them...John and Adelaide Colton?"

Jordanna waited for the recognition to hit the woman. She looked old enough to be her aunt's age if she were still alive. Surely everyone knew of the Coltons, Jordanna reasoned. The lady's face remained stoic.

"My aunt and uncle are the founders of Colton College. It's soon to be a university. They donated the land and had the school chartered after they died," Jordanna said a bit louder.

"I'm sorry, Ms. Bronson, but as much as I'd like to help you, I'm still not permitted to give out any information," she said, clasping her hands together in the form of a steeple on the smooth counter.

Jordanna chewed her bottom lip and put the picture back in her purse. She tried not to let the woman's pragmatism sway her, but it seemed like a losing battle. "Okay, I understand," she acquiesced. "But may I ask you one last question?"

"Certainly," the woman said with a clipped kindness.

"Well, I just want to know if the records go as far back to the fifties. Do you keep records for that long?"

"Oh, yes, of course. We have a list of the memberships from all of the fifties," the woman said as though she were speaking of a grand masterpiece.

"Well, thanks for your time," Jordanna said.

"You're quite welcome. I'm sorry I couldn't help you further, but rules are rules, you know." Her eyes danced behind her glasses.

"I understand." Jordanna nodded and turned back toward the main entrance.

A short and stocky man with white hair stood under an alcove a few feet from the door. He raised a thick finger in the air as though hailing a cab. "Miss," he said as he came toward her, "may I speak with you?"

Jordanna moved toward him as he limped to her.

He cleared his throat before speaking. "Miss, please excuse me for eavesdropping, but I couldn't help but hear you mention a name I haven't heard for years," he said with a winsome smile for a man his age. "Adelaide Colton. I heard you mention her name when I walked by just now."

Jordanna's spirits lifted. "Yes, she's my aunt."

"I once knew an Adelaide Colton." He smiled. "There can be only one…auburn red hair and green eyes." He studied her for a moment. "Eyes like yours! Just like yours." He looked surprised as though this moment weren't real.

"You knew her, sir? From here, at the club?" Jordanna grew excited.

"Yes, she was a friend of ours, my wife and I."

"What's your name, sir?"

"Franklin Biddle. Althea Biddle is my wife."

"Althea Biddle," Jordanna said. She formed the name slowly, hoping it would conjure up a recollection. "Hmm, I wonder if this is her in the picture," she said as she rummaged through her purse. She pulled out the black and white and handed it to the man. He brought it close to his face. A smile grew as he examined it. He pointed a thick finger onto the picture. "Yes, that's my wife! The blonde on the end there. She's the one holding the tennis racket!"

"What a small world this is, Mr. Biddle! I'm so pleased to make your acquaintance," she said with a smile. "I'm Jordanna Bronson."

"Indeed, a pleasure!"

"Is she here? Your wife?" She glanced around the perimeter of the lobby. "I'd love to meet her."

"No, I'm sorry she's not," he said with reservation.

"Will she be here tomorrow? I can come back."

Franklin Biddle's smile disappeared. A shadow fell across his face. "Actually, my wife is in a nursing home."

"Oh, I'm sorry to hear that."

"Yes, I am, too. It's the best place for her, though. She needs 24-hour care."

"Where is she staying?"

"Waynesboro Manor House."

"Oh, I've been there. I'm a part-time volunteer in the rehab. Well, if she's up for visitors, I'd still like to meet her."

Franklin Biddle looked at Jordanna and a smile returned to his face. "I think she'd like that."

"Great!" said Jordanna. "I will definitely stop by to see her!"

37

Early fall, 1982

A THRONG OF STUDENTS POURED OUT OF MAGINESS HALL as thick patches of cotton-white clouds shredded across the sky.

"Jordie!" Beth called from across the courtyard.

"Hi!" said Jordanna.

"Going to lunch?" Beth joined her and marched in step with her.

"Yes, I'm starved."

"I guess you heard the latest—about Kingsley?" Beth said.

"No, what about him?"

"He was kicked out of school."

"Really? What for?"

"Something to do with killing an animal—one of the ducks, I think."

"Oh, I'd heard someone found a dead duck. I didn't think that anyone actually killed the innocent thing. I just thought it died in a fight with another animal or something. How awful!"

"Yeah, it's a shame," said Beth.

"He's messed up, that's for sure."

"I guess."

"I can't believe it. How'd he do it?" said Jordanna.

"Apparently, with his bare hands."

"Oh, gosh, that's gross. How do they know he did it?"

"I don't know for sure, but I heard someone say he was bragging about it."

"Seems like something he'd do."

They made their way through the lunch line and found a table by the windows. Jordanna couldn't shake the news about the duck.

"I don't know what Debbie Hale sees in him," Jordanna said as she took a forkful of stew. "By the way, what are you doing this afternoon?"

"Aside from studying? Nothing. I'm free for the rest of the day."

"I was wondering if you could go on a field trip with me."

"To where? And please don't say the third floor."

"No, not there. Not this time. But it's not far from here."

"Okay, but I have to be back by dinnertime," said Beth. "I'm trying out for the play."

"Yeah, I was thinking of doing it too, and I have a meeting with Dr. Morgan."

"So where are we going?" Beth said.

"You'll see. I'll tell you along the way."

*

Waves of sunlight played on the damp ground as Jordanna and Beth walked along the tree-lined streets into Waynesboro. Large leaf piles nestled at the curbs. The leaves that hadn't been gathered lay strewn on the sidewalk like wet cereal. Jordanna closed her eyes and savored the woodsy bourbon-soaked aroma. Passing through town, up and down the quiet streets, they eventually came upon the circular driveway in front of the nursing facility. A large fountain littered with fallen leaves lay in the middle. Various shades of mums bloomed on either side of the walkway leading to the main entrance.

"This is where you volunteer," said Beth.

"Yeah, but I haven't been able to work in a while," said Jordanna. "I feel so horrible, but I've been so busy with the newspaper and schoolwork."

They stepped into a hushed lobby tastefully decorated in muted shades of green and gold.

"This place is so nice." Beth scanned the lobby.

"I know," said Jordanna, looking around for Doranda Welling.

In the corner, a man sat reading the newspaper to someone in a wheelchair. A white-haired lady in a sky blue sweater sat nearby engrossed in a book she held in her lap.

"May I help you?" a tall woman said as she methodically wiped the long leaves of a plant with a cotton ball.

"Yes, hello, we're here to see Mrs. Biddle," said Jordanna.

She studied Beth and Jordanna for a brief second. "You may have a seat," she said, still holding one of the leaves. She put the cotton down and went behind the desk to pick up the phone.

"This place looks like an upscale hotel," said Beth in a whisper.

Several minutes later, Mr. Biddle hobbled through the door. "Jordanna!" he said as he slowly approached.

Jordanna rose. "Mr. Biddle. Hi, how are you? This is my friend, Beth."

He smiled and nodded. Beth extended her hand.

"How is your wife today?" Jordanna said.

Franklin Biddle's sparse white hair fluttered like a cockatoo. "Oh, not bad today. Not bad at all," he said with a twitch of a smile. "I told her you'd be coming. So sorry you were not able to speak with her at your last visit."

"Well, it's kind of hard to talk when you're asleep," she said with a chuckle. "Would it be okay if we both visited with her today? Is she up?" Jordanna glanced at Beth and then back to him.

"Oh, yes, that would be delightful," he said. "Why don't we go in now?" He spoke as if talking to a deaf person and turned for the hallway.

Jordanna offered her smile as she passed by the elderly residents lined against the wall in wheelchairs, their vacant eyes glazed and searching. Jordanna's heart pulled at the sight. A few smiled at her, but most just stared straight ahead.

"I wonder if Mr. Upland is in there?" she said as they passed the exercise room. She craned her neck to catch a glimpse of him. Farther down the hall in the dining room, a few people perched at tables with half-eaten plates of food on orange trays in front of them. Most sat with their eyes closed. At the far end of the hallway, Franklin turned the corner and entered the last room on the right. Jordanna and Beth followed him and lingered at the doorway.

Inside, a woman lay on the bed by the window. The window shade was half closed, and a crusty African violet plant sat on the windowsill. Jordanna felt a stab in her stomach and crossed into the room.

"Come in," Franklin gestured with his hand, his voice still loud.

Jordanna felt suddenly awkward at approaching Mrs. Biddle, feeling the warm pocket of air of the woman's personal space, like walking into someone's bedroom.

Althea's eyes opened as they neared her bed.

"Althea," said Franklin, "Jordanna Bronson is here."

"Who?" Althea said, somewhat perplexed.

"You remember, the young lady I met at the club…Adelaide's niece. The girl I met at the cricket club?" he said more loudly.

"Adelaide's niece? Oh, yes." She looked over at them. "Oh, I'm sorry, I've been napping all morning."

"And this is Jordanna's friend. What was your name again, dear?"

"Beth."

"Oh, yes, Beth."

Jordanna stepped closer to the bed. Althea lay fully clothed in a navy blue pantsuit and black leather laced shoes.

Her eyes fell over the girls. Althea's watery eyes softened and she stared as if in disbelief. "Oh, my." She shook her head. "You look just like her." Her soft voice quivered. "I can't believe how much you look like her." Althea continued to stare in amazement.

"Did you know my aunt well, Mrs. Biddle?"

"Oh, yes. She was one of my closest friends," Althea said. "I'll never forget the first time I met her. She practically saved my life!"

"Really?" said Jordanna.

"If I recall...my memory isn't what it used to be...it was at the train station when my car wouldn't start. She gave me a ride...a lovely woman. We had such fun together," she said with a smile.

"What did you do together?" Jordanna asked.

"Ah, what didn't we do! We did everything together." She giggled. "We went to parties and to the city...tennis, of course, we played every week."

"Sounds like a nice friendship." Beth smiled her best smile.

Suddenly a shadow fell over Althea's eyes. When she spoke again, the lilt had gone out of her voice. "But then...after a while...something happened." She shook her head and looked out the window.

Jordanna shifted her eyes to Franklin, who watched his wife, his face soft with love.

"Right before our eyes," Althea said as she stared out the window.

"Mrs. Biddle, what do you mean?" Jordanna asked. "What happened to my aunt?"

"I don't know, dear," Althea said after a long pause. "I really don't know. But the sweet woman I knew at the train station changed. After her son died, she became depressed, and I don't think she ever recovered from it." Her tiny eyes resembled a frightened bird's.

Jordanna looked over at Beth. "That would be my cousin, Jennings, I told you about."

"And then she had another child. Oh, what was that child's name?" she said, squeezing her eyes shut.

"Susie," Jordanna said.

"Ah, yes. Now I remember. Little Susie. Such a darling girl. As I recall, she adopted the child."

"Yes, she did," said Jordanna.

Althea smiled with recollection. "I told her it would be good for her to have a little girl to take care of." She paused and looked back out the window. A bird sat low on a thick branch by the stone wall nearby. "And she did take care of her, with all of her heart she did." She paused and shook her head. "If only she'd taken care of herself."

"What do you mean, Mrs. Biddle?" said Jordanna.

Althea looked up, her tiny bird-like eyes glassy. "I don't think she knew how to forgive herself."

"You mean when Susie died?" said Jordanna.

Althea nodded.

"Forgive herself for what?" said Jordanna, puzzled.

Althea's smile faded. She folded her arms across her chest and curled her legs up into a fetal position. Franklin poured some water into a glass and set it by her bed table.

"I'm cold, Franklin," she said to him. "Where's my blanket?"

Franklin went to the windowsill where the blanket had been folded and placed it over her legs. "Al, we have company," he said a few minutes later, his voice still loud.

Althea remained curled up and silent.

"I'm sorry," Franklin said to Jordanna. "It seems she's closing down again."

"Does she do this often?" Beth asked.

"Only when she's troubled. She must be upset by something." His eyes explored Jordanna's face. "I'm sorry."

Althea stirred under the blanket and turned over while trying to sit up.

"Al, are you all right?" Franklin said.

"I...I want to tell her something else," said Althea.

Franklin came to her side. He bent down lovingly, as though tending to a newborn as he smoothed her blanket with his thick hands and reached over to help her sit up. When she finally managed to find a suitable position, she summoned Jordanna with her long thin finger.

Althea leaned over the side of the bed and said in a loud whisper, "Don't forget forgiveness, young lady." She lay back down on the bed and closed her eyes.

Jordanna looked at Mr. Biddle as if to ask him to explain, "What did she mean by *forgiveness?*"

He shrugged. Beth and Jordanna turned for the door.

"Be right back, Al," he said to his wife.

Once they were outside of the room, Jordanna touched him gently on the shoulder. "Mr. Biddle, I hope I didn't upset your wife too much."

"Oh, please don't be alarmed at her behavior. It's something I'm trying to get used to myself," he said with kindness.

"I'm sorry, if I...we disturbed her." She paused. "But do you know what she was referring to?"

Franklin Biddle looked down at the linoleum.

164

"You know," she said, trying to remind him. "What had she meant when she said the part about forgiveness?"

His gaze remained fixed on the floor. "I'm not sure," he said, slowly shaking his head. "I'm really not sure what that means."

Jordanna struggled to read his face. The creases were deeply etched. She sought his eyes. Did he know something? She couldn't be sure. "Well, it really was a pleasure to finally get to talk to her this time," said Jordanna, trying to change the mood.

"Thank you for coming...thank you both," he said with a half-smile and hastily went back inside his wife's room.

On their way out through the lobby, Jordanna stopped at the information desk. "Hi, is Dorrie working today?" she said to the woman behind the desk.

"No, she's off today. May I help you?" the woman asked.

"Yes, I'm Jordanna Bronson. I work here as a volunteer."

"Hello," she said with a smile.

"Actually, I haven't been here in a while, but I was just wondering how Mr. Upland was doing?"

"Mr. Upland? Let me see what room he's in." A moment later, she looked up with a slight frown. "I don't see his name here...let me check somewhere else." She picked up the phone.

A few minutes later, one of the occupational therapists came out. "Hi, Jordie, how are you?" said Lucy Parisano.

"Lucy, how are you?"

"Good to see you!" said Lucy, her round almond eyes flashing.

"Same here. Oh, this is my roommate, Beth. Listen, I haven't been here in a while, and I was curious to know how Mr. Upland was doing."

"You didn't hear? Just last week, he was discharged," said Lucy.

"Discharged, really? That's great news!"

"Yes, it really came as a surprise to all of us, his recovery. He was just so determined to walk again...and he did!"

"I remember." Jordanna wistfully recalled his struggles and the time she spent with him.

"Well, his progress was slow there for a while, as you know. But he kept pressing on...pushing himself. You could tell he really wanted to get better. And he improved so much, we all were amazed, just amazed. It's a miracle, really. The hand of God just reached down on him."

"Miracles do happen," Jordanna murmured to herself.

As they left the nursing home, Jordanna wished a miracle for everyone at the nursing home. Especially Althea Biddle.

38

January, 1983

JORDANNA PEERED OUT HER WINDOW onto the cold, overcast morning. In the image of an old-fashioned painting, the campus looked resplendent blanketed in white. Children slid over the frozen ponds in skates with crayon-colored scarves and mittens while others slipped down the hills in sleds and saucers. Jordanna wanted to join them and wished she had the time to spare. The little girl inside of her was still alive and well. But her Winterim course was a heavy study in old medieval English that left her little extra time for anything but studying.

By evening, another fresh snowfall dusted the campus. She moved closer to the window where flakes and frost clung. The falling snow began to recoat the already white grounds. White on white. She glanced around the room; the clutter on Beth's side annoyed her. She wondered how anyone could function in such a state of disarray. Beth was a straight A student, yet her side of the room couldn't have been less organized. How did she do it? She could rarely find her lunch pass or keys, yet every semester her name found its way onto the Dean's list.

All of Jordanna's side of the room was orderly and uncluttered. Perfume bottles stood symmetrically tiered. Books all faced the same direction. Pens and pencils always remained together in one section in her desk drawer, separate from thumbtacks and paper clips. Jordanna wondered with all of her own attention to detail why it was that she herself couldn't make the Dean's list. She recoiled at the disparity and hated herself for not being as smart as her roommate.

With her room clean and orderly, she wished the rest of her life could be so pristine. Her thoughts again turned to Jeff, who always hovered somewhere in the back of her mind. She couldn't seem to shake the memory of what they'd had together. Although he'd tried to get in contact with her over the past year or so, she felt better not taking his calls. She also wondered about Kingsley Willoughby. She hadn't heard his name since he'd been kicked out of school. Maybe he'd enrolled somewhere else by now. Although she never held the slightest fondness for him and was glad he was gone, in a weird way, she felt sorry for him. He'd always rubbed her the wrong way, yet she couldn't help but wonder what drew her so far to dislike him. She rarely disliked anyone. Other than his snarky comments, he'd done nothing to her. She knew some people's sensibilities clashed with others, but it was more than mere personality. She never really spoke more than a few words with him. It was more than that.

Alone in the quiet of the evening, the snow eventually began to tumble down in thick flakes. A layer of frost glazed the window. She lit a candle and settled in front of the bookcase. Nestled between her textbooks and composition journals, there were a couple of paperbacks she'd been meaning to read but hadn't gotten the chance. The old brown leather diary she'd found in Walden caught her eye. She had picked it up countless times, reading it over and over as she envisioned the happy life of Adelaide Colton. It beckoned to her once again.

She perused the first few pages, reading the entries and feeling the warmth of the words. Adelaide seemed delirious with joy, as though it could barely be contained in the ink and paper on which she wrote. Turning the pages, Jordanna vicariously engaged herself in the happier life and times of her aunt and uncle when they were young…before the tragedy.

As it got late and Jordanna began to tire, she closed the diary and placed it back on the bookshelf. The strong light of the newly installed desk lamp revealed a layer of dust beside some of the books that she hadn't noticed before. And something looked different about the diary. Picking it up again, she saw the binding had torn a bit. A loose thread dangled from the tear. Behind some frayed pieces of cloth, a closer look revealed something stuffed inside. With a pair of tweezers, she pulled out the paper that had been wedged inside. It was three sheets of stationery. There were initials in gold filigree font at the top. The initials, AWC, belonged to her aunt. Adelaide Walden Colton. Jordanna began to read the words.

August 3, 1967
I am sorely grieved. It has been one year since my beloved daughter has been laid to rest. My daughter died because of me.

Jordanna felt her stomach tense as she sat riveted to the page.

I began my life here on the Colton estate a very fortunate woman. I've wanted for nothing in the material sense, although in the spiritual sense, I lacked much, God knows. I forgot my first love, the love of the

One who created me, at one point, not even believing that He really existed. I cast him aside for the riches of the world, and what a happy world it was for me...yes, for a while, I didn't know anything but happiness. But happiness did not sustain me. It is not enough just to be happy, I've come to know. For happiness alone is sure to disappoint. Lord, I ask your forgiveness, even now, for straying from your side.

I write these words at the end of my life on this earth. I feel it is the end. I don't know for sure what the will or the way of God is with me, but surely now with my family gone, I have nothing to care for. It seems that everyone I love is soon taken from me. It's as though I kill everything that is good for me. Not that I deliberately killed anyone, although with my daughter, Susie, that remains to be seen. I was never punished for her death, at least, not on this earth. John saw to that. His power and influence had all of the scuttlebutt silenced, never to erupt again. Yes, he saw to that—as much for me as for himself. His law practice was most likely to have suffered if the truth were to come out.

I loved you, John, but where did you go all of those nights? I hated the fact that you were always away from the house so much. I could never understand why you had to leave me so often. What drew you to Baltimore? Did you remain faithful to me? I don't know for sure. I just know that Sarah lived in Baltimore before she lived with us.

I always felt guilty thinking that you may have fathered my sister's daughter, Jordanna, although it's never been proven, and I'm not certain of it. It's just a feeling that I've carried with me. To say it's just my imagination is something that I've told myself over and over again, yet the thought still surfaces. I had wished to suppress my suspicions and the anger it caused within me and, hopefully, my hatred toward my sister and niece wasn't obvious after I began thinking this way. But as I am not perfect, who knows what anyone saw or thought. All I had was my heart and mind and the emotions in them were wracked with a pain that I could not ameliorate. Rather than take issue with them and confront the situation, I turned inward and began to hate myself.

John, I know you thought you failed me when you couldn't give me another child after Jennings passed away. I tried not to show the hurt and frustration not being able to conceive brought to us, at first, thinking it was my fault. When Paul offered me his beloved daughter to adopt and raise for him on the estate, I couldn't have been happier to accept the child. How fortunate we were and how generous of Paul! The child brought life back to my bones ever so slowly as I thought the memory of Jennings would remain an indelible mark on my heart. But I kept it a secret...at least the details of whose child it was.

I felt led to cover up the truth mostly to protect you. Yes, John, I did it for you. I knew that you felt bad enough as it were, and being that the little girl was Paul's flesh and blood and not your own would only be adding insult to injury. I know you knew of Paul's feelings for me. You were not so much jealous of Paul as proud. The gift of his child, in your eyes, would have been just too much to bear. As a prideful man, you thought yourself invincible. I didn't want to remind you that you weren't.

On the day that Susie died, I felt so ill. It was not a good day for me, even before the accident. I was in the midst of preparing the food and games for her birthday party. My heart was heavy with grief, as I had just overheard Sarah talking with you earlier that morning. I was reminded all over again of my suspicion of your infidelity that had haunted me. I had been at a breaking point for months, maybe years, even. I do not know for sure. I do know that I regret even waking up that hot August morning.

After I found the broken lamp in Susie's room, the beautiful lamp we had purchased in Spain, the rest of the day became much of a blur. I remembered hearing the crashing sound, and I ran upstairs to see what the clatter was about. Finding Jordanna and Susie alone in the room, I went in and found the lamp completely shattered. It must have been an omen.

Afterward, I went downstairs for a drink and then couldn't find my diamond bracelet. Upstairs again, I walked into Susie's room, thinking it may have gotten lost while I was there earlier. All I could see through the glare in Susie's room was the blonde figure of Jordanna by the windowsill behind the curtains. At least, in my stupor, that's what it appeared to be, as I didn't have my glasses on and was feeling very faint. It appeared that Susie was nowhere around.

Struggling on my hands and knees to find the bracelet, I ended up on the floor—looking under the bed and behind the dresser. Then I spotted Jordanna, still behind the curtains, begin to move toward the window. It seemed to me that she was hiding for some reason.

I told her, "Come out, Jordanna."

She said she wasn't Jordanna, that she was Susie.

I said, "You're not Susie. Susie doesn't have blonde hair. You're a liar—a liar, just like your uncle. Come out!" I screamed. "Come out right now!"

The reality of what happened slowly sunk in. My desperation was swift upon me, and I could not make sense of what had happened at first. But the truth had taken ahold of me to the degree that I eventually realized that my own daughter must have backed out of the window and fallen onto the veranda, three floors below.

Yes, it was indeed my own Susie wearing a blonde wig from her playtime in the attic shortly before. She was hiding from Jordanna while they were playing Hide-and-Seek. I caused my own daughter to back out of the open window in fear of the crazed monster who was about to descend on her.

My child fell to her death, and it should have been mine.

Jordanna sat rigid on the floor. Her hands trembled against the delicate yellow pages. Like molten sparks, the words popped off the paper and insulted her sensibilities. Her eyes burned at the impact. She wanted to scream to purge the words from the pages, but it was too late. They'd already gotten into her mind and were drifting down into the pit of her, falling deeper and deeper. A cold draft slipped under the door on the other side of the room and up her spine. Ignoring the cold, she turned the page.

In my delirium, I barely noticed anything was amiss until the scream broke through to me, and I looked outside the window. I saw what resembled a ragdoll lying in a red puddle. Then I turned around and, standing in the room with me was Sarah, clutching Jordanna. I then realized just how far I had gone wrong.

The news that the child we adopted came from Paul was devastating to you, when you found out. I still do not know how you came to this news, but I have a suspicion it was my sister who may have told you. Life afterwards became difficult for us because nothing I could say or do would change the hurt I had caused you when you found out the truth. You never forgave me for keeping the real father a secret from you all those years although I begged and pleaded for your mercy. There was no going back for you, John Colton. The distance between us grew, and it spread so far, the middle ground turned up fallow.

When you found out about Paul and forced me to fire him, I didn't want to do it. Susie died nearly a month before, and it was altogether a dreadful time for him and all of us. Paul did not understand and was overcome with grief at my cold, callous words. It was all a feigned anger. I had grown to love him dearly, and left up to me, I would have never let him go.

As I sit here at the desk looking out over the grounds where he used to tend, I think about him with great feelings of contentment and also loss. My heart aches for a nobler life for him...wherever he is.

170

I know I am forgiven by God, for I have asked for His forgiveness, and I know that I shall see my daughter again in another life. But the damage has been done here. My life will never be the same, and the relationships that I've broken in the meantime will probably never be reconciled.

I look forward to the time when God takes me home to a future in heaven where all of my tears will be dried and all of my hurts will have been swallowed up and my pain will be gone. I look forward to seeing my Jennings and Susie again. As for you, John, I have forgiven all of your unspoken trespasses. That is, if they are true. I've been told never to trust my feelings too much. Perhaps it is all in my head. I do not really know for sure. I'm not sure about anything anymore.

I'm feeling a little weak now, and I must lie down. It is a beautiful day on the estate. The blackbird's call is sweet and mellow, and I feel much like flying away on its wing.

The snow stopped falling, and the moon's sharp crescent hung like a scythe. Jordanna picked up the pages she'd read and shoved them back inside the diary. She snapped the windowshade down, climbed into bed, and cried herself to sleep.

39

IT SNOWED THROUGHOUT THE NIGHT IN ST. DAVID'S. The relentless cascade fell and drifted until, by morning, the town looked suffocated by its white trappings. A dismal hush enclosed the campus. Jordanna didn't want to face the day and was glad Beth would be away for the weekend. She didn't want to talk to anyone.

Sharp sunlight cut into the room as she lifted the shade. Moving slowly to get dressed, she felt her arms and legs wrought with stiffness as though her blood had drained and all that remained was shell and bones. The memories of the happier times she had led with her family on the estate were now tainted with a soil that would take a long time to wash away. She wanted to run back to it, take her life back to the times when the days, it seemed, would never end. Her childhood. Her family. Her father. She wanted to bring it all back.

The crisp, cold air cut into her lungs like tiny knives. Her lungs strained with each breath as the cold air swept in and out. She wished she hadn't found the diary and tried to make sense of it. The words her aunt wrote—the revelations—portrayed a dark, troublesome picture. It was not the world she knew. It couldn't have been. The story was so unsettling that Jordanna had trouble finding any balance between the idyllic world she knew as a child and the story as it was laid out from her aunt's perspective. Should she reveal what she knew to her mother…question her on the verity?

But what would it gain to know if it were true? It wouldn't change anything. Whether her real father was John Colton, what would it gain in the long run?

*

The following day, she went downstairs to the kitchen in the student lounge. The air reeked of old grease. The wooden drawers on both sides of the chipped sink no longer fit tightly into their grooves and hung off kilter. She felt dirty just standing in the room. The dusty floor hadn't been swept, and she felt crumbs underneath her slippers. While most of Key Hall was kept clean, this part of the campus had been overlooked.

She put the diary on the table. The leather binding looked as sickly brown as vomit. The only redeeming thing about it was that it cleared her of the murder of her beloved cousin. Other than that, the words were an unwelcomed intrusion that threatened to destroy the memories of the happier times in her life. She'd known of her aunt's alcoholism but never dreamed that it would lead to such a tragic ending.

Her eyes fell upon a long silver knife in one of the drawers. Just the sight sent a rip through her stomach. She pictured herself pulling it out, holding the cold metal. While she could never kill herself and thought it was wrong, she imagined how people would view her death…when the medical attendants came and placed her on the gurney and had her body removed from the room, one arm dangling. How long would the arm drag before someone noticed? Would they bother to move it, place it back by her side? Who besides her mother would really care if she were dead? Jeff? Hardly, she mused.

She rummaged through another drawer and came across a matchbook. Did she have the nerve to burn the dorm to ashes? It had happened before. How innocent it would look. Fires happened all the time. Surely being killed in a fire, there'd be plenty of sympathy. She'd be known throughout the town. Another Colton tragedy.

The light coming through the small window cut across the room, landing on the stove. Under her robe, her body flushed at the sun's warm teasing. The moment she moved out of its path, the coldness drew in like a dagger. She picked up the matchbook and pulled out a single match. She struck it and held the flame up to the flat side of the diary, where it fizzled out. Taking a second match, she tried again. It would not light. Taking match upon match, her efforts proved futile until there was only one match left.

She changed her course. She grabbed the diary and began to tear the pages. One by one, she ripped each one from the old leather binding. Each tear came faster and more vehement until nothing remained in the tattered leather binding. She threw the binding with both hands into the trashcan. It landed with the thump of an old hard husk. She gathered the pages into a pile and moved to the sink.

Pulling paper towels from the rack, she wrapped them around the pages like a small mummy. With the last match in hand, she struck it hard against the empty matchbook. It roared with a hiss. The orange-blue flame fanned out under the paper towel, and soon the fire began to consume all of it. The flames licked and singed the paper, leaving bitter smoke behind.

She rinsed the charred remains down the drain as quickly as possible until the sink was spotless. Feeling weak and remorseful, she turned to go back to her room…and jumped at the sight of Kingsley Willoughby standing in the doorway behind her.

"Kingsley, you frightened me!" she said, holding a hand to her heart.

His eyes looked hard at her, filled with misgiving. "Hi, Jordanna," he said in an odd tone. "What are you doing? Cooking something?"

"It's none of your business," she said. "What are you doing here? I thought you were suspended—for killing that duck." She braced for his reply.

He didn't answer.

"Did you kill it?" A tremor sounded in her voice.

"Ah, you have your secrets, and I have mine," he said coolly.

She folded her arms across her chest. His frame blocked the doorway.

"You look frightened, Jordanna. You always do when I'm around," he said, peering down at her. "Why?"

Her throat tightened. She closed the lapels of her robe over her chest, crossing her arms over them.

"Don't worry, I won't hurt you, Jordanna." He eyed her. "In fact, I've always had kind of a crush on you...ever since we were kids."

"What are you talking about, Kingsley?"

"Yeah, don't you remember...KC, KC, you drink monkey pee?" He grinned peevishly.

She stiffened.

"KC, KC, you smell like stinky wee. Remember that, *Jordie?*"

Her eyes grew large as bits of her memory of him filtered back. She pictured a scruffy little boy with dark messy hair wearing a striped T-shirt and blue shorts. He stood by his beat-up bicycle with tears in his eyes. She struggled for a moment until it all came back—the little boy smell, bubble-gum breath, the echo of their voices with which they'd taunted him.

She tried to summon the words but they caught in her throat. "You're... KC?" she stammered.

"That's right. Kingsley Charles. My mother worked for the Packetts down the street. That is, after your Auntie Adelaide fired her. I came over a couple of times to play, but your gimpy little cousin and you would have nothing to do with me."

"She wasn't a gimp," Jordanna said.

"No? Oh, I guess it was you that limped?" he said smartly. "That's probably why she jumped out the window."

"She never jumped out the window, Kingsley. That's the rumor. And it's a lie!" She felt the blood rush to her face. "Are you the one who's been telling people that?"

"What's the big deal, Jordanna? Why do you take it so personally?"

174

"Why do *you* still take it so personally after all of this time? We've all gone through tough childhoods, Kingsley."

"Some tougher than others," he growled.

"And how did you recognize me after all these years? I was barely six or seven years old when I moved away from here."

"I saw your name up in the Dean of Students office one day and some people talking about it. Jini Davis and someone else mentioned your name along with the Waldens and Coltons. How many Jordanna Walden Bronsons could there be?"

"But, Kingsley, we were only little kids."

"Every time I came over, your bratty cousin would shout at me and call me names."

"That doesn't sound like Susie, unless maybe you'd made fun of her first."

"Even your aunt was mean to me."

"My aunt?"

"Yeah, the last time I was there, I knocked on the back door by the kitchen, and I saw your aunt sitting at the table with her head in her hands."

"My Aunt Adelaide was upset?"

"Yeah, and she just shooed me away, told me to come back another time—that she was busy. Her face was all red. She looked like she'd been crying or something. That's when I spotted the diamonds—when I left."

"What diamonds?"

"I saw something shiny at the bottom of the steps outside."

"Something shiny…like what? Was it a bracelet?"

"I guess. I don't really remember. When I found it and brought it to her, she just shooed me away again like she didn't care. I took it home and my mother asked me where I got it, like I stole it. I told her I found it at the Coltons', and she made me go back and return it."

Jordanna stood frozen, listening to his revelation.

"When I went back, I saw a lot of flashing lights, and an ambulance pulled up to the house. I got scared and just threw it and ran."

"You just threw it on the ground?"

"What was I supposed to do?" he said emphatically.

Jordanna felt her blood pressure rise in her head and began to tremble. "Kingsley, you're the reason my cousin is dead!" she cried.

"What are you talking about?"

"If you hadn't taken the bracelet, my aunt probably would have found it where she'd dropped it, and she wouldn't have gone upstairs looking for it."

"So how does that make me responsible for your cousin's death?"

Jordanna's throat ran dry. Her emotions swirled and scattered. Suddenly feeling dizzy, she leaned against the wall and took a deep breath. For a moment, she felt about to drop onto the floor. "I don't know. Kingsley, I don't know," she said, looking up at him.

He looked down at her, his eyes sad.

"I'm sorry. I don't mean to blame you, Kingsley, I know it's not your fault." For the first time in her life, she became remorseful for her attitude toward him. "In fact, it's a relief knowing that it's not my fault either," she said, her voice thick with emotion.

A screech pierced out from across the darkened lounge. The silhouette of a figure stood holding open the door at the far end.

"Jordanna, phone call for you," Karen Kraemer said from the doorway.

"Who is it?"

"I think it's Jeff."

"Jeff? Why would he be calling?" She'd told him months ago that the relationship was over. Something surged within her. "Tell him I'm not available."

"Jordie, he's been calling for days now," she said with her hand on hip.

"What for? More lies?"

Jordanna let out a sigh and rubbed her temples. Her head throbbed and her throat felt like sandpaper. She walked toward the door. Before leaving the lounge, she turned around. Kingsley was gone.

40

THE SNOW COVERED THE GROUNDS for the next few weeks, dressing the landscape in pure, blinding white—stark by day, and with the evening's twilight, a more tempered white—softened in purple shadows. By late winter, Jordanna received another call from Jeff. At Beth's prodding, she finally spoke to him, more so to assuage her roommate than anything as it seemed Beth, herself, had a stake in the relationship.

When Jordanna heard Jeff's voice break on the phone, she begrudgingly acquiesced to see him, knowing this would be a hard fight. Although her heart ached for him and their former relationship, she had no intention of getting back together with him. But she thought it only fair to give him a chance to speak what had been on his mind. No one had ever fought this long and hard for her attention.

She let him in through the fire exit door of the basement lounge. They settled onto opposite ends of the beat-up sofa. She averted his stare and looked at the floor, realizing the pain she was inflicting by her indifference. At one time, this would be something she'd savor. Now she didn't feel anything. She didn't want to hurt him. Not like before. She felt different now.

"Jordie, I..." Jeff's voice faltered. "I want you to know something." His eyes fixed on her. "Jordie, I never lied to you."

The room seemed to expand. Her emotions were at bay, and peace enveloped her as though she were talking with just a friend, not an old flame. She let him continue and felt in control like never before.

"Jordie, it's true about Maryann. I did go back to see her the weekend you went away," he said. "But I only went there to tell her something. It was important enough to tell her face-to-face. I needed to talk to her." He reached for her hand. "About you."

"What are you talking about?" she said, pulling her hand away.

"I went to Sicklerville to tell Maryann that I'd have to break things off with her. I went there to tell her I'd found someone...someone I was in love with. I thought it best to tell her in person. It was the right thing to do."

The balance of power she'd felt earlier was now waning. A circle of warmth hovered somewhere just outside of her body pushing to get inside. It floated up and around her head before settling near her heart. Was it his charm or was this genuine? She didn't know whether to let it in.

"It was what I had to do," he said, reaching over to take her hand once more. The skin on the back of his hand looked like porcelain. She always admired his hands, claiming they were too pretty to belong to a man. It wasn't fair. With all of the hand lotion she'd applied to her own, his seemed to look smoother without it. She let it linger a moment before looking up at him. His brows knit as his blue eyes washed over her face before locking into hers.

"Jordanna, you never let me explain to you. You kept me at such a distance for so long."

She immediately thought of Dr. Bradley. His words to her in their counseling sessions came back once more. For so long she'd been lied to and deceived by people, especially men. Not having spent quality time with her own father, nor having him to rely on, she learned her own inner weakness had set her up for troubled relationships. She laid the groundwork for meeting the wrong kind of men, the kind who had taken no thought to treating her or any woman with respect. And in her weakness, she had allowed it. That's what he meant, although at the time she didn't see it.

"I needed my own space, Jeff. When I didn't think you took our relationship so seriously, I decided it was time for me to grow up myself, not to be tossed around by every wind of doctrine, like the Bible says. I interpret that to include people and their words." She spoke slowly, trying to absorb the meaning of the biblical wisdom and drive it home to herself as much as to him. "So I took a leap of faith and I let it go. I figured you were like the rest. I thought you were being dishonest in your treatment of our relationship— sending me mixed signals, implying that we were...I don't know...different, somehow. If we were meant to be, God would have to restore the relationship. Not me."

"Jordie, I believe God brought us together. I've been smitten by you since the first day I saw you on that lifeguard stand," he said.

Her feelings were beginning to shift. What began with indifference toward him seemed to give way to loving him all over again. The tightness in her body began to drain away. She wanted to concede, but she held back. She knew he had more to say, and she wanted to hear the words.

"Jordie, when I first saw you talking to Sarge a couple of times, you know, back then...I was actually...well, jealous of that old man...wishing you'd talk to me the way you did to him." He grinned sheepishly. "I'd watch you for a while before I asked you out because I knew that you were, well, special."

"Special?" she said, trying to sound matter-of-fact.

178

"Well, I didn't know at first. Later on, someone mentioned that you were from society and all. They said you were related to the Coltons."

She felt her face flush. "Who told you that?"

"Does it really matter?"

She bit the inside of her lip.

"Kingsley Willoughby." Jeff hesitated. "Was he right?"

She looked down at her hand and straightened her ring. "Well, I'm related to them, but I'm not a deb. I never went through with the cotillion and the coming-out stuff. I always felt it was hokey anyway."

He bent closer to her, his eyes shiny. When he reached out to embrace her, she felt electrified.

"Can you understand how much I love you, Jordanna? Deb or no deb, it doesn't matter to me."

His words stunned her, and she didn't know how to respond. Seeing his emotions so clearly left her puzzled, weakening her resolve. Fearful of being too anxious, she held her answer inside. The pressure of her bottled-up feelings had filled her to capacity, almost more than she could take.

"How could you have doubted me, Jordanna?" His eyes, like blue-black lakes, glistened brighter, inviting her in. He held her by her shoulders, looking her squarely in the eye. "Please don't ever doubt me again, Jordie."

Her throat tight, she attempted to swallow. Then her tears, which simmered on the surface, began to leak until she released them completely. He pulled her in and wrapped his arms around her. She clung to him, shaking.

"I love you, Jordanna. I want you to be with me...now and forever." His voice cracked with emotion as he held her in his arms.

It felt like a dream. His words weighed heavy. Jordanna let his words settle into her. *I love you...now and forever.*

She had wanted to hear these words for so long. Were they real? She didn't know if she could ever believe him, even now. They ebbed and flowed within her mind like sea waves out of control. Thoughts of him sometimes brought her to sadness so deep it swallowed her. She wanted to be with him, to connect with him on every level, yet there was so much she hadn't told him about herself. How would he react if he knew everything?

41

THE TRAIN STATION BRONZED IN THE LATE AFTERNOON LIGHT. Jordanna darted to the ticket counter as a low rumble came from somewhere underground. There were two people in line ahead of her. An older woman stood first at the counter, her head bowed as though she were praying. Behind the woman were two men. At 5:09, Jordanna's body tightened as the minutes ticked. She needed to board the 5:12 out of Philadelphia to get back in time to meet Jeff back at campus. The train schedule in the atrium hung forebodingly as it announced the status of the Paoli Local in flashing white letters: BOARDING. A person in another aisle eyed his watch. Time. It had such control. She tried not to look at the clock. A voice on the loudspeaker announced the last boarding for the Paoli Local.

"May I help you?"

The smoky voice of the ticket clerk couldn't have come sooner. *Thank you, God.*

"One ticket for St. David's, please."

With a quick thank you, she grabbed her ticket and change and raced for the stairs. When she got to the bottom and rounded the stairwell, she met with a thick blast of warm diesel fumes. Two silver trains idled—one on each side of the tracks. Taking a gamble, she turned right, where a conductor stood in the far distance. His strident voice called for last boarding before he turned to enter the car. The door clunked shut. *Oh, please... wait!* She jetted down the barren platform, tucking her head low—anything to save precious seconds. *Please... don't pull away!*

Relief flooded as she got to the door and managed to heave it open. Inside, the train was packed with commuters. Sandwiched three abreast, row after row, it wouldn't be easy to walk down the narrow aisle crammed with briefcases and men's pointed trouser-knees poking out. From where she stood, the odds of having to remain standing for most of the commute were certain. But it was a small price to pay compared to missing the train all together.

As the sun flashed strobe-like onto the commuter's faces, she thought about what she'd wear to dinner tonight. This would be the first real date with Jeff in so long. Had it been nearly a year since they'd been together? She had to look good, but she didn't want to try too hard. Or, at least, look as though she did. Among several women seated on the train, one stood out, sitting in the third row. She wore a tweed suit with flecks of gold and an ecru silk blouse. A strand of pearls graced her neck. The colors in the suit brought out the gold in her blondish hair. The woman looked ageless. She'd love to look as nice as the woman in the third row. Refined, yet down-to-earth at the same time.

*

Jeff waited in the corner of the dorm's lounge by the window with an eye on the television. When Jordanna approached, he stood and walked toward her as if drawn by an invisible thread.

"You look nice, Jordie." He lent a discreet smile as his eyes locked onto her.

She'd never seen him in a suit and was glad she didn't overdress.

"Thanks. You don't look so bad yourself," she said. "By the way, where are we going for dinner, Minnella's?"

He smiled before reaching for his coat. "I think I can do better than Minnella's."

"Why, what's so special?"

"It's our first time together in a while. I just thought you might want to go somewhere nice is all."

She put on her coat and they headed for the door.

"So, where are we going?" she asked as the car pulled onto Chaminoux Road.

He glanced at her for a second before turning back to the road. "Ever hear of the Four Seasons?"

*

After a quiet dinner, they came back to her dorm room. Jordanna lit a candle and placed it on the windowsill. He sat on her bed, a quiet contemplation in his features.

"Jordie, nothing's changed. You're still who you are—the girl I fell in love with," he said, taking her hand.

"I hope you understand where I was coming from for so long. You know, why I may have seemed...well...," she muttered under her breath.

"It's fine, Jordie. It's fine. Don't punish yourself. You've already done enough of that."

He reached over to embrace her. His skin held the familiar, warm scent of musky cologne.

"My mother didn't want me to come to school here," she said. "Too many memories. She told me later that she was afraid I'd sink into the depression again."

"You never seemed depressed to me. But you had something going on inside. That's probably what propelled you, pushed you. It was your drive to help the underdog, you know? You channeled it into fighting other's battles."

"I guess," she said with a shrug. "I guess all things do work together for good for those who love God and are called according to His purpose."

He nodded slowly. "God works in mysterious ways."

"I kept things buried for so long...kept the swirling sharks at bay. But there were days when thoughts of my cousin almost took me over the brink. And then with Kingsley and the rumor and everyone laughing about it..."

"I'm so sorry," he said. "About everything."

"I know."

"It's too bad about your aunt."

"She had some deep issues, that's for sure." She shook her head. "It's weird. All this time on campus I couldn't dodge the feeling that Susie was trying to get my attention. I know it sounds nuts, right?"

"You're very sensitive. Maybe she was. Not that I've ever experienced anything like that, but..."

"As much as I hated reading that letter, I'm glad, in a way, that I found it," she said. "It's bittersweet, really."

"It's helped you move on, put the shadow of doubt behind you. I can see it in your eyes. You've changed, Jordie."

"I hope there's a compliment in there somewhere."

"Compliment? It's more than a compliment," he said as he embraced her.

As they sat together, she longed to be closer to him and knew he felt the same way. But she'd seen couples on campus over the semesters that had grown close both emotionally as well as physically. Sadly, the couples who'd given into their passions too early often broke up. Jordanna didn't want to become a statistic of a broken relationship.

"Let's go for a walk," Jeff said while cradling her in his arms. "I'm feeling a bit stir crazy."

"It's probably getting cold," she said.

"There's not much wind, though. I don't hear it howling anymore."

They bundled themselves up in scarves and hats and stepped out into the night. The moon—high and bright—lent just enough light to guide them.

Through the winding paths, they ended up at Walden Pond. As the crisp air blew across the frozen water, lending a winter-cold sweetness, she had a strong urge to glide across the pond.

"It would be so great to be on that ice right now," she said, remembering her box of winter things was on the top shelf of her closet back home in Mullica Hill. She loved the rush of the wind in her face and hair. "It smells like snow," she said as they looked out over the pond. "I wish I had my ice skates."

"So do I."

"You don't skate!" She playfully punched his shoulder.

"I know. I meant you. I wouldn't mind seeing you pull off a double axel," he said with a grin.

"I wish. But let's leave the double axels to Dorothy Hamill."

Jeff stood from behind and held her. As he pressed into her, she felt the burden she'd been bearing gently lift. He pulled her around to face him.

"But I can *dance*," he said and placed her hands in his.

Scattered snowflakes lightly descended under the moonlight as they spun together waltz-like on the pavilion. She melted in their embrace, feeling his love sweep around her, giving her peace like a gentle waterfall. All the memories she'd tucked into the back of her mind, buried deep within the folds of time over the years, she now had the power to cast away. All of the matters that she took to heart...everything that had been obscured by the seasons and faded through the rest of life's struggles and storms, she could let go of. God was near. Her world had been so rough at times, filled with shadows of something she couldn't quite see or touch, yet she fought through the doubts and depression, boxing in the darkness. She waited so long for God to reach up through the doubt of her uncertainties to give her the strength to let go. But now she felt the clarity of God's hand upon her. Her prayers had been answered. She felt the charity of his grace. She let her feelings flow out and away as she danced by the pond.

What remained now was another enigma. What was her mother's part in all of this? Jordanna remained haunted by the accusations her aunt had made in the letter. Her mother's impropriety loomed large in her mind.

42

AT SIX A.M., JORDANNA LAY COMFORTABLY UNDER HER BED SHEETS. Although awake, the feeling of half-sleep fused in her bones. She remained still, relishing the comfort and content that had escaped her for so long. In the midst of her morning prayers, she stopped short at the sounds of loud, static clicking along with flashing red lights coming from outside the window. She pulled herself out of bed, startled to see two police cars in the parking lot while two more cars screeched around the corner and pulled in beside them.

"The police are here!" she said to Beth, still in bed.

"The police?" Beth said groggily from under the covers. She got out of bed to join her by the window.

Four police cars sat parked outside at the back entrance of Key Hall.

"Must be serious," said Jordanna.

They rushed to get dressed.

*

A low murmur emanated from the crowd in the upstairs lounge of Key Hall.

"What happened?" asked Jordanna, approaching a group by the vending machine.

"Someone got attacked," said Fuzz, who stood sweeping nearby.

"Again?"

"Yep."

"I heard it was Sharon Reese," someone said.

"Sharon?" Beth cried. "Oh, that's awful!"

Jordanna's encounter with a potential attacker came alive once more as she mentally relived the day she ran away from the man in the clearing.

"I hope she's all right," Beth said to Jordanna.

"Well, you're never all right after these things happen," said Jordanna as they headed for class.

A sense of fear permeated the hallways and pressed in all around as the somber-faced students milled around the lobby in Maginess Hall. Their murmurings all seemed to focus on Sharon, or something else just as serious. A number of classrooms had signs posted on the doors indicating that classes were cancelled for the day.

"Dr. Inwood's class is cancelled," said Beth as she approached the empty classroom. "I'll see you later, Jordie."

"Okay, see ya." Jordanna wondered if Dr. Morgan's class was cancelled as she headed for the second floor where she bumped into Jeff.

"Hey," he said and looked at her intently, his caring eyes searching. "I just heard about Sharon."

"I feel terrible for her."

"Belden's class is cancelled. There was a note on the door," said Jeff.

"I was just going to see if Dr. Morgan cancelled. Want to walk with me?"

"Sure. Everyone's class is probably cancelled."

Snippets of conversation converged as people murmured together in small groups.

"Sounds like everyone is talking about it," she said as they squeezed through the crowded hallway.

Outside Dr. Morgan's classroom a few of her students gathered.

"Hey, Laurel," said Jordanna. "I guess you heard?"

"Yes, it's unbelievable," she said.

"I'm guessing we don't have morning classes?" Jordanna looked at the sign on the door.

"No, it's been cancelled and rescheduled for this afternoon," said Laurel.

"I hope she's okay. Did they take her to the hospital?" asked Jordanna.

"I would think so," said Laurel.

"Do they know who did it?"

"The police are still looking into it."

Jordanna turned to Jeff. She noticed his face looked pale.

"Are you okay?"

"Yeah, why?"

"You look tense," she said.

"I'm fine."

"You don't look yourself. Did you have breakfast?"

"Actually, I'm feeling a little lightheaded. I could use some carbs. Let's go to the cafeteria."

*

Jeff took the last bite of French toast and wiped his mouth. He crumpled a napkin and pressed it between his hands. He rolled it over and over until it began to shred.

"What's wrong?" said Jordanna.

"I've been thinking."

"I'm listening."

He glanced furtively around the dining hall before he leaned in across the table. "When I first came to this campus, I felt weird at first. I don't know why, just around a few of the guys, I felt uneasy."

"Really? Why?"

He shrugged. "Just a feeling I had."

"Uneasy around who?" she said.

"Some of the rich guys, Tom and PJ. They boarded in Guffing, on my floor, so I got to know them pretty well. Some of them encouraged me to pledge the fraternity, but I wasn't sure if I'd fit in with those guys, you know? They were all from a different social class, and I wasn't sure. So I hung back and watched from the sidelines for a while."

"Rich, not rich, what's the difference? We're all just people. Besides, your parents aren't poor."

"I know, but…"

"What's class distinction have to do with getting an education? It's ridiculous." Jordanna studied her glass of iced tea, deep in thought for a moment. "I'm sorry, go ahead."

"Like I said, I wasn't keen on it in the beginning."

"But you did eventually join the fraternity, didn't you?"

"Yeah, but once I did, I really regretted it."

"Why?"

"Well, mainly because of Kingsley."

"Kingsley?"

"Yeah, there was something about him." Jeff's pale face now appeared strained in the dining room light. "I didn't feel comfortable with him. Like he talked out of both sides of his mouth, and you never knew where you stood with him."

"You didn't know if you could trust him, you mean?"

"Exactly."

"So why didn't you quit?"

"Well, I didn't want to look like a quitter, you know, or worse—a wimp. I didn't want to get harassed by anyone, especially Kingsley, so I simply dropped back and stood in the shadows, you know? I've been wary of him ever since."

"So, he's been bothering you?" said Jordanna.

"No, nothing like that."

186

"So what is it?"

"Wait, just wait," he said as he leaned in closer. "One day, I overheard some of the frat guys talking by the gym lockers, and it sounded like they were talking kind of cryptic."

"What do you mean? Like they were talking in code or something?" Her insides tensed with anticipation.

"Uh huh, and I couldn't make heads or tails out of the conversation. Anyway, from then on, it seemed like Kingsley changed. He became wrapped up in his own world. He didn't hang out as much with the frat guys and didn't seem to be around campus all that much. At least, I didn't notice him."

"I wish I could say the same thing...seems like wherever I am, there he is," she said.

"And when I did see him, he seemed depressed or something. Just wasn't himself."

"Well, he's always been a bit off. I mean, look at the duck incident." Jordanna took a sip of iced tea.

Her thoughts turned to her last conversation with him in the kitchen. Should she tell Jeff? Was this a good time to tell him about all she knew about Kingsley from her childhood? She glanced at the clock. "I have class in a little while. That is, if it's not cancelled."

"Okay, let's table this for now. Are you heading back to Maginess?"

"Yeah, let's go."

As they approached Maginess Hall, Jordanna paused before going inside. "I have something interesting you might want to know about Kingsley," she said.

"So do I," Jeff replied.

*

Jeff paced back and forth in his room.

"Jeff, you need to say something to someone," Jordanna said emphatically. "How long are you going to keep this to yourself?" She sat on the windowsill.

The bed on the other side of Jeff's room lay stripped. The drawers and closets were empty. Kingsley had moved out over a month ago when he was suspended for the duck incident. Only a box remained inside his former closet.

With his head in his hands, Jeff looked up with a beleaguered expression. "I'm not sure anymore. I'm just not sure." He got up and walked to the window. "But I think I know what I need to do."

43

May, 1983

THE FRESH SCENT OF LILAC PERCOLATED IN THE MORNING AIR. The sweetness drifted into the sun-splashed dorm hallway. Most all of the rooms were open wide—both doors and windows—as though on cue to receive the passing ambrosia. People in the throes of moving and clearing out their rooms for the summer, or forever, went in and out in the manner of worker bees. Boxes and suitcases lined the hallways along with bags and piles of clothing.

Jordanna moved down the hall and heard the intermittent muffled murmurs of well-wishers as people on their way out said their last good-byes to each other. As some tearfully hugged and promised to write or call, a wave of nostalgia hit her. She felt at peace, yet a glimmer of sadness hovered not far behind. She always felt closest to people when she knew she'd never see them again.

"Christy!" Jordanna said to a tall girl coming out of the girl's room.

Christy turned and smiled. "Hi, Jordie!"

"Are you all packed?"

"Yeah, just about. I'm waiting for my father to pick me up," said Christy. "I've got so much stuff...my stereo and mini-fridge and all." She gestured with her hand. "I think I have more to bring home than I brought here."

"I can see." Jordanna peered up and down the hallway. She shoved her hands into her pockets, searching for a way to extend the last moments with her. "Well, I guess this is it, huh?"

Christy nodded. She pulled a section of her long, red hair and began to curl it around her finger. "I won't be back next year. I'm transferring to the University of Virginia."

"Really? Good for you," Jordanna said.

"Thanks." Christy shot a quick smile.

An awkward silence grew as Jordanna longed to say something more than just idle small talk. She felt the precious moments tick by. She didn't know Christy that well and hadn't said much more than hello or good-bye to her during the past year. She felt compelled to make up the lost time. She looked down at Christy's dusty Earth shoes.

188

"I've always wanted to know—are those Earth shoes comfortable?" Jordanna pointed to Christy's shoes. "I've seen the advertisements in magazines and just wondered…"

"These? Oh, yeah, they're great. These are my third pair."

"I've wanted to ask you that all semester," Jordanna gave her a self-conscious smile. "I was thinking of getting a pair but ended up with these." She kicked one foot up to reveal the stylish platform shoes she would always choose over the plain or practical.

"Well, if you ever decide to get a pair, you'll love them for sure," said Christy.

Jordanna hung on Christy's every word. She remembered someone telling her that Christy had liked Jeff at one point, the year before she'd transferred to Colton. Jordanna studied her long oval face in the morning light washing in from the window, wishing her own skin could look as nice, and wondering what Jeff saw in her. Her long red hair shone like a new penny. Dressed in jeans and a plaid cotton shirt, she looked like a gentrified version of the farmer's daughter.

"Well, good luck!" Christy said, quickly filling up the dead space.

"Same to you!" Jordanna waved as she turned around and walked down the hall.

*

Throngs of people descended on Walden Hill. Friends and family of those graduating mixed and mingled while pausing to stop and pose for pictures. Rows of white chairs filled three quarters of the hillside, and people pressed in on all sides to find a seat. The graduates, all draped in black, gathered on the path by the waterwheel to walk in together as soon as the cue was given. The waterwheel rolled and splashed in the warm spring air, churning methodically like gentle background music. The first time Jordanna saw it, her cousin Susie was by her side. Now, as Jordanna stood on the path just above it, a flash of memory sparked her curiosity as to how Susie would have looked at this moment.

Searching through the sea of bodies on the hill, she spotted her mother in the crowd, a white handkerchief in her hand. In the distance, she saw Fuzz, the dormitory custodian, standing under a sycamore tree. At his feet sat Sarge's dog, Toby.

As her fellow graduates went to receive their diplomas, she felt a wave of emotion and fought to keep back her tears when one of the students came up to the podium in a wheelchair. TJ Harkness, one of Jeff's fraternity brothers, had been in a car accident. No one thought he'd ever come back to school afterward and were surprised when he had the courage to continue. Despite his setback, he'd never given up and graduated with honors.

When she heard Jeff's name called and the *cum laude* that followed, she felt prouder than she ever had about him. As he stepped down from the podium, he winked at her. While she received an honor for Outstanding Achievement from the English department, it didn't match the pride she felt to be graduating from something bigger and better than just college. She felt as though she'd graduated into being a step closer to God. For he had been her teacher all along.

She looked around and soaked in the beauty all around her. *This moment. This place.* How much she'd come to appreciate her time here. Jordanna had come so far. How blessed she felt to have so much. She didn't deserve it, she felt. God had been so gracious to her. Certainly, it was He who called her to this place.

44

One month later

"Mom, what's all this?" Jordanna said. "You moved all these boxes by yourself?"

"I had them in my closet, and a few were up in the attic," she said matter-of-factly.

"You should have called me before you did all this, or gotten some help from Mrs. Higgins, at least."

"I know it appears I've exerted myself, but really, Jordie, I haven't."

"How'd you get all this stuff down?"

"I just paced myself. It was exhausting, but I took my time." Sarah sighed as she plopped herself on the sofa next to a tall pile of boxes.

"So what is it that you wanted to show me? Did you find a diamond necklace, or your long-lost opal ring?" Jordanna asked while taking a seat on the floor.

"Actually, I've found a lot of things that you might like to see," Sarah said as she opened one of the smaller boxes. Her arthritic fingers moved stiffly. "This is a necklace that your grandmother gave to me. I want you to have it." She held it up, her eyes brightening as she handed it to Jordanna.

"Wow," she said, holding the 24-kt. diamond necklace. "You want me to have it, Mom?"

"Yes. I haven't worn it in years and I thought you'd like to wear it for your wedding."

"Wedding?" said Jordanna, stunned at her mother's candor.

"Yes, I thought you and Jeff were serious. At least, that was the impression I'd had," said Sarah. "What? You don't want to get married now?" Her brows furrowed.

Jordanna blanched at having to explain the details of her relationship with Jeff. She'd burdened her mother so much already. It might come as a shock to let her know that her heart was still not settled on the idea. At least, not like before.

"You're not going to just...just live with him, are you?" Sarah's eyes flashed.

"Mom, you know me better than that."

A hush came over the room. Jordanna felt a deep appreciation for all of the effort it took her mother to find and gather the things she thought Jordanna would need for the wedding. It broke her spirit to have to admit to her mother than things might not work out like she'd planned.

Jordanna went to the mirror in the foyer and put on the necklace.

"I like it on you." Her mother smiled admiringly. "It's classic and refined. Just like your grandmother."

"It's nice," she said. Turning back to her mother, she leaned over and kissed her on the cheek. "Thanks, Mom."

Sarah shifted and stooped to check the contents of one of the boxes at her feet. "There's something else here, I want you to see." She rummaged around and brought out another box. Inside was a satin bag that contained a lacey pale blue garter. "Here's the something 'blue,'" she said, "I'm going to assume that this fits." Sarah stretched it wide. "Okay, yes, it looks like it will, but since you won't need it." Her features turned taut as she put it back in the satin bag.

"I'm guessing you have the 'borrowed' and the 'new,' as well?"

"Does it matter at this point?"

"I don't know, just asking. You seem to have everything," Jordanna said as she cast an eye around the boxes that sat side by side across the entire length of the hearth. It looked like Christmas without the colorful wrapping paper.

"Just a minute, I think so. Let me see where I put them. Oh, yes, here they are." Sarah picked up a black velvet case that contained a strand of ivory pearls. "These are real, Jordanna—another gift from my mother to me when I was about 15."

"They're beautiful."

"You may borrow them, should you need them, but I would like them back."

"They must be expensive." She fondled the pearls for a few moments, examining them under the light. "They're so luminous! You can tell they're real."

"They are."

Jordanna carefully placed them back into the velvet box. She lay back against the sofa with her hands behind her head. "Okay, you have something old, something blue, and something borrowed. So what's the 'new'?"

"Well, I figured it would be your wedding gown," her mother said with a quiet deference. "And I also have something else for you." She handed Jordanna a manila envelope. "Make sure you keep this with you. You'll need it when you go to get your marriage license."

"Mom, please. I'd really like to table that topic for now, okay?"

"It's your life, Jordie. I don't mean to take over."

"I know, Mom, but…"

"I just want what's best for you."

"I know. I'm still trying to work things out…"

"You still love him, don't you?"

"Mom, please don't ask me that right now."

*

It was only a short time ago when her only child was just a little pixie-haired girl who worried so much about her, Sarah thought. Through the years, their worry for each other shifted between them. They passed it back and forth like a heavy stone. Now her daughter had become a grown woman, yet Sarah still imagined her daughter as a young child.

Jordanna picked up a photo album sitting by one of the boxes. "Oh, look, here's a picture of you and Aunt Adelaide!" said Jordanna. "You guys look like twins!"

"Oh, I remember those dresses…your grandmother made them," she said. "As a girl, I had always looked up to Adelaide…wanted to be like her…dress like her… I learned from imitating her. All my life, she was my guide, really. I copied her so much that it nearly drove her crazy." Sarah paused to pour more wine for herself.

"Where was this picture taken?" said Jordanna.

"I believe that was on her spring break from college, I think," she said, taking a sip. "I missed her so much when she went off to school, although I'm sure she was glad to get rid of me. When she'd come home for Christmas and Easter breaks, I'd drag her by the hand upstairs so she could tell me all about what she'd been doing in school. You know, things about her social life and such. She always had her eye on one boy or another, or maybe it was the other way around. She attracted them like flies to honey."

"I'm sure she did," said Jordanna.

"But our personalities were so different. I was shy, and she was so outgoing, like you."

"You were both so beautiful." Jordanna turned the pages of the photo album.

Sarah smiled as the memories surfaced. "Oh, but she was the more beautiful, I always thought. I remember one evening in Prague when Mother called us down from the bathroom. We were practically at each other's throats trying to prepare for a formal where your grandfather would be speaking that evening. She practically threatened us to get ready, or we'd have to take the Metro in our formals."

Jordanna grinned.

"When she came down the steps in that red satin gown with a single red ruby hanging from a gold chain around her neck, she looked so striking, I nearly lost my breath. It was then that I knew that the world would revolve around your Aunt Adelaide, and I'd always be a shadow in it."

"Mom, you're hardly a shadow. Why do you say that?"

"Addie seemed to have it all in the way of grace and beauty...womanly charms. I guess it was her personality, too, that colored her so much larger than life. I never had her self-confidence. But I thought through imitation, I'd come into my own, so to speak." Sarah stopped and studied Jordanna. "You've always reminded me of her. You have her looks and something of her personality."

Hopefully, you'll have a better ending to your life than she did, Sarah thought, watching Jordanna as she stroked Pudding's head while she purred softly.

Sarah tried not to show her emotion. In the back of her mind, she had often worried about the past, how much of her daughter's memories of living with the Coltons had stuck with her. How much of that dreadful morning did she retain? Her psyche was so young and fragile. Was it wise to send her back to the scene, the scene that changed their lives? So many years had passed since the summer of 1966 where the death in the Coltons' mansion had traumatized the family.

Jordanna had taken the shock of her cousin's death the hardest. The youngest always did. *"She seems to have repressed it,"* the psychologist said. He told Sarah that Jordanna would eventually be all right. The school counselor had concurred. They all assured her that Jordanna would heal. It would just take time. As Sarah watched her daughter, she found the psychologist was right. Her daughter was fine. Even more than fine. She had matured into a beautiful young woman.

The sun dappled at the edge of the horizon, sending trickles of light onto the hardwood floor as Sarah and Jordanna sat by the fireplace.

"Tell me more about Daddy," Jordanna said as she came to a picture of her father and mother. "Look at his suit. So handsome! He seemed to be very much in love with you, Mom."

"I think that was the first day I met him. What a wonderful time we had.

We met on a blind date. I think it was Lois Ferrier who introduced us and we became smitten almost from the start. When you were born, his whole world came to life, it seemed." Her eyes misted a bit, and she forced a smile. "And when he died, that's when mine came to an end."

Sarah wiped her eyes. "Oh, I'm sorry, Jordie. I guess my feelings are always right on the surface." She took a sip of wine. "I sometimes think that I'll always have a bit of grief lingering in my heart for your father. It's been so hard. Addie had always tried to set me up with other men, to help me fill the void, but I didn't take any interest in them. I think my life with Jordan was as good as it could ever get for me."

"I remember Uncle Milton coming to call," said Jordanna. "He always wore a hat, remember? That hat with the green feathers!"

"Yes, after his dear wife died, he'd come calling on me—on both of us really. He wanted to take us both to dinner and to the theater. He was such a gentleman, really, and loved you dearly, but..." Her lips trembled as she attempted to smile. "But I didn't feel the same way."

Jordanna saw why men had flocked to her mother, with her china-like skin and vulnerable expression. Her soft blue-gray eyes reflected a fragile core that she swiftly masked with her quick smile. She heard them remark about her mother...speak of her with words such as *natural beauty...so down-to-earth*. Her beauty came from the inside and spread outward. Jordanna always had been compared to her mother's sister, Adelaide, but she hoped that one day, people would see more of her own mother in her.

"What about Uncle John?" Jordanna said.

"What about him?"

"Did he...you know, ever approach you?"

"Why would he do that, honey?"

"Well, when Aunt Adelaide began to decline..."

"Oh, Jodie, no, never! That wasn't even an option."

Jordanna blushed. "I'm sorry to have —"

"John only had eyes for Addie...," Sarah said wistfully of her dead sister. "How much that soul has gone through. She went through so much more than any woman should. I often spoke to John about her and told him how I felt. Her depression got so deep at times. We both wondered how far she'd go."

Sarah wiped her eyes. "With each passing year she seemed to get worse. Her once vivacious spirit waxed over to someone so unlike her old nature. Everyone saw it." She shook her head sadly. "And not only her friends but some of the other townspeople saw it, too. They gossiped terribly that she was no longer the same person as before. Some asked how she was doing, but most of them didn't. They wouldn't have such pity, not for someone like her."

"Why not?" Jordanna asked.

"Well, your aunt was not so gracious in her last years. She'd changed. Became so demanding...ever since she'd been a young girl, she'd always gotten her way. Even with me, when we were children, she'd be bossy."

"How?"

"Oh, well, being the older sister, she kind of took charge. She relished being in control. When your grandmother had a dinner party or such, Addie would end up sitting at the adult table—always. Even though she was only a few years older than the rest of the others at the children's table, she managed to place herself with the adults."

"They had children's tables when you were a kid, too?" Jordanna said.

"Oh, yes!"

Jordanna laughed.

"Nothing could change my feelings for her, but when I saw that living at the estate was no longer good for you, I took you away," Sarah said. "I always felt coddled by her—every move thwarted—like having a bird's wings clipped. And as she got older, it seemed her need to dominate took over all the more. It eventually became too much for me to bear."

"Did Uncle John love us?"

"Of course. Why do you ask?"

"He seemed, oh, I don't know, so...aloof, I guess."

"Oh, he was very reserved. Still waters ran very deep with him," Sarah said. "He was a good man, a good lawyer, too, just like your father. He was a very loving man. He loved Adelaide more than words can say."

Pudding slunk over and rubbed her head against Sarah's legs.

"Jordanna," Sarah said softly, "no matter what happens with you and Jeff, or you and any man, I want you to know one thing."

Jordanna lifted her eyes to meet her mother's. Sarah reached over and embraced Jordanna tightly. "I want you to know that you're loved more than you realize."

"I know, Mom."

"Love comes from knowing your place with God. You never had a real father for very long. I'm sorry for that. But God has always been right here for you. He's your father, Jordanna. He's everything you'll ever need. Do you understand?"

"I'm beginning to see that now," she said, knowing she'd have a long way to go to fully understand the scope of God's love for her. "I'm taking it one day at a time."

196

Jordanna's heart grew light. Clearly, through her mother's wisdom, she could see that she was still the chaste woman she had revered her to be all of these years. If there were anything between her mother and her uncle, she could see now that it was merely platonic and most likely for the sake of Adelaide's mental health. Her heart ached, though, for her Aunt Adelaide.

Jordanna was glad she did not let on about the pages she had found inside her aunt's diary. The false assertions were too cruel and would be too dreadful for her mother to bear. She'd been through enough in her lifetime and didn't need to know any more about Adelaide, especially her misguided thoughts that had no real basis other than the fabrications of her own imagination. Obviously, her addictions had altered a part of her mind and her assumptions about her own husband and sister were all manufactured through the perverseness of her waning faculties. It felt right then and even more so now that she had burned the diary and the pages she found in the binding. The remembrance of the words would, hopefully, fade away as far as the ashes had spread.

*

Later on, back at home while going through a stack of mail, she opened the contents of the envelope her mother gave her. Inside, she found her birth certificate. Jordanna's heart filled with lightness. Overwhelming her beyond joy was the next line she read: *Father, Jordan Bronson.* The black letters on the yellow paper almost popped off the page. She took them in as if it were a love letter, reading the words over and over. Her father was, indeed, Jordan Bronson!

Oh, Mama, I didn't know. I didn't know for sure. I just didn't know.
She cried for joy.

*

Jordanna stepped out into the chill of the morning to pick up the morning paper from the doorstep. The bold headline held her eyes as a shiver ran up her legs. A short while later, her phone rang.

"Morning, it's me. Did I get you up?" said Jeff.

"No, it's okay," she said.

"Did you read the paper yet? They caught the Colton attacker. The story is on the front page of the *Waynesboro Times.*"

"I know. I read it. You were right."

"Yeah, I knew it was him."

"How did you figure it out? When did you suspect it was Kingsley?"

Jeff remembered the day when Kingsley had gone to class, leaving him alone in their room. While sitting on his bed trying to study for his history final, something looked odd about the bed across the room. Kingsley's bed. It was unmade and, under the mattress, something unusual stuck out. Jeff got up and took a closer look.

Under the mattress was a man's black hairpiece and beard.

Epilogue

One year later...

STRAINS OF HANDEL FILLED THE AIR as the guests, refined in suits and hats, murmured quietly. Garlands of peach, ivory, and warm pink roses draped along the front row of chair backs and echoed at the stone pillars at the altar by the pond. Jordanna waited by the waterwheel for the bridal march to begin. She surveyed the landscape...the guests who'd come to celebrate...the pavilion where the minister and her betrothed stood...the masses of roses.

She'd planned her wedding day as far back as childhood. While bike rides and playing dress-up were the girly pastimes she had embraced as a child, even then, her mind wandered to a future time. Living on the estate with the Coltons, she and her mother were welcome; this was what her mother had told her.

But in her heart, Jordanna always felt a gap between the welcoming arms of her aunt and uncle and her place in them. There were the requisite hugs and kisses, and surely their smiles were genuine. Uncle John opened his arms wide when they arrived; his rosy lips always curled up around his cigar as he gave her a gentle hug. Yes, their affection was there, but only for a time. It never seemed to linger for long. Like seeds scattered on hard ground where the birds plucked and gathered, they were sucked up before she was able to grab hold. So fleeting. The love was displayed, it seemed in theory, and it was so irretrievable at times and always remained a question in Jordanna's mind. Was it aimed at her? Was it real?

In her vivid imaginings, Jordanna painted a wedding for herself—one that would fill the gap of her empty heart and beyond. A day where all of the love she'd have for her intended one would bounce back to her...blossoming up and over her and spilling from her heart to his and back again. The reverberations would ripple out onto Walden Pond and everyone at the wedding ceremony would feel the love she had found in her betrothed. While she didn't know who she would marry at the time, she wrote down the names that he might have. She loved the alliteration she'd created, the pairing her own name and her intended's...Joseph and Jordanna...or John, Jerrold, Jason.

So when she met Jefferson James, she sensed this was a good omen.

Jordanna walked down the path toward the altar. Her ivory silk and satin train rustled behind her. Jeff and his best man—his cousin, Michael—stood next to the minister, and Beth Brisco, her maid of honor, glowed in peach chiffon as she stood waiting on the opposite side. In the first row, her mother bore the appearance of royalty, resplendent in an emerald green dress. Seated in the row behind her was Dr. Bradley; his robust face held the glimmer of a smile. Dr. Morgan and her husband, Ron, were seated next to him.

As Jordanna rounded the lake, Jeff was overcome with emotion. His eyes shone bigger than she'd ever seen them before. Through all of their starts and stops at love, she was grateful for the path that led to this day.

The ceremony flowed as beautifully as Jordanna had planned. In the end, the only thing missing was her father. While moved with joy over the occasion of her marriage, Jordanna felt a pang of sadness that her father was not there to walk her down the aisle, yet all of the stories and pictures her mother had shared about him brought his presence alive. Thinking of him, even now, she was grateful that her mother had found such a wonderful man and that he was, indeed, her biological father— her mother's first and last real love. Named after her father, Jordanna always felt a bond with him, and although she buried the ache of never knowing him fully, the memory of his spirit left a tangible presence in her mind and heart.

The minister smiled and closed his Bible.

"Now you may kiss the bride," he said with a broad grin.

She felt the strength of Jeff's arms around her as they embraced in a warm kiss. Turning in unison toward the crowd, he took her hand as they moved forward up the aisle. After a few steps, she felt the warmth of strong, yet invisible, arms still around her like a band of protection from which she couldn't break free.

The calm green water of Walden Pond looked inviting. The ducks paddled in silence, rippling the water behind them while the Mute swan with her ethereal grace sat off to the side, alone and content by the reed grass. High on the hill, Walden Hall stood tall and prominent among the surrounding trees, its stone and mortar swelling with pride. The daylilies swaggered in the breezes, and the waterwheel's spinning buckets churned methodically in a sprightly rhythm. Amid the cadence of St. David's, the gentle *con-ker-reee* call of the red-winged blackbird resounded over the water. Her mother's words echoed in her mind—the words her mother had said to her not so long ago: *"Love is knowing your place with God."*

Author's Note

The protagonist's story in this book is not too far from the truth. The campus where the story is set is a real institution of higher education on Philadelphia's Main Line where the true-to-life rumors still linger on what really happened one fateful summer day.

Acknowledgments

First, my utmost thanks go to Ramona Tucker and Jeff Nesbit, for their kind acceptance of my work and for their vision for my story. I owe you both my sincerest appreciation.

Many thanks go to my mentor, Joyce Magnin, who brought me into the world of writing through teaching and engaging me in the art of creating a novel. Thank you for raking through my manuscript at all hours and entertaining frantic emails with a sane response.

To Dr. Betsy, the first professor to introduce me to concrete writing. Thank you for your gracious editing of an entire pile of loose pages we called a novel.

To Cec Murphy, Rowena Kuo, Tim Shoemaker, Diana Flegal, Bill Jensen, and Priscilla Strap, whose candor, advice, and keen eye brought me that much closer to honing my writing skills— a big thank you to each of you as well as my writer's critique group, including Terri Gillespie, Nyla DiGiorgia, and Diane Rosier.

To Trayce Duran and Vickie Bickhart, my sincerest thanks for your interest in my work long before it was a work. Your contributions were worth a million.

To my Boss, Frank Quattrone, your support, kindest encouragement, and continual praise over the years have made me a better writer in one way or another.

You all have my fondest appreciation.

About the Author

"Mary will never be a mathematician," were **MARY CANTELL**'s third-grade teacher's words to her parents at the PTA meeting upon their meeting Mrs. Langen. Taking this as a cue, the eight-year-old wannabe writer adopted the self-fulfilling prophecy and began pursuing her natural love of language.

Graduating with a B.A. in English Writing, she later became a radio/TV broadcaster and sidelined as a newspaper columnist. Her day job found her reporting Philadelphia's traffic conditions as well as hard news, weather, and sports inside an 8x8 foot booth. It was not so glamorous—at least, not from her vantage point.

When she was laid off after 16 years in the news biz (and lost her newspaper column as well, all in the same week), it was obviously a blessing from God now to have the time to write a novel. *Her Glass Heart* is the result.

While resuming another newspaper role as a syndicated columnist of all things A&E related for the past five years, her freelance writing of every genre has found publication in various magazines and book anthologies.

Along with her love for chocolate and playing chess, Mary enjoys mountain hiking with her husband and watching black-and-white film classics.

www.marycantell.com